HAVOC

ALSO BY CHRIS WOODING:

HAVOC

CHRIS WOODING

ILLUSTRATED BY DAN CHERNETT

SCHOLASTIC

First published in 2010 by Scholastic Children's Books
An imprint of Scholastic Ltd
Euston House, 24 Eversholt Street
London, NW1 1DB, UK
Registered office: Westfield Road, Southam, Warwickshire, CV47 0RA
SCHOLASTIC and associated logos are trademarks and/or
registered trademarks of Scholastic Inc.

Text copyright © Chris Wooding, 2010
Illustration copyright © Dan Chernett, 2010
The right of Chris Wooding and Dan Chernett to be
identified as the author and illustrator
of this work has been asserted by them.

ISBN 978 1407 10511 6

A CIP catalogue record for this book
is available from the British Library.

Typeset by M Rules
Book printed by CPI Bookmarque Ltd, Croydon, Surrey

Papers used by Scholastic Children's Books are
made from wood grown in sustainable forests.

1 3 5 7 9 10 8 6 4 2

www.scholastic.co.uk/zone

THE CITIES

Storm Warning

1

Seth had never seen a storm gather so fast. It felt as though it was reaching towards him, a vast, dark hand to snatch him up. A choking sense of dread was growing inside him.

Thunder rolled across the sky as he ran down narrow roads and lanes. Black clouds slid over the horizon like spilled ink. A fine mist of cold rain began to speckle the tiny village of Hathern, deepening the chill of the October afternoon. A bitter wind had sprung up, whipping his untidy black hair around his ears.

He carried the ornament wrapped inside his jacket, held against his stomach as he ran. Something told him to keep it hidden. As if the darkening sky was full of unfriendly eyes.

The rain was falling hard by the time he got to his house. He shut the front door behind him and leaned against it, catching his breath. Mum and Dad were in the living room, in front of the TV as usual.

"It's really coming down out there, isn't it?" Mum commented. Dad made a half-interested grunt of agreement.

Didn't they feel it? Didn't they feel the terror of the storm, the awful sense that it was swallowing them up? No, they were unaware. Of course they were. If it wasn't on the TV or in the papers, they didn't want to know.

He hurried upstairs to his room. The wind was getting strong, rattling at his windows. Rain lashed the glass. It was getting dark as night outside, and it was barely four o'clock. He wasn't the kind of kid who scared easily, but he was scared now.

He pulled the curtains shut, took out the ornament and laid it on his bed.

It made his skin creep to look at it. A fearsome, squidlike monster stared at him with a grey, dead eye. Its stone tentacles were clutched tightly around an egg-shaped piece of whitish, cloudy mineral.

It sat there in the gloom, unremarkable except for its ugliness. Lightning flickered outside the curtains. In the distance, a cat was yowling.

Slowly, he reached down and picked it up. It was cool to the touch. He peered at the egg, clutched in the tentacles of the monster.

There was a light inside it. A thin worm of brightness that writhed and twisted like a restless serpent. The ornament became warm in his hand, and the light became brighter, until the egg lit up his face like a tiny sun.

It felt like life. Like there was something alive in there.

"They're coming for you, aren't they?" he said quietly. "They're coming for both of us."

Seth snatched up a backpack and hurriedly stuffed in a few clothes. He wrapped the ornament in a T-shirt and put it inside. The light faded as soon as it left his hands.

After that, he dug out the lockbox where he saved his pocket money. It was stashed behind a pile of junk that included a baseball bat, a basketball, and the front wheel of a BMX. Seth had always been an active kid, uninterested in computer games or TV, but he tended to give up on hobbies as fast as he started new ones. Nothing excited him enough, that was the problem. Everything was too regulated and safe.

Until he'd found out about the world of Malice. A world inside a comic book.

He opened up the box and stuffed a handful of crumpled notes into his pockets. No telling when he was coming back. Maybe never.

There was a skittering noise on the roof, as if a horde of little crabs had gone scampering across it. Seth looked up. Icy fingers gripped his heart.

I know that sound.

There was no more time to delay. Lightning flashed and thunder boomed again. The storm was almost overhead now. He shrugged on a waterproof coat and slung his backpack over his shoulder. He was reaching for the door just as his mum opened it.

"Have you *heard* this *storm*?" she cried happily, bustling in. "It's like the end of the—" She stopped abruptly as she saw him standing there with his coat and backpack on. "You're going out in this weather?" she asked.

She was wearing a sweat top and tracksuit bottoms, her plump, jolly face wearing an expression of puzzlement. Her blonde hair was greying more by the day, it seemed. She kept it cut short, so as not to be a bother.

This is how I'll always remember her, he thought, sadly. *Looking just like this. Not quite getting it.*

"I have to go," he said.

"Go where?" she asked.

"I don't know. Away."

She stared at him, uncomprehending. He could have made some excuse, just something to get past her and out of the house; but Seth prized honesty in people, and he was no liar.

"Mum, I don't have time," he said. She was blocking the doorway. "I have to go."

He saw tears gathering in her eyes and immediately regretted his tone. Most of the time, he only thought of his parents as a boring nuisance. Their lives seemed so dull to him that he couldn't imagine they had the same kinds of feelings as he did. It was easy to forget that they were people, too.

"No, you're not," she said quietly. Then, louder: "No, you're not! Not after what you put us through last time! You're not leaving us again!"

She hurried over to him and began clumsily pulling the backpack off. He struggled against her, but his arm was caught in one of the straps.

"Get off me!"

"You're not leaving us again!"

"Mum, I—"

He pushed her away, harder than he intended. She stumbled back into his wardrobe, banged her elbow, and burst into tears.

"Why are you *doing* this to us?" she wailed.

The sight of his mother crying made Seth feel loathsome. They deserved a kid they could be proud of, instead of one who could barely stand to be in the same room as them. He reached out towards her, to comfort her somehow, but he stopped before he touched her. How could he make her understand that he was doing it for them? That whatever was descending on them would destroy them all? How could he make her understand, when he didn't really understand himself?

"I'm sorry, Mum," he said. "I don't have a choice."

He headed through the doorway, on to the landing and down the stairs. Mum came out after him, calling for Dad.

"Mike! Mike! Seth's running off again! Don't you let him!"

Seth had the front door open and was halfway out of it when a strong hand grabbed his wrist.

"No, you don't!" said Dad. His face was stern and his small eyes flashed with anger. Seth felt a surge of anger in return. He yanked his hand away. Why was his dad only ever interested in him when there was discipline involved?

The two of them glared at each other in the doorway. Mum came halfway down the stairs and paused, her hand to her mouth, watching the scene. Seth wasn't old enough to take on his dad, but he was old enough to defy him.

"I'm going," he said. "I'll be back when I can."

"You're not going anywhere," Dad warned. "You broke your mother's heart last time, you ungrateful little sod."

"Some things are more important than staying at home and watching TV, Dad," Seth said, coldly.

His dad opened his mouth to reply, but just at that moment there was a blood-chilling howl from outside, drifting over the village. It was like the lost, agonized hunting call of a wolf, but a hundred times more terrible. Dad went pale.

"What was that?" Mum whispered from the stairs.

"They're coming for me, Mum," Seth said. "I have to run."

"Stay inside, eh?" said Dad. His face was slack, and he was looking out into the storm. The sternness had gone from his voice. Now he was just a balding, middle-aged man, afraid of the dark. "Get inside and shut the door. It's not safe out there."

Lightning stunned the village in white, and the thunder hit at the same time. The storm was on top of them.

"It's not safe anywhere any more," Seth said. And with that, he turned and fled from the house.

3

Seth pulled up the hood of his coat as he ran out into the street. The rain was coming down hard, washing along the winding roads of the village. It came pouring from the gutters of the church up the road, splattering on the window sills of the old Scout hut, dripping from the rusty climbing frame in the schoolyard. The storm hissed at him, and the cats yowled, and somewhere out there was something dreadful.

He looked back at his house to see if his parents were following. Mum was calling his name. Dad was holding her back, to prevent her from chasing after him. "You'll catch your death!" Seth heard him say.

But that wasn't really why Dad was keeping her inside. It was because of the cry he'd heard, rising over the rooftops. Maybe, at last, he sensed that there were things in the world that didn't make the papers and couldn't be explained by politicians. He sensed that, and it made him afraid.

Seth heard the door closing. His parents had shut themselves in their home, trusting to its safety. He hoped they were right. With him gone, they shouldn't be troubled. It was the ornament the enemy wanted. The Shard.

The lane where he lived was on a hill, and he followed it to the top, where it came to a crossroads. He had no idea where he was going, only that he had to get away. Lightning split the clouds in dazzling forks, and the storm roared in fury. The trees of the churchyard bowed and rustled as he passed. The shadows in the village were deep and thick, and he didn't know what might be hiding in them.

At the top of the road, he stopped and peered round the corner. He froze as he saw someone heading towards the junction. The other residents of Hathern had taken shelter, but not this man. He was huge, well over six feet, broad-shouldered and overweight. He was wearing a slicker, and his face was shadowed by a grey fedora jammed down on to his head.

But Seth didn't need to see his face to recognize Icarus Scratch.

Heart pounding, he ran back down the lane a little way and cut through the churchyard, keeping the ancient building between him and Scratch so that he wouldn't be seen. The trees that hung over the old paved path between the gravestones rustled and clattered in the wind, whipped up by the unnatural storm. Seth couldn't fight the suspicion that they were warning his enemies. *Here he is! Here! Here's the boy!*

He came out on the other side of the churchyard on to an empty, single-lane road that ran in front of a row of houses. Curtains were drawn, and lights shone between them. As he emerged, the lamp posts blinked into life, responding to the darkness. A yellow glow soaked into the village.

At the bottom of the road was a junction that led past the school and the recreational ground, and into the fields and woods that lay at the back of the village. Seth decided he would strike out in that direction. It was as good as any.

He took one last look around for signs of Scratch, then raced down the road towards the junction. He'd almost reached the bottom when someone stepped out in front of him.

It was a thin woman in a black blazer and pencil skirt, with blonde hair tied tightly in a bun, carrying a leather handbag. She had sharp, pointed features, and was hurrying with her head down, holding up a large umbrella to ward off the rain. She looked up and saw Seth, who had stopped still at the sight of her.

"Foul night," she said, in a crisp upper-class accent. "You look drenched. Here, I have another umbrella in my bag if you'd like." She came up the road towards him, holding out her own umbrella. "If you take this one for a moment, I'll get it out."

She was probably harmless, Seth thought. Just someone caught out in the storm. He could use an umbrella. He reached out to take it.

Lightning blasted the village in blinding white. Just for an instant, Seth saw something else in the place of the polite upper-class lady in front of him. A wizened, fanged thing, with burning eyes, slit horizontally like a goat's. Something out of a nightmare.

Too late, he realized his mistake. His friend Kady had told him about this woman. Her name was Miss Benjamin. If Scratch was bad, she was worse.

Miss Benjamin saw the change in his expression, and her face twisted into a snarl. She grabbed at his arm, but he pulled away from her just in time, and her fingernails only clawed his coat. He ran from her, plunging headlong through the rain, and as he went he heard her screeching.

"There's nowhere you can go where we can't find you,

Seth Harper! Give us the Shard!"

Panic seized him. The shock of staring into those demonic eyes had rattled him badly. He fled through the village, his face dripping with rainwater, the storm raging all around him. His pack thumped against his back with the weight of the ornament inside.

He took back alleys, dodging through gardens and along the sides of houses. Occasionally he caught a glimpse of a cat, running alongside him or shadowing him from a rooftop. The cats were still clamouring and wailing all over the village. Seth wasn't sure whose side they were on. Were they telling his enemies where he was, or were they warning him to get away?

At the edge of the village was a patch of allotments where the local gardeners grew their vegetables. The soil had turned to glistening mud under the onslaught of the storm. On the far side, over a narrow country road, were the woods.

Seth ploughed through the allotments, the mud sucking at his trainers, glancing over his shoulder as he went. Away from the streetlights, the dark closed in. He could hardly see where he was going as he made his way between rows of bamboo canes, past manure heaps and sheds.

That was when he heard the cry of the unseen beast. That awful, tortured sound that had disturbed his dad earlier. Except this time, it was much, much closer.

It sounded like it was coming from within the allotments.

He redoubled his efforts, forging through patches of vegetables. The wind and rain and mud all conspired to slow him down. He fought them, pushing on towards the road.

Lightning flashed, illuminating a clutter of sheds and fencing. Something large moved behind one of the sheds. Seth caught only a glimpse of its hindquarters, but that was enough.

Don't let that thing see me.

But it did see him. The beast howled again, a high note that deepened to a horrible cackle. Seth ran, as hard as his legs could manage.

He was almost at the edge of the allotment. The storm pummelled him. The beast shrieked as it broke cover and came chasing across the vegetable patches. Seth's lungs were burning in his chest and his thighs ached, but he knew that if he faltered for even an instant, the thing behind him would rip him to pieces.

He broke out of the allotment and skidded down the grass verge to the winding country road. There were dazzling lights, the roar of an engine, a screech of brakes. He'd landed right in the path of a car.

Seth threw himself aside as the beast came leaping down the verge and into the road. He caught sight of it, just for an instant, as it was lit up by the headlights. Enough to see that it was some kind of grotesque, mutated lion, with massive, crooked fangs and mad yellow eyes. Plates of bone and twisted horns burst out of its dirty fur, and it wore a metal mask over its muzzle that bristled with hooks and nails.

Then the car hit it, and the headlights went out with a smash. The beast was thrown several feet down the road, and rolled to a stop in a heap.

Lightning flickered again, illuminating the road. He could see a young brown-skinned man of eighteen or nineteen at the wheel of the car, wearing a stunned expression. In the back was a girl, half in shadow, mouth agape.

The beast was still for a moment. Then it began to stir.

Seth didn't waste another second. He ran to the car, pulled open the rear passenger door, and threw himself inside, next to the girl. Now that he saw her properly, he was surprised to find he recognized her. Her name was Alicia Lane. She was in the year above him at school.

"Drive!" Seth shouted.

The driver turned around in his seat. "Hey, what're you—"

"*Drive!*"

The driver floored the accelerator, responding to the urgency in Seth's voice. The car slewed around the beast, which was already getting to its feet. As they passed it, lightning flashed again. Alicia was pressed against the side window, and she got a good look at it before they sped off up the road. She turned from the window and stared at Seth, wide-eyed. Seth looked back at her for a moment, then slumped back into the seat and breathed a long sigh of relief.

The Lanes

1

"What *was* that thing?" cried the driver, as they turned off the country road and headed away from Hathern. He was clearly upset by the experience. "Was it a dog? That better not have been a dog!"

The rain was coming down across the windscreen as fast as the wipers could clear it. Streetlamps slid past them, casting bleary daggers of light through the water.

"It wasn't a dog," said Alicia quietly.

"What was it, then? A deer? I didn't even see it! Just came out in front of me!"

Alicia didn't reply. She just stared at Seth, as if he could provide answers. He didn't have any.

He knew her slightly, but only by reputation. They'd never spoken. She wasn't from the village, but from another one nearby. She had a reputation as something of a brainiac, but she was pretty and dressed well and hung around with the in-crowd, so she managed to stay out of the geek pit where the socially disabled lived. In fact, she was surprisingly well-liked for an overachiever, mainly because she kept quiet about her grades and never said a bad word about anyone.

She was half-Jamaican, with a shock of frizzy brown hair framing a coffee-coloured face. Rectangular glasses from some designer Seth had never heard of were perched on her nose. She was wearing a black roll-neck cardigan and jeans tucked into her Uggs.

"You alright, boss?" the driver asked Seth. "You hurt?"

"I'm okay," said Seth. He'd worked out by now that this must be Alicia's older brother Lemar. He'd left school years ago. He'd had a reputation for terrorizing the juniors when Seth had been in year seven, although as far as Seth could remember they'd never crossed paths.

"That thing was chasing you, yeah?"

"Yeah," said Seth wearily.

"So what was it?"

"It was dark," said Seth. "Maybe you're right. Maybe it was a deer."

Alicia gave him a look, but she didn't say anything. She'd seen what it was, and it wasn't any deer.

Lemar was satisfied with his answer, though. As long as it wasn't a dog. You were supposed to report it if you ran over a dog.

"Dad's gonna kill me when he sees the car," he muttered. He was looking for a place to pull over, but they were on a dual carriageway and there was nowhere to stop.

"It was an accident," said Alicia.

"It'd have been an accident if *you* were driving," Lemar said sourly. "Since it's me, it's somehow gonna end up being my fault."

Alicia rolled her eyes and gave up trying to comfort her brother. She turned her attention to Seth. "You're Seth Harper, right? You used to hang out with Kady Blake and that other kid."

"Luke," said Seth.

But Luke was dead. Malice got him.

Kady, though -- she was a different matter. Kady was alive. Kady was still in there somewhere, in the world inside the comic. Kady and Justin.

He heard his own voice, echoing out of the past. *I'll find you. I'll get back somehow and I'll find you guys. I won't forget. I promise.*

But he *had* forgotten. He'd made that promise to Kady, and he'd broken it. He'd forgotten her. He'd forgotten everything.

When you left the world of Malice, you forgot you'd ever been there. That was the way it worked. That was how Tall Jake could keep snatching kids. The ones who made it back didn't remember a thing.

But Kady had given him a post-hypnotic command, using a technique learned from her mother. They knew he'd forget when he escaped Malice, but he was supposed to remember when he came across the trigger that Kady had planted in his mind. That trigger was the Shard.

Except that it had been weeks until he found it. He'd

wasted more than a month drifting around Hathern, unable to remember what he was supposed to be doing there. A month! Who knew what might have happened to Kady and Justin in that time?

Seth took his promises very seriously. He never promised if he couldn't deliver. He believed in a world where someone's word was their bond.

I have to get back to her. I have to find her, and bring her the Shard.

I have to get back to Malice.

He remembered it all now. The grimy corridors of the Clock Tower. The polished chrome of the Menagerie. The Timekeeper, the Conductor, the Chitters. The endless Oubliette, that choked light and hope. Skarla's den.

And his friends. Kady. Justin. A clockwork sabretooth tiger called Tatyana.

The car slowed suddenly as Lemar found a lay-by and pulled the car off the dual carriageway. He yanked the handbrake and got out, then walked around to the front to inspect the damage. Seth heard him swearing.

"Alright, what was it really?" Alicia demanded of him, the moment her brother was out of earshot.

"What was what?" asked Seth.

"You know what!" She was scared, and it was making her snappy. "He might not have seen it, but I did."

There was a fragile look in her eyes. She wanted him to make it make sense. But he couldn't. He could only tell her the truth.

"You ever hear of Malice?"

"Oh, come on. . ." she said.

He shrugged. "You asked."

Seth noticed that the storm seemed to be clearing. The thunder and lightning had stopped, and the rain was easing up. Outside, Lemar was tugging at the front bumper of the car, which had come loose. He was muttering angrily to himself.

"You're seriously telling me that whatever was chasing you came out of a *comic*?" Alicia scoffed.

"You wanna tell me where *else* it came from?" he challenged her. "Seen anything like that on any nature programmes lately? Read about it in *National Geographic*?" She said nothing. "Didn't think so."

"I heard you disappeared," she said at length. "When they found you, you were all messed up. Couldn't remember where you'd been."

"I've been to Malice," Seth said. "I got out, but my friends are still in there." He pulled open his backpack and showed her the ornament nestling inside a cradle of rumpled clothes. "I was supposed to find this and bring it to them. I need to get back to Malice." He zipped up the pack and slumped in his seat, his head lolling back, looking up at the roof of the car. "But I've no idea how."

"Well, how did you do it the first time?" Alicia asked. Her tone made it clear that she was only playing along for now. She hadn't bought into his story yet.

"I said the chant, did the ritual. You know it, right?"

"Course I do. 'Tall Jake, take me aw——'"

He lurched in his seat and clamped a hand over her mouth. She squealed in surprise.

"Don't," he said. "Honestly. Just don't."

He let her go. She edged along the seat, away from him. He was worrying her now.

"I can't do the ritual again," he said. "He's the last person I want to know where I am. Calling him to come get me would be pretty stupid."

She adjusted her glasses and gave an exasperated sigh. "Don't you know how nuts you sound, Seth?"

"It's the truth," he replied. He looked out of the window, at the other cars swooshing past on the dual carriageway. The rain had thinned to a drizzle, and the sky was lightening. The streetlights began to go out as the afternoon sun threatened to break through the clouds. "Look, I don't care if you believe me or not. I'm not trying to convince you of anything. Because if you saw that creature with your own eyes, and you still think there's a rational explanation, then you're an idiot."

Alicia was hurt by his bluntness, but Seth didn't care. He had far more important things to worry about than whether or not this girl thought he was crazy. Lemar threw himself into the driver's seat and slammed the door. It was clear by his expression that the damage to his dad's car was going to be expensive. He swore one more time, then twisted around in his seat to address Seth.

"Listen, is there somewhere I can drop you, boss?"

Seth looked lost. He still didn't have any idea where he could go. He belatedly realized that he didn't have his mobile with him: he'd left it behind when he fled his parents' house. He couldn't even call anyone. Not that there was anyone who could help him.

"Where do you *live*, mate?" Lemar persisted, getting impatient.

"I can't go back there," Seth said quickly.

Lemar threw up his hands. "Then where do you *want* to go? Or you just want to get out right here in this lay-by?"

Alicia leaned forward. "Can you drop us on Narborough Road?" she asked suddenly.

He frowned. "I thought I was taking you to Sally's place to study?"

"Change of plan," she said.

"Dad'll roast you if he finds out."

"Only if you tell him. And I'll make sure to tell him there was no way you could have avoided that deer that jumped into the road. You know he won't believe you otherwise."

"Yeah, yeah. Little Alicia, good as gold." He shrugged. "Whatever. Narborough Road it is."

He dropped the handbrake and pulled out of the lay-by and back on to the dual carriageway. He turned on the radio and began slapping his hands on the steering wheel in time to the beats.

"What's on Narborough Road?" Seth asked Alicia, keeping his voice low.

"A friend of mine," she said. "He's obsessed with Malice.

If anyone knows anything about it, he does. Maybe he can help you."

"I thought you didn't believe me," he said.

"I don't," she replied. Then she gave him a pointed glare. "But I'm not an idiot, either."

Seth sat back in his seat and allowed himself to relax. He had a destination, then. That was good. He would see where this new development led. For this brief time at least, he was safe from those who hunted him.

He looked out of the window. The rain had stopped entirely, and the sun had emerged, shining on the wet tarmac. The leaves of the trees on the roadside glistened.

The storm had passed for now, but Seth was still uneasy. Because his friends were still in Malice somewhere.

Kady. Justin.

Where are you now?

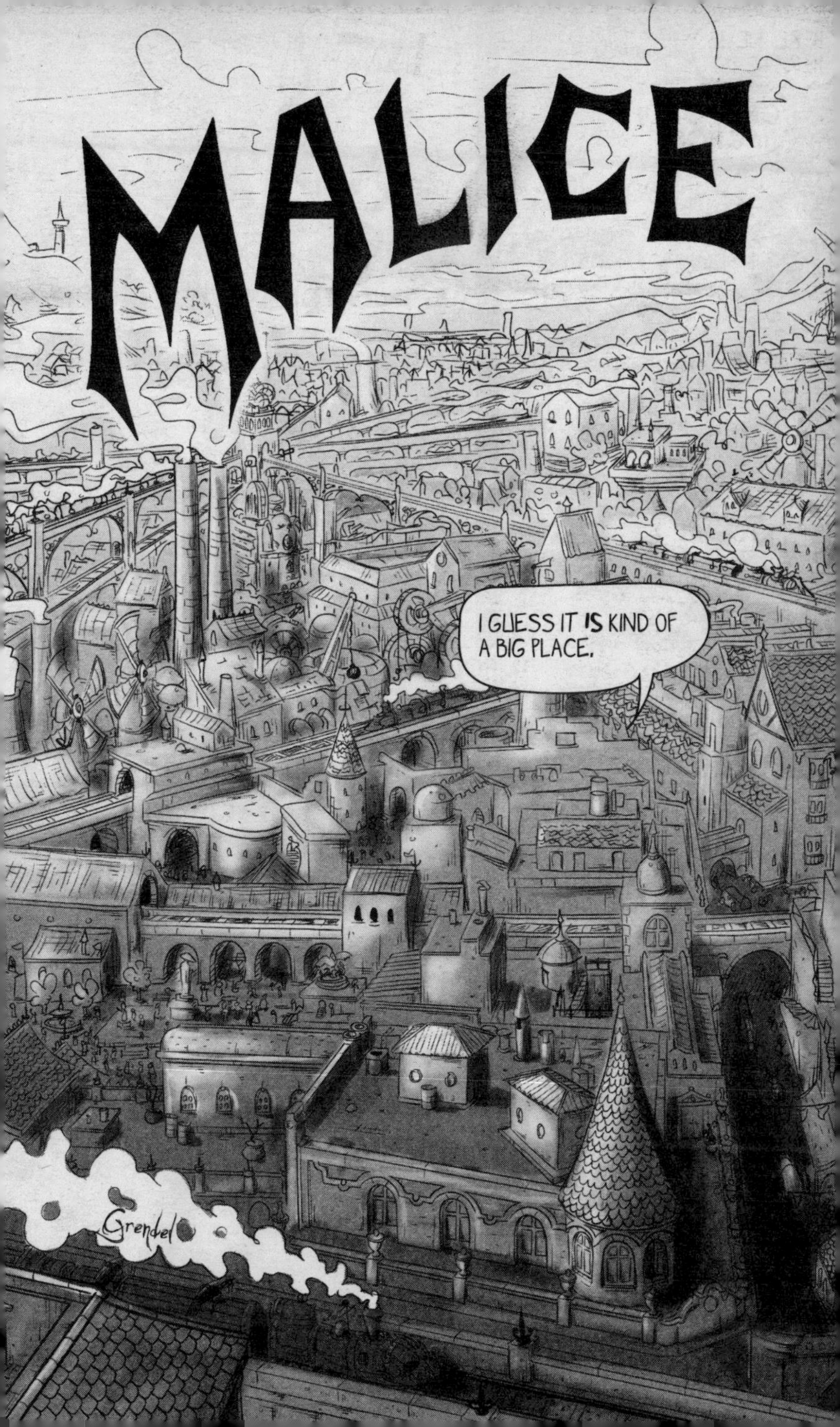
MALICE
I GUESS IT IS KIND OF A BIG PLACE.
Grendel

Scab's Row to Cog Park Station

1

"Someone want to explain to me what's going on?" Justin demanded impatiently.

"Hell if I know," Kady said. She was just as shocked as Justin to find herself being hugged by a stranger with a Boston accent. She'd been expecting a guarded and suspicious meeting, with lots of questions being asked of her. After all, this was a member of Havoc, the underground organization that Kady and Justin wanted to join. Havoc had devoted themselves to bringing down Tall Jake, and their guerilla tactics and acts of sabotage had made them a painful thorn in the tyrant's side. They were a beacon of hope for all those children who had been snatched from their homes by Tall Jake, and who were now lost in the strange world he ruled over.

She'd expected someone a bit more impressive, to be honest.

The kid let her go and gave her an uncertain grin. He

looked like he was of Chinese descent, with an open, honest face that wore a smile easily.

"What, you forgot me already?" he said. "It's only been a year! Well, maybe a little over, but who's counting?" He slapped her on the shoulder.

"Ow," she said, rubbing the spot where he'd hit her.

His grin faded and his face became harder as he realized she wasn't joking. "Scotty!" he said. "Scotty Chen!"

Kady made a face to indicate that the name meant nothing to her. "Did I know you from before or something?"

"What is *up* with you?" he asked, getting angry now. "Scotty Chen! You know!"

Justin rolled his eyes. "Can I butt in here? Kady, this is gonna go on for ever unless you tell him you've lost your memory."

"She *what*?" Scotty cried.

Kady glanced around the Pin and Shackles. They were drawing attention from the patrons. "Okay, let's lower our voices and sit, huh?" she said. "Before we get the Regulators coming down on us."

They did as she suggested. Tatyana positioned herself next to the booth, erect, guarding them.

"The Regulators don't come round here," said Scotty. "That's why I picked this place."

"Well, good," said Justin. "But all the same, we're kind of looking to keep a low profile, know what I mean?"

"Yeah, sure," said Scotty. "Sorry. I just got excited." He looked at Kady. "You really don't remember me?"

"I really don't," she said with a shrug. "Sorry."

It was an unpleasant sensation, to come face to face with somebody she'd obviously met before and not remember him. She tried as hard as she could, but her brain insisted she'd never seen him. Yet she knew that there was a gap of four months in her life, the summer of last year, when she'd gone missing from her home. She had no recollection of that time, but she'd guessed what had happened. She'd been inside Malice, and somehow got out. This was her second time inside the world of the comic. She still had no idea what she had done the first time around, but she figured the boy in front of her did.

"So were we friends or something?" Kady asked Scotty.

"Yeah," he said dismally. "We were really good friends. I can't believe you don't remember."

"Hey, don't feel bad, mate," Justin said. "It happens to everyone. When you leave Malice, your mind gets wiped. You don't remember a thing."

Scotty's eyes went wide. "Is that true?" he asked Kady.

"It's true. Happens to everybody. Why do you think nobody's tried to close down Malice from the outside? It's 'cause all the kids that escape don't remember where they've been."

She thought of Seth. Seth, somewhere on the outside. Had her post-hypnotic command been strong enough to bring his memories back? Or had he forgotten her completely?

No. She wouldn't believe that. Seth had promised

to come back, and he never broke a promise, no matter what.

Scotty was chewing over the new information. "That explains a lot," he said. "No wonder nobody ever came back." He looked at them helplessly. "We never knew."

"Course not," said Justin. "Who'd tell you? That's how Malice works. That's how it keeps its secrets." He gave a dry half-smile. "You gotta admit, it's clever."

"*Clever?*" Scotty exclaimed.

"Justin is just crazy enough to *like* living in Malice," Kady explained, with a patient glance at her companion.

"It's better than Kilburn," Justin said. "At least my dad ain't here." He sat back and swept out an arm to indicate the collection of bizarre folk who inhabited the tavern. "And look at the locals. They're interesting, you gotta give 'em that."

Kady couldn't argue. *Interesting* didn't begin to cover it. Ever since they'd arrived in the City, Malice's great metropolis, they'd come across new people every day. Some were human, or nearly so; others were not even close. There were people with scales and tails, with multiple eyes or faces like horses. There were people who walked on all fours, and muscly ogres with mechanical arms. There were people who disappeared in an explosion of leaves when you talked to them, and others that changed shape as fast as switching a TV channel.

Strangest of all was how quickly Kady had become used to it. Not long ago, she would have said that Malice wasn't real. It was just a stupid comic book, another dumb rumour for bored kids to spread around the playground at school. But here she was, sitting in a booth in a rickety tavern in a seedy part of the City. She could smell cigar smoke and roasting meat in the air. She could hear the jabber of the bizarre folk that filled the tables and lounged at the bar. She could feel the muggy warmth of sweaty bodies and the fires from the kitchens. She was wearing clothes that would have her laughed off the street back in the States. Here, they didn't seem odd at all.

She was living inside a comic book. And it was every bit as real as the world she'd come from.

Justin leaned his elbows on the table. "Before we get into the reunion," he said to Scotty, "can you take us to Havoc or what?"

"Sure I can!" said Scotty, brightly. He looked at Kady. "We'll be real glad to have you back."

"Back?" asked Kady. "You mean I was part of Havoc before?"

Scotty made a stupid-face. "*Duh*. You were the leader."

Kady was stunned. Justin just stared at her, his jaw on the floor.

Scotty got to his feet, suddenly businesslike. "I'll explain on the way to the hideout. Let's get going. I think, under the circumstances, we can skip the new recruit assessment." He stepped nervously around Tatyana. "Nice tiger, by the way."

"Hey," said Kady. "You haven't had some kid named

Seth turn up recently, have you? Maybe he was asking about me?"

Scotty looked blank. "Sorry. No one with that name at Havoc."

Kady looked sad for a moment, then forced a smile on to her face. "Just wondering," she said.

2

It had been a long month since they said goodbye to Seth in Skarla's den.

Kady hadn't been there to see Seth walk through the doorway that had taken him back to the real world. She'd been too upset to watch him leave. When he'd gone, Justin came to fetch her. Skarla, the strange plant-lady who lived at the bottom of the dreadful dungeon known as the Oubliette, had led them through a series of tunnels back to the surface which avoided the traps and monsters they'd faced on the way down. Once out of the Oubliette, she'd wished them good luck, pointed them in the direction of the City and retreated back to her den.

They'd found themselves in the countryside, beneath a pale, cloudy sky. The hills and scattered woods had a sad, empty kind of beauty to them. After the horrors they'd experienced in the Oubliette, Kady thought it all very peaceful.

They set off towards the towers of the city that they could see in the distance. On the way they came to a village, where strangers took them in, gave them food and urged them not to travel at night. So they slept in the barn that the strangers offered them, and in the morning they set off again. The kindness of the villagers encouraged Kady. Maybe Malice wasn't all horror and misery, after all.

Justin found them jobs by the end of their first day in the City. He'd lived his whole life in inner London, and he knew how to deal with a metropolis. He walked into a workshop where they fixed machinery, and with a bit of fast talking he managed to impress the owner. Justin had skills that the natives of Malice didn't. He'd grown up with a mechanic for a father, working on cars and motorbikes, and he'd picked up a thing or two that amazed the men in the workshop, who had no experience of that kind of technology.

The owner was a man called Shaddly Bletch, who took Justin as an apprentice on the spot. They shook hands on it. Justin shook a little too hard and Bletch's arm came off. He laughed and told his horrified new apprentice not to worry. He'd have a new one in a couple of days.

Shaddly Bletch was a kind fellow, but an unusual sort. He was permanently wrapped in rags and bandages, and always looked a mess because bits and pieces of him kept falling off and regrowing – a nose, an ear, a hand. *Regenerative leprosy*, he called it. Apparently, it was quite rare. Kady was thankful for that.

Bletch also allowed Kady to stay, but she had to work for

food and board as a dogsbody. She had to take orders, carry messages and make lunch for the workers, among other things. Kady had never had a job before, but she found she quite liked it. The workers were friendly, and she got to explore the city while out running errands. She would chat with Nibscuttle, the baker, who she visited every morning to pick up rolls for the workers' lunches. Nibscuttle had six legs and two heads. She liked the left head more; the other one complained a lot.

But for all that she'd come to enjoy this place, she missed home. She missed her family and her cat Marlowe. She missed spending hours on Facebook or playing CounterStrike. She even missed school, sort of. It was always funny listening to the girls backstabbing each other in chemistry class. It was *normal*. And there wasn't a great deal of *normal* in Malice.

With food in their bellies, a roof over their heads and money in their pockets, they used their free time searching for Havoc. It was the only way Seth would be able find them again, if he made it back to Malice. They'd told him they would try to seek out Havoc. That meant he would do the same.

They hung out in cafés. They listened to gossip and rumours. They asked questions. It took them a long time, but finally someone approached them. Someone who'd heard they were asking questions about Havoc. Someone who could arrange a meeting.

That was how they met Scotty.

Kady was impatient to learn more about Havoc, but Scotty said it wasn't safe to talk on the street. "Too many eyes and ears," he said. Justin raised an eyebrow as a creature with eight eyes and two sets of massive, batlike ears shuffled past.

"He's not wrong," Justin quipped, proud of his comic timing. The creature stopped and glared at him, and he hurried on.

They headed out of Scab's Row towards Cog Park station. With Tatyana guarding them, they could walk in safety through the slums. Soon the streets became cleaner and wider, and the population was better-dressed. The buildings didn't lean any more. Shop windows were full of gadgets and displays of coloured cakes. Carriages passed them often, and they saw a clockwork automobile that clicked and rattled as it made its way up the street.

Following Scotty through the City, they passed the Fire Gardens, with their rows of beautiful dragonplants that burst into flame each dawn. In the distance, on the hillside, was Maze Park, where the were-hounds lived. Behind it was Foggen Rise, where you could listen to ghosts play their music when the moon was right.

Cog Park station stood on four stout pillars that lifted it above the rooftops. It was a small, suburban stop on the aerial railway that ran all over the City. Spiral stairs led up to a simple platform inside an arched shell of iron and brass. A few other people (Kady used the term loosely) waited on the platform with them.

Scotty gave them both a black ticket. "These are good for one journey to any station in Malice," he said.

"We've been here a while," said Justin. "We know how it works. Black for a journey within Malice, white for a journey anywhere. Even back home."

"Where did you get these from?" Kady asked, taking her ticket.

"I bought them," said Scotty, with a shrug. "Black tickets are easy to get. It's white tickets that are hard."

"Didn't know you could just *buy* them," Kady said.

"I thought you'd been here a while?" Scotty asked, with a triumphant look at Justin. Justin mumbled something unpleasant under his breath.

"What about Tatyana?" Kady asked, tickling under her chin. Tatyana purred like a tractor.

"She's just a machine. She doesn't need one."

Tatyana snarled, making Scotty jump. Kady folded her arms. "Tatyana is *not* 'just' a machine," she said primly.

Scotty held out his hands to placate the clockwork sabretooth. "Sorry. My bad. I meant, she doesn't need a ticket because she's not ... because she doesn't count as being alive. Not to whoever makes those decisions, anyway."

"She's luggage." Justin grinned.

"Exactly!" said Scotty, snapping his fingers.

"Can't you be even a *little* sensitive?" Kady was on her

knees next to Tatyana, stroking her neck soothingly. Tatyana growled. "Don't listen to them," Kady told her. "Boys are all dummies."

"What are you complaining about? She gets a free ride, doesn't she?" said Justin.

The train pulled into the station a few minutes later. It was a nightmare of steel and spikes and steam, with gun turrets on either side and an angled front like a snowplough. The sight gave Kady a chill. The last time she'd ridden one of Malice's trains, it had been taking her to the Oubliette. She never wanted to think of that place again.

"All aboard!" said Justin, who was feeling perky after scoring a point on Tatyana.

They clambered into one of the carriages. It had round portholes and coiled-metal seats. Two other passengers got on with them, and moved to the end of the carriage. There was nobody else.

The doors sealed shut with a hiss and the train started to move. Justin looked around the carriage as the others sat down.

"Now where's that creepy conductor? I bet he's around here somewh*aaAAAH*!" He yelled in fright as he turned and found himself face to face with the Conductor, who had apparently materialized out of thin air. The Conductor's empty eyes were black pits of shadow in his blank white mask.

"TICKETS, PLEASE."

IRC

1

It was only twenty minutes' drive up the motorway from Hathern to Leicester. Sitting in the back of the car, with Lemar driving and Alicia silent next to him, Seth felt peaceful. Things made sense at last. For a month he'd been confused, bored and listless, but now he knew what he had to do. He was going back to Malice.

They came off the motorway and buildings began to rise up around them. They were on Narborough Road, heading into the city. It was a cold and cloudy day, but there was no sign of the storm that had troubled Hathern. The pavements weren't even wet.

Seth stared out of the window at the rows of houses passing by. He didn't like cities. All that tired Victorian brickwork and peeling paint. All those quietly rotting window frames and shabby gauze curtains. The crisp packets skipping along the gutters, the narrow, suspicious glances from people on the street, the graffiti hidden in every corner like the remains of luminous spiderwebs. Cities made him feel shut in and trapped.

Lemar pulled up at the place Alicia told him to, and the two passengers got out.

"You gonna be alright?" Lemar asked Alicia, casting a threatening look at Seth. He knew Seth was behind his sister's sudden change of plans, and he didn't like not knowing why. "Sure you don't wanna go to Sally's?"

"I'm fine," she said. "Tell Dad I'll call him later."

"Okay," he said. "I'll see you, yeah? You'd better back me up when Dad asks what happened to his car."

"I will."

Lemar gave Seth one last glare and drove away. Alicia sighed and gave Seth an apologetic smile. "He's very protective."

"So I see."

"Come on." She led him up a side street and then took him along a cramped, dark brick alley that ran between two terraced houses. They went through a wooden gate into a dusty back yard. Alicia knocked on a door that was made of two big panes of rippled glass set in a plastic frame.

"This is one of those back-door-is-the-front-door houses," Alicia explained. "I used to come over and play when I was younger. We were friends in primary school."

"What about now?"

"I still see him at school a bit. He's in my art class. That's why I know he's obsessed with Malice. He's always talking about it."

"I didn't know you did art," said Seth. "I thought you were, y'know, a maths and science type."

She gave him a sharp look, in case he was making fun of her. When she saw that it was an honest observation, she adjusted her designer glasses and said: "I am. And that's *all* I'd be if Mum and Dad had their way. It's all 'doctor' this and 'professor' that with them. But I do art because I want to be an illustrator. Not that it matters to them what I want."

A light came on behind the door, and she shushed him, even though she was the one talking. It was opened by a dumpy, tatty-looking woman with brown hair in a lank ponytail.

"Alright, Alicia?" she said. "Haven't seen you in a long while."

"Hi, Mrs Gormley. Is Philip in, please?" Alicia asked politely. She was very well-spoken, Seth had noticed. It was hard to believe she and her older brother were related.

"He's always in," Mrs Gormley replied. She stepped aside to let them past. "Up the stairs. Follow the machine guns."

Alicia thanked her and went inside. Seth trailed after. As he passed over the threshold, he slowed suddenly and frowned.

"What's wrong?" Alicia asked.

He shook his head. "Nothing," he said. How could he explain the strange feeling of dread that had settled on him the moment he set foot inside the house?

He tried to tell himself it was just his imagination, but he didn't *have* much of an imagination. Besides, the feeling was too strong for that. It was as if an icy blanket had been laid on his shoulders.

I want to get out of here, he thought. But he couldn't do that. Alicia had said that Philip could help him, and he needed all the help he could get right now. If this kid Philip knew all about Malice, then Seth had to see him.

They went through the kitchen into a small hallway and up a cramped set of stairs to a darkened landing. They could hear machine guns now, as Philip's mother had promised. There were screams and explosions coming from a bedroom at the end. The white light of a computer monitor shone beneath the door.

Alicia knocked. The machine guns stopped as the game was paused.

"What is it, Mum?" came the irritated reply.

"Philip?" she called. "It's Alicia."

"Who?"

She glanced at Seth and looked embarrassed. "Alicia Lane," she said.

Seth heard the creak of a chair and the sound of footsteps and huffing. Then a bolt was drawn back and the door opened.

Philip Gormley filled the doorway, lit only by the sharp glow from the screen behind him. He was fat (Seth couldn't think of any nicer way to say it, because he was *really* fat) and he wore an outsize Ramones T-shirt. A mop of scruffy blond hair fell across his brow. He brushed it back and looked at them uncertainly, puzzled at having his house invaded.

"Hello?" he said.

"Seth, this is Philip," said Alicia. "Philip, Seth."

They greeted each other warily. "I think I've seen you at school," Philip said.

"I'm in the year below you."

"Right."

Before the moment could get any more awkward, Alicia began to explain. "We were wondering if we could ask you a favour?" she said. "You know how you're always talking about Malice in art class?"

Something skittered across the attic, tiny clawed feet tapping on the ceiling. Seth looked up, alarmed. He felt the icy blanket beginning to soak into his bones. Something was very wrong in this house.

"It's just a mouse," Philip said, noticing his reaction. He looked at Alicia. "What about Malice? I don't have a copy, if that's what you're after."

"You said there was a forum or something that you sometimes posted on. Where people swap hints and rumours about Malice."

"Not a forum," he corrected her. "It's an IRC channel." He saw Seth's blank look and elaborated for his benefit. "Internet Relay Chat. It's like Instant Messenger but dozens of people can talk at the same time."

"Oh, okay," said Seth, still not sure where this was

going. "I don't know much about computers," he added, apologetically.

"Do you think you could show us the forum . . . uhh . . . the *channel*?" Alicia asked.

Philip frowned. "Look, what's this about?"

Seth stepped in. "Alicia says you're interested in Malice. That right?" Philip nodded. "Well, I've been there."

Philip snorted in disbelief. "Sure you have."

"I'm serious."

"Sure you are."

"I need to get back there."

"Sure you do."

Alicia looked exasperated. "Philip! I'm just asking you if you wouldn't mind showing us this IRC channel you're always talking about."

Philip sighed and shambled over to his computer. He lowered himself into a well-worn office chair. "Come in, then," he said. "Lock the door. Mum's always barging in."

It was a big room, and every surface was covered in mess. A dozen dirty mugs stood in various places. Plates were covered in biscuit crumbs. Comics lay on the floor. The bedsheets were rumpled and tangled, and the curtains were drawn to close out the last of the afternoon light. The air in here was stale and smelled unhealthy, but Philip didn't seem to notice.

"You're gonna have to perch on the bed," Philip said, twisting his monitor so they could see it. Alicia locked the door behind them and they made space on the bed to sit.

Seth had to move a Peperami wrapper that was occupying his spot.

Philip began booting up programs and clicking through menus. "I better warn you, we might not find it. The channel opens and closes in different places, moves about, comes and goes. It's weird. Doesn't happen on any other channel." He clicked through a few more menus and then grinned. "It's your lucky day. There it is."

2

* Now talking in #Grendel
* Topic is "Only Malice talk here. Type /**umode-mH** for private chat. Ops, deop when you leave. No AOLers, we hate you guys."
* Set by angel_buster on Sun Oct 12 16:11:56
* jester_003 (tongkay@121.120.7.aM475=) Quit (Ping Timeout)
<angel_buster> sure y not?
<Griff> I mean, he's gotta have some hidden away
<Griff> It's a comic shop
<angel_buster> you'd think
* jester_003 (tongkay@121.120.7.aM475=) has joined #Grendel
<jester_003> i swear guys, my router borks like all the time on this chan
<jester_003> gremlins
<angel_buster> i bet it doesn't work like that tho

<angel_buster> its not like mail ordering a copy of the Hulk
<saffron> gremlins
<ka_787> gremlins
<Griff> Well, someone's gotta have one
<saffron> don't feed your router after midnight
<ka_787> or get it wet
<jester_003> well duh
* jester_003 rolls his eyes
* tintype (benaQi@117.47.81.vT256=) has joined #Grendel
<tintype> waaaaaaasssssssuuuuuuuuuuupppp????
<saffron> shhhhhuuuuuuuuuuuttttttuuuuuuppppp
<tintype> downer :(
<saffron> hugs!!!

Seth and Alicia exchanged a glance.

"Do you *understand* any of that?" Alicia asked Philip.

Philip laughed. "It's a bit confusing at first, I suppose. You've gotta learn to keep your eye on who's saying what. There's usually two or three conversations going on at once. And ignore all that computer gibberish, it's for techies." He slapped the desk. "So here it is. The famous IRC channel. Impressed? Didn't think so."

"Can you ask them questions?" Seth asked.

"Course I can. What do you want to know?"

"I want to know how to get to Malice."

"Pffft. That's easy."

"No, I mean without doing the ritual."

Philip thought about that for a moment. "I heard you can get there if you get yourself a special ticket. I mean, they say the kids in the comic have to find these tickets that are scattered around Malice to escape. Stands to reason they'd work both ways."

The rumours were right. Kady had done exactly that, when she followed Seth into Malice. But Seth didn't have any idea where to get one. "Can you ask them where I can find a ticket?"

Philip studied him closely with his dark eyes. "You don't really buy all this stuff, do you?"

"Don't you?" Seth asked. "I mean, you seem to know a lot about it."

"Well, yeah, but y'know . . . it's interesting. I'm *into* it and stuff. I'd like to get my hands on a copy of the comic to see what all the fuss is about. But you're saying you've *been* there?" He waved it away.

Seth didn't chase the matter. It was strange how people could believe in something so strongly and yet they didn't *really* believe. They couldn't take that last step. They didn't want it to actually happen. You could spend your whole life believing in fairies, but if you *saw* one, you'd check in to therapy. If Jesus made a second appearance he'd be mocked and hated for claiming to be the son of God.

Philip had gone back to the keyboard. "My nick is Breaker, in case you're wondering."

"Nick?"

"Nickname," Philip sighed. "Try to keep up, eh?"

<breaker> alright all

<jester_003> sup breaker

<saffron> hey hey

<breaker> got a noob here says hes been to Malice and
come back

<saffron> ORLY?

* Griff scratches his chin

<ka_787> is he telling the truth?

<Griff> Of course he's not, you moron

<ka_787> ok ok, calm down

* jester_003 (tongkay@121.120.7.aM475=) Quit (Ping
Timeout)

<breaker> he wants to know how to get back again

<breaker> without saying the chant

* jester_003 (tongkay@121.120.7.aM475=) has joined
#Grendel

* jester aims a hammer at his router

<mim> whos the noob?

<mim> ASL noob

<tintype> oh god you woke up mim

<tintype> thought she'd fallen asleep

<mim> I never sleep

<breaker> ANY SUGGESTIONS KTHX?

<saffron> mememe

* Griff calls for silence

<mim> ASL noob?

<tintype> for gods sake will someone cut off her fingers?

<saffron> kid I know told me a story

<saffron> theres an abandoned factory near where he lives

<saffron> all kind of spooky stuff goes on there

<saffron> some older kid went there with his g/f one night

<saffron> came back scared out of his wits face all scratched up

<saffron> g/f never came back

<saffron> police and everything

<saffron> he said there were like all these creepy people down there

<saffron> says they took his g/f

<saffron> they didn't find anything in the factory so they arrested him

<saffron> in his pocket they found a ticket

<saffron> WHITE ticket

<saffron> he said he found it in the factory

* jester_003 (tongkay@121.120.7.aM475=) Quit (Excess Flood)

<ka_787> brrr

<Griff> So this was a "friend of a friend," right?

* jester_003 (tongkay@121.120.7.aM475=) has joined #Grendel

<jester_003> aaaaaaaargh

<saffron> just saying

<saffron> doesn't it seem like there's more and more stuff like this happening lately?

<angel_buster> you mean like the old trainyard in Lewisham?

<saffron> yeh

<tintype> they reckon two kids got killed there

<mim> hey noob, what's your name?

<tintype> they said it looked like dogs had got them

<tintype> but the autopsy said the bites weren't dogs

<tintype> more like human bites

* ka_787 is scared

<mim> NOOBY NOOBY NOOBY

<saffron> breaker, your friend should check it out

Philip sat back into his office chair and swivelled to face Seth and Alicia. "They're always talking about stuff like this," he said. "You know how people say that Tall Jake is behind these kids that are disappearing all over the place? Some of these guys jump on every little unexplained thing and say it's about Malice."

"They're probably just urban legends," said Alicia. "Like the one about the scary guy who keeps calling this girl when she's alone in the house. They trace the call, and it turns out to be coming—"

"—*from inside the house!!!*" Philip cried in a fake wail of terror. "Yeah, like that."

"What does 'noob' mean?" asked Seth, reading the

conversation on the screen. "Why's everyone calling me that?"

"It means newbie. New kid," Alicia said.

"Who's that Mim person?" Seth asked, pointing. "Does she want to talk to me or something?"

Philip groaned. "Mim. She's always around, being annoying. She keeps trying to make friends with people, trying to get them to meet up with her in real life so they can swap notes on Malice. She's pretty desperate. Nobody likes her much."

"Can you ask where that factory is?" Seth prompted.

<breaker> saff where's the factory?

<Griff> It's MADE UP! Doesn't anyone get it? Only the COMIC is real. The rest of it is all hype!

<saffron> shut it griff, go back to FunChat

<saffron> Mackenzie Street in Birmingham

<Griff> You're all falling for the hype, losers.

* angel_buster sets mode +b Griff*!*@*.*

* Griff has been kicked by angel_buster (smite all doubters!!!)

<angel_buster> bored of him

* ka_787 claps

<mim> noob I bet I can guess your name

<saffron> Go at night tho

<saffron> or don't

<saffron> that's when he saw the creepy people

<ka_787> yes! yes! guess the name

<ka_787> breaker you have to tell us if we're right
<ka_787> I bet it's . . . Paul!
<mim> I bet it's Seth Harper

Seth felt an unpleasant jolt at seeing his name on the screen. A mouse ran across the attic. Alicia was staring at him. Philip turned in his chair.

"*Is* that your name?" he asked. Seth nodded.

"Can she *see* us or something?" Alicia asked. "Have you got a webcam running?"

"I don't have a webcam," Philip said.

Alicia leaned closer to the screen. The lines of text were reflected in the lenses of her glasses. "Then how does she know?"

Philip typed something. At the last moment, Seth lunged forward to stop him. Suddenly he was struck with an awful certainty. Telling this Mim person who he was would be a very bad idea. "Don't!" he cried; but Philip had already hit RETURN.

<breaker> you must be psychic
<ka_787> omg
<ka_787> mim how you know that?
<mim> hello Seth
<mim> I have a message for you
<ka_787> wait how you know who it was?
* ka_787 (moomin@219.64.126.TR69=) Quit (Excess Flood)

```
* saffron (saffypoo@121.97.202.Fr384=) Quit (Excess
    Flood)
* jester_003 (tongkay@121.120.7.aM475=) Quit (Excess
    Flood)
* angel_buster (angelo008@125.163.11.DM554=) Quit
    (Excess Flood)
* tintype (optimustwine@219.159.67.Rg523=) Quit
    (Excess Flood)
<mim> there's nowhere you can run Seth
<mim> you have something that belongs to us
<mim> we're going to kill anyone that helps you
<mim> we're going find you
<mim> and then we're going to
<mim> RIP
<mim> OUT
<mim> YOUR
<mim> EYES
* Disconnected
```

Seth stared at the screen. He couldn't breathe. The mouse in the attic had been joined by several friends (although Seth thought they sounded more like rats than mice). He was so cold that his legs were trembling.

"I've got to go," he said.

"Hey, wait, does she *know* you or something?" Philip asked, aghast. "She's never done anything like that befo—"

"I've got to go!" Seth said again, getting to his feet. He

felt like the walls and ceiling were pressing in on him. Alicia got up too, a worried expression on her face.

"What's up with you? She's just some weirdo."

"I'd stay off that channel if I were you," said Seth. "And I'd stay away from her."

"Pfft. As if I'm scared of Mim," he said scornfully.

"You should be," Seth replied.

"Right. Whatever."

Seth got up and unlocked the door. Alicia said a quick goodbye to Philip and followed him. In the doorway, Seth stopped and looked back at Philip.

"Why don't you believe?" he asked.

"'Cause I did the ritual, and I said the chant, and nothing happened," Philip replied. There was a note of bitterness in his voice. He felt cheated. "It took me weeks to work up to it. After all that, it just turned out to be some stupid story."

There was a skittering noise from overhead. Seth looked up, his heart sinking.

"Was that when you first heard the rats in the attic?"

"Mice," Philip corrected. He frowned. "I don't know. It was around that time. Why?"

Seth shook his head. "I have to go."

With that, he hurried away. There was nothing he could say to Philip that would make any difference. He knew now what was wrong in this house. Philip had called on Tall Jake. He hadn't come yet, but he'd been called. Maybe he'd never come. Maybe it would be ten years from now. But once you said the chant, you were under Tall Jake's shadow until he chose to take you. That kid wouldn't last an hour in Malice.

Philip was doomed. He just didn't know it.

The moment Seth was out of the house, he felt a weight lift from him. He didn't stop until he was some way up the street. He sat on a low garden wall and took a few breaths.

"What's wrong?" Alicia asked. "Seth, what is it?"

"Couldn't you feel it? Couldn't you feel . . . the *evil* in that house?"

Alicia looked helpless. "I didn't feel anything."

"He called on Tall Jake. I could *sense* it hanging over that house. One night, when he's alone, he's just gonna disappear. And there's nothing anyone can do about it." Now he'd got over being scared, Seth was beginning to get angry. It was all so unfair.

Alicia was horrified. "You mean there's no way to take it back? After you've called on Tall Jake?"

Seth shook his head. "That's why we've got to stop him."

Alicia sat next to him on the garden wall. Her head was hung, her frizzy curls falling over her face. It was dark now, and the streetlights tinted everything in yellow.

A middle-aged couple walked up the street. The woman stared at them with a sour expression as she passed. She suspected they were somehow up to no good. Kids their age always were.

Seth couldn't help remembering that moment when he'd met Miss Benjamin, when that flash of lightning had revealed the demon behind the mask. What if there were more of her kind, watching him right now? How would he ever know, until it was too late?

"Promise me you're not making this up," said Alicia quietly.

"Sorry?" Seth didn't understand her at first.

"Promise me you're not lying. That you really went to Malice. That Tall Jake is real."

There was something desperate in her voice that puzzled him. "I promise," he said. "I know it sounds crazy, but it's true. Malice is real."

She took a shuddering breath and sat up. She bunched her hair back and slipped a hairband over it to keep it in place.

"We've still got time to get to Birmingham and back tonight."

It took Seth a moment to work out what she was saying. "You want to go check out the factory?"

"We have to, don't you think?"

Seth shook his head. "*I* do. Not you," he said firmly. "You've already done enough. They said they'd kill anyone who helps me. I can't put you in any more danger."

She got off the wall. "I called on Tall Jake," she said.

Seth closed his eyes in despair.

"I just did it for a dare. It was a bit of fun, that's all. But I don't suppose that matters."

"It doesn't."

Alicia looked down the street. She was scared, and

trying to hold it together. Seth knew that her bravery was fragile. She didn't want to get involved in this. She wanted to turn her back and go home and forget all about it.

But she couldn't. Because she'd seen the monster that chased him. She'd read those terrible threats on the screen. She believed him now, and Seth knew what that meant. It meant she would spend every night of the rest of her life afraid that Tall Jake was coming to get her.

That, or she could try to do something about it.

"You sure?" Seth asked.

"Of course I'm not sure!" she said. "So come on, before I change my mind. Birmingham's only an hour on the train."

Seth slid off the wall and adjusted his backpack. The Shard felt heavy now.

"Let's go," he said.

Talon Fells

1

The train took Kady, Justin, Scotty and Tatyana out of the City. Kady watched through the portholes of the carriage as the metropolis fell away behind them, to be replaced by a grand, empty wilderness of rocky hills and valleys. The train ran on an elevated track, supported by pillars. The weak light of the Malice sun gave the scenery a sombre tint, but the view from so high up was breathtaking. She marvelled at it for a short while, before the rocking of the train sent her to sleep.

Some time later, the train pulled into a stop. Scotty signalled that it was time to get off. It was an elevated platform, like the one they'd embarked from. The metal sign on one of the pillars said:

They stepped on to the platform, along with several other passengers. Too late, they spotted two Regulators waiting by the exit.

Justin swore under his breath. Kady froze. She wondered whether they should jump back on the train before the doors closed. Justin grabbed her arm and urged her forward.

"Keep walking," he said. "They'll chase us if we run."

They set off down the platform towards the stairs that led down to ground level. The Regulators were standing on either side of the exit. They were scrawny and dressed in battered black uniforms, and their faces were half-covered by grimy visors. They carried gas-powered spear guns, which fired four-inch slivers of metal like bullets.

"Are we in trouble?" Scotty asked. "Are you wanted or something?"

"Not sure," said Justin. "Let's just say we've been staying out of their way just in case."

There was no way to avoid them, and nowhere to run to. The train doors closed and it moved off with a hiss of steam. They kept walking, closer and closer to the stairs.

Now they were close enough to see the tight white skin of the Regulators' faces. Their jaws and mouths were visible beneath the visors of their helmets. They looked bloodless and dried up, lips thin and cheeks hollow.

Don't let them be waiting here for us, Kady prayed.

She kept her eyes fixed on the exit. She was doing her best not to seem nervous or suspicious, but she found that it made her worse. Her stomach was tied in knots. She could smell them, even at this distance: a dusty, earthy smell, like mould and graves. And beneath that, a vinegar scent, sour and sharp.

One of the Regulators hissed through his teeth. It came stalking up the platform towards them, its companion close behind.

Kady's heart sank. The game was up. So close to reaching Havoc, and they'd been caught. She squeezed her eyes shut.

When she opened them again, the Regulators had passed by. Ahead of them, the exit was clear. A set of spiral stairs lay beyond.

She blinked in surprise, and looked over her shoulder. The Regulators were heading towards a small, elderly passenger who had got off further down the carriage. He had reddish, wrinkly skin and wore goggles and a smock.

"Don't stop," Scotty muttered. "Don't look."

But Kady couldn't help it. The elderly man began to back away as he saw the Regulators were coming for him. They bore down on their victim, seized him, and threw him to the ground.

"I haven't done anything!" he protested, as he scrambled away from them. "What is this about? I haven't done anything!"

The Regulators weren't interested. They raised their guns. The man gaped in terror.

"Wait! This is about my book, isn't it? I'll write a

retraction! I'll tell everyone I was wrong to say those things about Tall Jake!"

Kady turned away, unable to watch. Behind her, the man's begging was cut short by the hissing clatter of spear guns.

Kady felt sick.

That could have been me.

The stairs were made of metal, and wound around one of the pillars that supported Talon Fells station. Tatyana went down first, padding gingerly step by step. Nobody said a word about what they'd seen. They were all numb. It wasn't the first time they'd witnessed the Regulators murder someone in cold blood. It happened often in the City. The death sentence was applied to any crime, from stealing bread to feed your children to begging in the wrong neighbourhood. Kady had swiftly learned to walk on by. Best not to get involved. She'd only end up dead herself. Each time, she bit her lip and promised herself that somehow, they would destroy Tall Jake and end all this. But it never made her feel any better.

At the bottom of the stairs was a crude road that led towards a village in the distance. "There used to be people in that village," said Scotty. "Then someone spoke up against Tall Jake. They took everyone to the Deadhouse. Every one of them. Women and children too."

Scotty struck out in the opposite direction, towards the brow of a stony hill. The sun was sinking and it was getting chilly. Wind blew through the grass and rustled the unfamiliar shrubs of Malice. The plants that grew here were tough and hardy, and many of them had thorns or nettles. They reminded Kady of thistles, with coloured petals hiding amid the sharpness.

Scotty pulled up the hood of his cloak against the wind. "I feel sorry for them, sometimes," he said.

"Who? The Regulators?"

"Yeah."

"You feel sorry for *them*?" Justin said.

"It's not their fault," Scotty said. "It's what Tall Jake does to them in the Deadhouse. Nobody *volunteers* to be a Regulator, you know. They're prisoners. He has the Meat-Men cut out all their pity and mercy. They become slaves to his will." He spat on the ground angrily. "If I had my way, we'd be hitting the Deadhouse instead of—"

He stopped suddenly. Justin raised an eyebrow. Scotty had a guilty look on his face. He'd said more than he was supposed to.

"The Deadhouse is Tall Jake's seat of power," Scotty explained. "It's where he builds his armies. Makes sense to mess it up."

"I didn't know that," said Kady.

"Before he took over all of Malice, each of the Six had their own domain and they ruled the land between them," Scotty said. He seemed happy to be showing off his knowledge. "Tall Jake was master of the Deadhouse. Crowfinger lived in the Crags. The Cripplespite had the Black Arbours. The Lack was down in the Oubliette, the Queen of Cats had the Acropolis, and the Shard ruled from the Burning Lakes.

"Then Tall Jake ambushed them all. Crowfinger's dead, we know that much. The rest are hidden or in exile."

"Skarla mentioned the Six, back when we were in the Oubliette," Kady said. She frowned as she remembered the words of the strange plant-woman who lived at the bottom of that terrible dungeon. "She said that once we find the Shard we might be able to get the rest of the Six to join us against Tall Jake."

"You went to the Oubliette?" Scotty was aghast. "And you survived?"

"Barely," said Justin. "We had a brush with the Mort-Beast."

"I heard about that thing," said Scotty. "He sent it to destroy the Lack's temple and her followers, but he lost control of it."

"Well, it did the job," Justin said. "Mate of mine killed it, though. *Re*-killed it, I suppose you'd say."

"He killed the Mort-Beast?" Scotty cried. "I gotta meet this guy!"

"You will," said Kady, but her voice was more certain than her heart. "You will."

2

On the far side of the hill was a gnarled old wood. Scotty led them into it.

It was an eerie kind of place. After only a few metres, the trees closed up behind them, sealing them in. There was a damp hush everywhere, broken by distant, lonely cheeps and caws. The ticking of Tatyana's clockwork gears seemed unusually loud. Kady caught glimpses of things darting through the underbrush, but they disappeared too fast to see what they were.

The trees here were not like oaks or elms. Some were like colossal thorn bushes, with many thin trunks that tangled up in each other, and sharp spikes three inches long. Others were big, shaggy things that rustled their leaves menacingly when the intruders got too close. They followed Scotty as he picked a path through the wood.

"So how about we talk about me?" Kady said, to break the silence. "Like, what I was doing in Malice when I was here the first time. I don't think we need to worry about being overheard now."

Scotty looked over his shoulder at her. "Yeah, I suppose I'd better bring you up to speed." He thought for a moment, then began.

"Havoc, well, it wasn't much to start with. A bunch of kids who'd all found their way out of Tall Jake's traps and got loose in the City. A lot of them were just troublemakers at first, you know. The kind of kids that just wanted to cause a problem."

"I like 'em already," Justin said, from the back of the group.

"So why did you join up?" Kady asked. "You don't seem like the sort."

"I'm not. But I was smart enough to know I wouldn't

have made it long in Malice on my own, and they sorta liked me, I guess. So I stuck around." He grinned. "But then you showed up one day, and straight away you started bossing everyone around."

"Sounds like Kady," Justin agreed.

"Hey!" Kady protested. Then she thought about it a moment and said: "Actually, that *does* sound like me."

"God knows why, but they listened to you," Scott went on. "'Cause you had ideas. You got them to see how pointless it was, just smashing up things for the sake of it. You got us organized."

"I did?" Kady was bewildered.

"So we started looking out for other kids to rescue. We got talking to other groups who had a grudge against Tall Jake. They're everywhere in Malice, hidden all over. He did a lot of damage when he took over this land, made a lot of enemies. Pretty soon, we had a bunch of members, and we had good relations with the rebel gangs."

"I really organized everyone like that?" Kady asked. "Seems more like something my mom would do."

Justin sighed. "When you were in London you tracked down Icarus Scratch and Black Dice Comics. You found your own way to Malice and rescued us from the Oubliette. I think you're just about capable of organizing a bunch of kids."

Kady gave him a pixie smile. "That was dangerously close to a compliment."

"Yeah, well, it's as close as you're gonna get," Justin muttered.

Kady had a new bounce in her step. She supposed she'd never really been tested back home. You never knew what you could do until you had to.

It was something Seth used to complain about. "We're never *tested*," he'd say. "Everything's too *easy*. Our great-grandparents went to war, for God's sake. We went to World of Warcraft."

Well, Kady wasn't averse to an easy life. But it was nice to know she'd risen to the challenge, even if she couldn't remember anything about it.

"Okay, so now we've established how awesome I am," Kady asked. "What happened next?"

Scotty looked over his shoulder towards Justin, who rolled his eyes. "Yeah, she's still the meek and modest girl you knew," Justin said sarcastically. Tatyana shook her head in despair and grumbled deep in her throat.

Kady beamed at them all, unfazed. "Well, come on! Me, me, me!"

Scotty brushed aside a creeper that was trying to get a hold on his arm. "Through our contacts we got intelligence that there was a weapon we could use against Tall Jake. It was supposed to be hidden in an old temple, but there was something guarding it. You set off to get it, and you never came back."

Kady frowned. She remembered having bad dreams back in Hathern, after Luke disappeared. Dreams of running through a temple, chased by a hunched and cowled thing. It had cool blue lenses for eyes and carried a flamethrower. She remembered the smell of burning hair.

"There *was* something guarding it," she said. "I found the Shard, but afterwards . . . somehow I found my way out of Malice. There must have been an exit, like the one in Skarla's den that Seth went through. I must have escaped, to get away from the guardian. . ."

"And you turned up at home," Scotty finished.

"I must have thought I could get back. . ." Kady said. "I mean, I had a ticket with me. I just didn't count on having my memory wiped."

"And so the Shard ended up sitting on your bookshelf," said Justin. "*Now* I get it."

Scotty's eyes went wide. "So you *do* have it?"

"Not with me. Seth went back to get it. He'll bring it to us. You have to look out for him. He'll be searching for Havoc."

Scotty's excitement suddenly faded. "I'll do what I can. But Jan's not keen on too many new faces. He gets paranoid."

"Jan?"

"He's leader now. Swedish kid. Since you left, we lost direction. It's not like it was. It's more like a gang now. A lot of kids have drifted away. The others . . . well, we get by." He made an apologetic face. "I don't think he's gonna be very happy to see you back, Kady."

3

The shadows were long and the sun had almost left the sky when they reached the lake. The woods surrounded it, crowding up close, and there were mountains visible in the distance. The water was still and dark, and nothing disturbed it.

Scotty led them down to the shore, where they found a small boat hidden in the undergrowth. Justin eyed it uncertainly.

"Let me guess," said Kady. "You can't swim."

"I'm thinking of the cat," he said. "If we tip over, she's going straight to the bottom."

Scotty studied Tatyana, who sat on her haunches, patiently waiting for them to sort out the problem. "You know, I can't see her getting into the hideout anyway, even if Jan would let her in. She's too big to get down the ladders."

"Ladders?" Justin asked. "Where are we going, anyway?"

"Over there," said Scotty, pointing. Kady squinted. It was just about possible to make out a smooth hump breaking the surface of the water, out in the lake. A round metal island in the twilight.

"That's your hideout?" Justin asked, unimpressed. "It's kinda *bare*, isn't it?"

"It's under the water, doofus," Scotty replied. "That's just the hatch."

Kady had knelt down in front of Tatyana and was stroking the side of her face. "Are you gonna be alright out here for a while?" she asked. "We'll come back as soon as we can."

Tatyana butted her in the shoulder and purred.

70

"Ah, she'll just go to sleep," Justin said. "She'll be okay."

"You sure? I guess so," said Kady, giving the tiger an uncertain look. "Well, let's get going."

They climbed into a boat. Scotty took up the oars and began rowing them over to the island. Tatyana settled down on the shore, yawned hugely and closed her eyes.

"Told you," said Justin.

As they got out into the lake, Kady saw that there was a metal landing on the far side of the island. There, a dozen more boats floated, tethered to mooring poles.

They moored their own boat and got out. The island was wide and smooth and featureless, except for a small hatch in the middle. There were several dials set into the hatch, with numbers on them. A combination lock. Scotty worked the dials until the entrance code was right, and the hatch popped open with a hiss.

Inside, a narrow ladder led down. Kady could see why Scotty thought Tatyana would have to stay outside. She searched for the sabretooth on the shore, but it was too dark to see her now.

"Everyone in!" Scotty said. "Ladies first. Welcome to the Bathysphere."

Kady climbed down, and found herself in a chamber with riveted metal walls. It was like being inside a submarine. There was a sighing sound, like bellows, from deep beneath her. Dim oval lights glowed. A pressure door, with a wheel in the middle, stood ajar. She could hear footsteps approaching from behind it.

Justin came down after her, and Scotty. Scotty was just pulling the hatch shut when the pressure door opened.

The newcomer was a tall, handsome blond boy dressed in a heavy jacket and boots. There were several other boys with him, some almost as old as eighteen. All of them were large and none looked especially friendly.

"Jan, you remember Kady," said Scotty, nervously.

The blond boy stared at Kady in surprise. "Hi!" Kady said.

Jan looked over his shoulder at his companions. "Grab them," he said sharply. "Throw them in the brig!"

"Hey!" yelled Kady, as the boys crowded in to seize them. "Get off me!" She was dragged out of the room.

As she left, she saw that Justin wasn't going quietly. He punched one of the boys hard on the jaw. His attackers wrestled him to the ground. She didn't see what happened after that, but she could still hear them punching and kicking him. Tears of anger sprang to her eyes as she was manhandled away down the corridor.

Birmingham

1

It was almost dark by the time Seth and Alicia arrived in Birmingham, even though it wasn't yet six o'clock. The nights were getting longer. They'd get a lot longer yet before the day began to fight back.

Seth had bought his ticket with the savings he'd taken from home. Alicia paid for her own with her pocket money. The carriage was only half full when they got on. They took their seats next to each other, and watched the station slide away as the train began to roll.

They sat in silence for some time. Neither was sure what to say to the other. Before this afternoon, they'd been virtually strangers. Now they were travelling together to explore an abandoned factory, in an unfamiliar city, in the dark. It would have been frightening at the best of times. The fact that there might be something dreadful waiting for them made it even worse.

Somehow, they'd ended up being in this together, Seth thought. That was what happened when you started messing with Malice. People got tangled up in it. Luke hadn't wanted to get Seth involved, but he did. Seth hadn't wanted to get Kady involved, but it happened anyway. And now, just because Alicia's brother happened to be driving down a country road at the wrong time, Alicia had been sucked in too.

Then there were the families. Seth thought of his mum and dad, who had probably called the police by now, even though he'd only been gone a few hours. He felt a stab at the memory of his mum's teary face. Even Dad, who had the emotional range of a wheel of cheese, would be upset in his own strange way. He hated having to hurt them.

But it wasn't only them. What about Kady's parents, ruined by her disappearance? What about Luke's mum? They'd all suffered terribly after their children vanished.

He had to stop it. He had to stop Tall Jake.

Seth didn't want to be responsible for Alicia. He didn't want her getting hurt. But he was glad of her company all the same.

"I can't believe this is happening," she said, eventually.

Seth didn't know what to say to that. He'd found it hard to believe himself, at first.

"It's all crazy. This whole thing is crazy," she went on. She shook her head sorrowfully. "I lied to my parents. I *never* lie to my parents. If they knew I was skipping study and going to Birmingham with some boy I barely know, they'd kill me."

Seth laughed. "After everything that's happened tonight, *that's* what you're worried about? I nearly *was* killed! *Actual* death, by the way, not just a stern telling-off."

"I don't like lying," she said fretfully.

Seth became serious. "Me, neither. But sometimes you have to. This is something your parents will never understand. They'll try to protect you by grounding you, or they'll send you to therapy, but they'll never *believe* you. That's why we have to keep them out of it. They'll just get in the way."

Alicia looked out of the window at the night-shrouded countryside. "I always did what I was told," she said. "Lemar was such a tearaway, and I was the good one. I was the one that got the grades. I was the one who was going to be a scientist or an engineer or something." She took off her glasses and cleaned them with the edge of her pullover. "It's not that they'd be mad. They'd be *disappointed*. That's worse."

Seth let his head tip back against the headrest, and looked up at the ceiling. "Wow. I disappoint my folks all the time." She gave him a sharp glare, and he realized he sounded flippant. "Look, you said you wanted to be an artist, right?"

"Illustrator."

"Right. And you're good at it?"

She shrugged. "I get A-stars in art."

"So be an illustrator. It's all very well your parents telling you what they want you to be, but it's *you* that has to live with it. Not them. There's more to life than grades, y'know."

"Yeah," said Alicia, grimly. "I learned that tonight."

2

Seth and Alicia bought a map of Birmingham from Tourist Information and some torches from a hardware store, then headed off in search of Mackenzie Street.

As they left the city centre behind, the streets became quieter and more desolate. Mackenzie Street was a long, curving road that ran between two large fenced-off areas. One was a building site, where dumper trucks and cranes sat idle in the glow of the streetlights. The other was a tumbledown factory surrounded by scrub ground.

"That'll be it, then," said Seth. "You want to wait here, or are you coming in?"

Alicia looked like she didn't much want to do either. With no houses nearby, the road was spookily quiet.

"I'll come," she said.

The fence was easy enough to climb over. Seth went first and helped Alicia down the other side. They headed towards the factory.

It had been abandoned for some time. Most of the windows were broken, the roof had holes in it and the brickwork was crumbling. No developer had wanted the land, so it had been left standing. It happened a lot in places like this. Empty buildings stood like rotten teeth that nobody could afford to pull. Just one more reason why Seth didn't like big cities.

The scrub ground around the factory was scattered with debris. Chunks of rubble, crushed beer cans. A bit of police tape flapped by, caught in a breeze.

Seth was getting that icy-blanket feeling again. As they neared, it became stronger. At first, he hoped it was his imagination, but soon it became impossible to ignore. It was the same feeling he'd had at Philip Gormley's house, except it was even stronger here. A sense of waiting evil.

"There's something in there," he said.

Alicia stopped. "What?"

"Can't you sense it?"

"I'm scared, that's all. I don't *sense* anything."

"I do," he said. "Look, it's a long story, but when I was back in Malice I was . . . well, I used a bow that belonged to some kind of . . . well, she's like a goddess or something, I suppose. They called her the Lack. And it . . . it sort of *affected* me. I don't know how. I just know that I could sense there was something wrong in Philip's house long before he told me he'd called on Tall Jake. And I know there's something wrong with that factory."

Alicia studied him carefully. "Are you going in anyway?"

"Yeah," said Seth. "Are you?"

Alicia took a deep breath. "Yes."

Abandoned places never stayed secure for long. Local kids and vagrants always got in sooner or later. It didn't surprise Seth to find a side door hanging ajar. Beer cans and cigarette butts lay around the doorway.

He pulled open the door and peered inside. There was a corridor beyond. The walls were peeling and the floor was dusted with chunks of plaster and stone. Light from the road provided a dim yellow illumination.

He went in. Alicia followed him closely. So closely, in fact, that she was almost pressed up against him.

Doorways led off the corridor into empty rooms. Some were old offices, with desks bolted to the wall or filing cabinets turned on their sides. Others were larger rooms, with tall windows that had been smashed by bricks, and holes in the floor where machinery had once stood.

"So we're looking for some kind of ticket, right?" Alicia asked.

"That's right. The way you beat Malice is to escape it. Nobody would want to play Tall Jake's games if there was no chance of winning. So there would be tickets hidden in certain places. *Dangerous* places. Some were black, which meant you could go to another domain in Malice – to try again, if you like. Others were white, which meant you could go home."

"So we're looking for a white ticket?"

"Right. The white tickets work both ways. My friend Kady used one. It can get me back to Malice."

Seth hefted the weight of his backpack again. The Shard seemed to be getting heavier and heavier. He wasn't sure if it was wise to carry it into a place like this, but he didn't dare leave it somewhere. He couldn't be certain it would be safe.

"You know, we'd search quicker if we split up," said Seth.

"No, thanks!" Alicia exclaimed with panicky haste. "I'm not in a rush! Haven't you ever seen a horror movie? I don't care if it takes twice the time, I'm not walking around this place on my own!"

She caught the grin on Seth's face and realized he'd been joking.

"Ha ha. Side-splitting," she murmured sullenly.

"Sorry," he said, not sorry at all. He'd needed to do something to lighten the mood. Otherwise he feared he might just turn and run, overwhelmed by the awful atmosphere that clung to this place. Whoever that Mim character was on the IRC channel, she'd seen the others giving Seth advice on where to go. She might be on her way here. She might be lurking in wait.

Might be, he reminded himself.

They explored some of the rooms off the corridor, but there was only rubble and junk to be found there. Nothing stirred, and the only sound was the scuffing of their shoes as they poked about. They returned to the corridor, and a little further along, Seth found a fire door. He pushed on the bar and let it swing open.

Beyond was a stairway, leading down into blackness. A rush of foul air blew up from below, the faint scent of rancid meat. Alicia turned her head aside and covered her face with her hand.

"Oh, God. . ." she murmured. "What is that?"

Seth turned on his torch and shone it down the stairs. He saw only a concrete floor at the bottom. He took a step inside, and Alicia grabbed his arm.

"You're not going down there, are you?" she whispered.

Seth just stared at her. She saw the determination in his gaze. "You really haven't ever seen a horror movie, have you?" she said weakly. "You *never* go down to the basement."

"I never was much for TV," Seth said, and went down. Alicia turned on her own torch and followed, muttering under her breath.

An underground corridor led away, with pipes running along the roof. There was no light from outside. Beyond the beams of the torches, it was pitch-black.

He hesitated at the bottom of the stairs. The darkness brought back uncomfortable memories of his time in the Oubliette. He felt his scalp prickle.

Alicia looked back up the stairs, towards the fire door at the top. "We can go back," she suggested. "There might be another way to get a ticket."

"There's no time," said Seth. He swallowed down his fear. "I've got friends in there. I need to find them."

They advanced up the corridor to a T-junction. Two identical, blank corridors led away. Seth took one at random. They came to a doorway, and he shone his light in. The beam played over a huge, rusty boiler that had been partly disassembled. They moved on.

They came to another T-junction shortly after, and another after that. Each time they were faced with more blank corridors. Seth could hear Alicia quietly reciting the route they needed to take to get back. *Left, right, right.* Seth found it strangely comforting. He dreaded to think what would happen if someone closed the fire door and shut them in down here. There would be no hope of rescue then. They would be left in the dark until their lights went out.

Seth couldn't handle that again. Not after the Oubliette. Once in a lifetime was enough.

Come on, where are you? I know there's something down here.

The smell of rancid meat was getting stronger. Seth heard rats scrabbling in the corners, and once he caught one in his torch beam, nibbling on a beetle. It sat up and stared at them, its nose twitching. Alicia gave a loud yelp of surprise when she saw it, and it fled. The sound echoed away into the silence.

"Sorry," she whispered.

But there was no further sound, and no indication that anyone – any*thing* – had heard them. After a while Seth realized he was holding his breath, and he let it out slowly.

They followed the corridors further. More doorways opened into empty storerooms and fuse cupboards. *Right, left, right, left, left, right, left, right, right.*

Then they saw a light up ahead.

It was only faint, a dull glow that spilled into the corridor from round a corner at the far end. Seth turned off his torch, and Alicia did the same.

"What's that?"

Seth didn't reply. He crept closer. The light was just enough to see by. There was a distant clanking sound, like machinery. The air was rank, and a sense of dread clutched at him.

It's around that corner. Whatever it is, it's around that corner.

Then Alicia grabbed his elbow. "The walls," she said. "Look at the walls."

He saw what she meant immediately. The walls were no longer blank concrete, and the rusty pipes had disappeared. The walls, ceiling and floor of this corridor were made of a grimy, tarnished metal, like copper.

"Did you notice when it changed?" he asked. She shook her head.

A loud screech, close by, made them both jump. It was the shriek of metal on metal, like the hinges of some huge gate.

Alicia's eyes were wide with fright. "There's something down here," she said.

WAIT.

SOMETHING'S **CHANGED**.

CHANGED? WHAT'S CHANGED?

I DON'T **KNOW**, BUT –

I THINK WE'RE BEING **WATCHED**.

SETH, I DON'T NEED TO BE **SCARED** ANY MORE THAN I ALREADY **AM**.

CAN WE **PLEASE** GET THIS **OVER WITH**?

WHAT **IS** THIS PLACE?

NO IDEA **HOW**, BUT I THINK WE'RE IN **MALICE**.

NOT ONLY THAT, BUT WE'RE IN THE COMIC **RIGHT NOW**.

RIGHT **NOW**?

HOW CAN YOU **TELL**?

I CAN FEEL THEM OUT THERE. THEY'RE **READING** US.

jnkfjhgiunnb,kfjbbj

DON'T **BOTHER**. YOU CAN'T COMMUNICATE WITH THE OUTSIDE. THEY **CENSOR** IT.

SO ASSUMING WE'VE SOMEHOW GOT INTO **MALICE** –

– WHERE EXACTLY **ARE** WE?

4

Left, right, left, right, left, left, right, left, right, right.

Seth's heart pounded hard in his chest. Torch beams wheeled crazily in the darkness.

"Right!" Alicia cried, as they approached another junction. There was a roar from behind them, and the heavy clump of boots. Seth turned right. He could barely see where he was going. He only caught glimpses of floor and wall and ceiling. It was hard to keep the torch still when sprinting.

"Left!" Alicia shrieked. She was on the verge of hysteria, driven by pure fear. If she'd had any doubts left about Malice, they were gone now.

The walls were no longer metal, but concrete. They'd changed again, without Seth noticing. The eerie feeling of being watched had faded, too.

They were out of Malice. But they were not safe yet. The ogre was close behind them.

"Right!"

It was a maze in the corridors beneath the factory. He silently thanked her for memorizing the route, and at the same time wished she would run faster. He was forced to slow down to her speed. Knowing what was behind them, he wanted to flee at full pelt. But he wouldn't leave her. Besides, without her, he'd be lost.

He flashed his torch over his shoulder to check on

her. He saw her terrified face for a moment. Behind her, something huge lumbered into the corridor with a snarl.

"Which way?" he called as they approached another junction.

Left, right, left, right, left, left, right, left, right, right.

"Right! No, left!"

"You're sure?"

"Left!"

They went left, and left again soon afterward. They turned and turned again, each corridor looking the same as the one before. Seth could hear that the sounds of pursuit were fading. The heavy footsteps became fainter.

"It's taken a wrong turn," he said. "It's lost the trail."

He looked back at Alicia. A desperate grin flashed across her face. She knew why. Because she'd memorized the route out of there, and the ogre didn't know it.

Left, right, left, right, left, left, right, left, right, right.

Suddenly they were at the stairs. Seth felt a rush of giddy relief as he saw that the fire door at the top was still open. They flew up the steps into the glow of the streetlights, and slammed the door behind them.

Seth leaned against the metal, panting. Alicia was bent over, leaning on her thighs, out of breath.

There was an echoing roar from the corridors below. They exchanged a glance and bolted. Through the derelict factory and out, over the scrubland. They clambered over the fence and kept running. They didn't stop until they'd left the factory far behind.

HAVOC

Prisoners

1

Kady was shoved into the cell hard enough to make her trip. She stumbled and fell to the cold metal floor of the brig. When she got back to her feet, Jan's thug was standing in the doorway, his arms crossed.

The brig was a small room, divided in half by a row of bars. Kady stood on one side, inside the cell. The thug stood on the other. There was a rhythmic sighing of air from the walls, as if the Bathysphere was breathing.

"What are we supposed to have done?" she cried. After searching for Havoc for so long, she hadn't expected to be met with violence. "We're here to join you!"

"Shut your mouth" came the blunt reply. His name was Parker. She'd heard the others call him that. He was a Brit, short and stocky, with squashed, blunt features. The shadows were thick on his face in the weak glow from the oval lights in the walls.

There was a commotion, and Justin was dragged in by two older boys. His face was bleeding and his eye and lip were swollen. They brought him into the cell and dropped him to the floor. Kady knelt down next to him, frantic.

"Are you alright? Justin? Are you okay?"

Justin slowly and painfully rolled over on to his back. He raised himself on his elbows and spat blood over his shoulder.

"That's the best you got?" he sneered at his tormentors. "My mum punches harder than you."

One of the thugs lunged at him, but his companion held him back. "Not worth it, mate," he said. They stepped out of the cell. Parker slid the barred door shut, locked it and took the key.

Kady helped Justin to his feet. They'd worked him over pretty good. She angrily wished Tatyana was here. The sabretooth would have shown them a thing or two.

Jan walked into the brig and stood on the other side of the bars, looking in at them. The sight of his calm face enraged her further. She got up and stormed over to the bars.

"What the hell are you doing?" she demanded. "Is this how you treat all your new recruits?

"It's how we treat strangers," he said, nodding at Justin. Then he turned his ice-blue gaze to Kady. "And possible traitors."

"Traitors?" Kady cried in disbelief.

"How long has it been since you went off to recover the Shard, hmm?" he asked. "A year? More? It took you a long time to find your way back, didn't it?"

"I've been back home," she said. "Back in the real world."

"This *is* the real world, Kady," Jan replied. He spoke in a maddeningly reasonable tone, in perfect English with a slight Swedish lilt. "At least, it is for us. You still don't have the Shard, I see."

"It's on its way."

"I'll bet it is," he said. He didn't believe her for a moment. "So where have you *really* been?"

"I told you, I—"

He spoke over her. "Yes, yes, you said. And now you're back, one year later, as if nothing has happened. I suppose you expect to be leader again, do you? You think I've been holding the position open for you?"

"I don't expect anything!" Kady snapped. "I definitely didn't expect to be attacked by a bunch of meatheads."

"Even if they do punch like pansies," Justin added, with a red grin. You just couldn't keep him down.

Jan ignored him. "I suppose you can prove your story?" he asked Kady.

Kady went blank. Everything she still had from home – her climbing gear, her purse – had been left in her backpack at the workshop. She hadn't given it too much thought. It had all seemed pretty useless until now.

Then she had an idea. She pulled off her beanie hat and turned it inside out to show him the label. It had washing and care instructions on. "Look!" she said. "Where did I get this, then? Huh? The Malice Wal-Mart?"

"To be fair, they probably do have a store here somewhere," Justin quipped.

"You could have taken that from any kid in Malice," Jan said dismissively. "The fact is, we don't know what has happened to you this last year. Maybe Tall Jake got hold of you, hmm? Maybe he's got you under his power even now? He's sent you here to spy on us?"

"Don't be an idiot," Kady said. "Where's Scotty? He can vouch for me."

"Scotty's not the leader here," said Jan. "I am."

Kady bit back a reply. Getting mad wouldn't do her any good against this guy.

Her mother had been obsessed with psychology – it came with the territory of being a hypnotist. Kady had picked up a lot from the magazines that were always lying around the house. She'd learned that sometimes you had to step back and figure out why a person was acting the way they were. So she took a breath, and she thought for a moment.

Jan saw her as a threat to his power. He was frightened that Kady's return would mean a challenge to his leadership. All those people like Scotty, who didn't agree with the way he ran things, would see Kady as a way out. A return to better times. Under Jan's calm façade, he was insecure and paranoid.

"That's right," she said. Now she was calm too. "You *are* the leader. And I'm not. That's all in the past. I'm not interested in taking over, Jan. I just want to be part of Havoc. I want to help fight against Tall Jake."

Jan's eyes narrowed slightly. He was suspicious.

"Things are different now. We do things my way," he said.

Kady held up her hands. "That's fine. Whatever. We do things your way. I'm not looking to cause a problem here. I just want to pitch in."

Jan's gaze switched to Justin. "What about him?"

Justin shrugged and wiped his swollen lip with the back of his hand. "Hey, I'm just along for the ride. As long as we stick it to Tall Jake, I couldn't care less who calls the shots."

"Just give us a chance to prove ourselves," said Kady. "That's all I'm asking."

Jan appeared to consider that. He must have known that he couldn't keep them locked up for ever, and he couldn't let them go either. Despite their unpleasant welcome, Kady didn't believe things had got so bad that Jan would consider killing them. So Kady was trying to reassure him that his only remaining option – to let them join – was a safe one. She really *didn't* want to lead Havoc. Taking over a gang of rebel kids was the last thing on her mind.

Maybe Jan would have let them out, maybe he wouldn't. But they never found out, because just then the door crashed open and a stranger loomed into the room.

His sheer size was striking. He was only sixteen or seventeen, but he was over two metres tall and built like a concrete bunker. He was black, his hair forced into cornrows, and he had a stern, glowering expression on his face.

"What you think you're doing, eh?" he snarled at Parker.

Justin recognized a London accent and called out happily. "Alright! An East End boy! Give us a hand here, mate."

The new kid turned on Jan wrathfully. "Someone wanna tell me why you got Kady locked up in there?"

Jan and his thugs were visibly intimidated by the newcomer. "We don't know where they've been or—"

"It's *Kady*!" he roared. "She pretty much *made* Havoc. If it weren't for her, none of us would be here!"

"Look, Dylan, you can't just—"

But Dylan wasn't listening. He snatched the cell keys off Parker, unlocked the door and slid it open. He beckoned to the prisoners. "Come on, then."

Parker grabbed Dylan by the shoulder. "Oi! Who put you in charge?"

Dylan swivelled, picked him up by his shirt and slammed him against the wall. One huge fist hovered under Parker's nose. "Don't put your hands on me, man," he threatened. He looked around at the others. "Any of you wanna try it?"

Nobody did. "Thought not," said Dylan. He let Parker go.

Jan and his boys backed away as Kady and Justin emerged from the cell. Justin couldn't resist a smirk and a cheeky little salute as he passed them.

"See you around," he said. He could still hear them

muttering swear words as he pulled the brig door closed behind him.

2

The infirmary wasn't much larger than the brig, but it had one interesting feature: a lozenge-shaped window that ran along one wall. Outside was darkness, but in the darkness there were lights.

Some were distant, bobbing globes of white, like lamps. Others were streaks of red that rushed across the blackness like meteors. Some floated past the window, flashing and strobing. Others were luminous patterns of yellow and green that flowed and shifted and melted away.

"It's the fish in the lake," said Scotty, who was applying ointment to cuts on Justin's face with a cotton swab. "This place was a marine observatory. No one knows what happened to the scientists. It was empty when we found it."

Justin was sitting on the edge of a surgical table, trying not to wince as Scotty attended to his wounds. He was holding an ice pack to his head. Kady stood nearby, observing. Dylan was by the door, a brooding, silent presence in the room.

"You look like you've done this before," Kady said to Scotty.

"I'm sort of the resident medic," he said. "Eldest of six boys. Lot of fighting, lot of knocks. I spent my childhood patching up my kid brothers." A sad expression crossed his face. "I miss the little douchebags."

"So why not go home?" said Justin.

"No ticket," he said. "Black tickets are easy enough to get, but a white ticket? You wouldn't catch me going after a white ticket. The places you find them are the places you get killed. The Labyrinth? The Crags? No way! And unless someone has a spare to give me, well. . ." He trailed off.

"How did you end up here in the first place?" Kady asked. "I didn't know the comic got out as far as the States. Or Sweden, for that matter."

"It doesn't, as far as I know," Scotty said. "At least, I never saw a copy. Nor did anyone I knew, although a couple of kids pretended they had one. It's the internet. Someone tells someone, they tell someone else. Rumours. I was friends with some kid on MySpace and he pointed me to some chat room. That's how I learned all about it." He stood back from Justin and examined his handiwork. "You'll live," he said.

"Thanks, doc," Justin replied, getting off the table. "It was touch and go for a minute there."

Scotty resumed his story as he put the medical supplies away in a cabinet. "So anyway, one day I did the ritual. The crow feather, the twig, the cat fur and all that. . . Just to see." He made a sweeping gesture to indicate the room. "Turns out it's all true. Who knew?"

Kady looked over at Dylan. "I owe you a big thanks," she said.

Dylan shrugged it off. "Scotty says you don't remember nothin.'"

"Dylan was the one who got everyone listening to you, when you first turned up," said Scotty. "He had your back from the start. Jan might have the other kids scared with his goons, but the goons are scared of Dylan."

Kady was trying to think of some words of gratitude for his support in the past, but it was difficult to be genuine when she didn't recall what he'd done.

"Why didn't you take over? After I was gone?" she asked in the end.

"Ain't my thing," he said. "I ain't one for telling people what to do."

"No, that's definitely her department," said Justin.

"I do *not* boss people around!" Kady protested. "Much."

Just then, a face appeared at the door. It was Parker. He swept the room with a sour glare, which settled on Kady and Justin. "Jan wants to talk to you. Just you two."

Justin indicated the bruises on his face. "He already talked to me."

Parker rolled his eyes. "I'm just the messenger. You wanted a chance to prove yourselves? Go see him." With that, he left.

"He might be thinking of clueing you in on our next raid," said Scotty.

Justin raised an eyebrow. "Seems like your little chat loosened him up a bit," he said to Kady.

"Seems so." She indicated the door. "Shall we?"

"Ladies first."

No Way Home

1

"I'm going to London."

Alicia looked up from her coffee. Seth was counting money out on to the table in the Starbucks where they sat. Bus timetables were scattered between them. Through the window behind him, she could see the busy platforms of Birmingham New Street station.

"Now?" she asked.

"I can get a bus from down the road. I'll be in London before midnight."

"And then what?"

"The tube might still be running, I don't know. I'm pretty sure there are buses that run all night, though. I'll figure it out."

"No, I mean . . . what's in London?"

Seth sat back in his chair, satisfied that he could afford a ticket. It would all but wipe him out, but he could afford it.

"Three things," he said, counting on his fingers. "First,

Black Dice Comics. That's the shop where Scratch works, where I got my first copy of Malice. Maybe I can find something there. Second, there's a house in Kensington. Kady went there. She told me the address. That's where Scratch was staying. She found another copy of Malice there. Either of those places might be somewhere I could find a ticket, or a clue, or *something*."

He might also find Icarus Scratch there, the sinister comic vendor who collaborated with Tall Jake. Scratch was a dangerous man, and Seth wanted to stay out of his way if possible, but he might have to take the risk if he wanted to find a way into Malice.

"What about the third thing?" Alicia prompted.

"The old train yard in Lewisham. You remember, they mentioned it on that chat forum?"

"Is Lewisham in London?" Alicia asked blankly.

"Yeah," said Seth. "In the south. Kady used to live in Greenwich before she moved to Hathern. It's pretty close by." He picked up the pen he'd borrowed from her and scribbled down some letters and numbers on the back of one of the timetables. He pushed it across to her. "This is a car number plate. It's Scratch's car. Kady made me memorize it before I left her. I don't know how much use it'll be – I mean, I don't know how to trace a car from its number plate, and I'm pretty sure the police won't do it for us."

Alicia held up her hands. "Seth. Stop."

"Stop what?"

"Have you thought about this at all? You're just going to London? Just like that?"

Seth didn't see her point.

"Seth, we're ... I mean ... face it, we're just kids! I mean, you know, nobody likes to think of themselves as a kid, but... Be real!" She tapped her fingers on the table, agitated. "That's all your money, isn't it? How are you going to eat? Where are you going to sleep tonight?"

Seth was bewildered by her argument. He couldn't see any reason why being young should stop him doing anything. Besides, forward planning was never his strong suit.

"I'll sleep on the bus," he said. "Or I'll find a park or something."

"You know how dangerous it is to sleep in a park in London?" she cried.

"No," he said. "Do you? You didn't even know where Lewisham was till a minute ago."

Alicia didn't have an answer to that. "Look," she said. "Come home with me. I'll sneak you in. You can stay at my place for the night. Then in the morning we can—"

But Seth was shaking his head. "I can't. I daren't. I don't want your family involved in this. God knows what I might bring down on them."

Alicia had a desperate look on her face. "Seth," she said. "You can't do this. You can't take on all of this."

"I can," said Seth. "I can, because I have to." He leaned forward, his face grim. "Don't you get it? There's no way home for me. Anyone who helps me is in danger. The only way is to keep going forward." He picked up his backpack and put it in his lap. "I have a responsibility now. What's in this bag could save lives. Every day I delay, that could be one more kid snatched up by Tall Jake. Next time it could be your friend Philip. It could be *you*."

Alicia's eyes filled with tears behind her glasses. He hated having to remind her that she'd condemned herself by inviting Tall Jake to take her away. Maybe one night she'd end up back in the Deadhouse, snatched out of her bed while she slept.

"You know. . ." he said, "I spent my whole life wishing that I had the chance to do something *worthwhile*. To be like Lewis and Clark, or Neil Armstrong or Columbus or something. Not like winning some stupid reality show and selling a load of records. Something *real*." He met her gaze and held it, letting her see the determination there. "Well, this is it. This is my chance. So don't tell me I can't do it because I'm not old enough. If I was an adult, I wouldn't even believe in Malice. This is something only a kid can do."

Alicia dropped her gaze to the table. She took off her glasses and wiped her eyes with her knuckles. "I can't," she said. "I'm sorry."

"You can't what?"

"I can't do this. I can't take the world on my shoulders like that. I'm scared to death."

"I'm not asking you to—"

"God, the things we *saw*!" she said. "It's not even *possible*!" Her voice was trembling, and just for an instant he saw how close to the edge she was. She'd been pushed far enough for one day. Maybe for one lifetime.

"Don't worry," he said. "I get it."

Her eyes brimmed again, and she said in a tiny voice: "I have to go to school tomorrow."

He laid his hands over hers. "It's okay," he said softly. "I'll take it from here."

"I'm just not like you," she said, and the tears spilled down her cheeks.

2

Seth saw Alicia to the train, and they said their goodbyes. He took her mobile number and promised to let her know how he was. There was no point giving her his number. He'd left his mobile at home when he fled the house, and he wasn't going back there until all this was over.

Once she'd departed for Leicester, he went to the coach station and caught the last coach to London.

As the bus was winding its way out of Birmingham towards the motorway, he tried to get some sleep. But sleep wouldn't come. There were too many thoughts whirling around in his head.

How had they got into the Deadhouse from that factory? How could it have happened? Neither of them had a ticket. Neither of them had been taken. He wondered if it might be something to do with the strange power he'd received from the Lack during his first visit to Malice. But that couldn't be right, because other people had done it too. Like that couple that they'd talked about in the chat room. The girl had disappeared, and the boy was left talking about "creepy people" who had taken her. Only he had come out, with scratches on his face.

Could Malice be leaking into the real world? In the lonely and abandoned places, places like the factory and the old train yard in Lewisham, was the comic bleeding through?

Seth didn't want to think about what that might mean.

He was sorry to see Alicia go, but a little relieved too. It had made him nervous having her along. Putting himself in danger was one thing; putting someone else in danger was quite another. Now he hoped she would be safe, at least for a while. But if someone didn't stop Tall Jake, she wouldn't be safe for ever.

Alicia had wanted him to slow down, but there wasn't *time* to slow down. He'd wasted so much time already. How many kids had been taken during that month after he returned from Malice? That month when he'd drifted listlessly around Hathern, bored, waiting for his missing friends to come back?

What kind of trouble was Kady in now? What if he was already too late? He couldn't live with himself if she'd been hurt, or worse, and he hadn't been there to protect her.

Sir Knight, she used to call him. She liked to make fun

of his old-fashioned ideas of right and wrong. He missed her making fun of him.

So, what now, Sir Knight?

He couldn't deny that his experience in the Deadhouse had frightened him. Enough so that he didn't dare go to the train yard yet. He might be able to find Black Dice Comics from memory, but he couldn't do it in the dark. So that left the house.

It wasn't a very attractive choice, but it was the best of the bunch. He had an address memorized. He would find it, somehow. He didn't know the city at all, but he'd find that house. Perhaps there would be something there that would help him get back to Malice. If not . . . well, one thing at a time.

He allowed himself to relax in his seat. Now that he had a plan (or as close to a plan as Seth ever managed), his limbs felt suddenly heavy. It had only been six or seven hours since he'd touched the Shard, and brought that dreadful storm to Hathern. A lot had happened in that time. He was worn out.

Holding his backpack to his chest, he closed his eyes for a moment. He didn't open them again until they'd reached London.

3

Seth was woken by the rustle and movement of people getting up around him. He blinked and looked around. The coach had pulled into an unfamiliar station. Beyond the station lights, it was dark, and there was condensation on the windows.

"London Victoria," the driver announced over the PA system. "All change."

Seth unzipped his backpack and peered inside, to check that the Shard was still with him. Then he wiped his bleary eyes, got off the bus and went into the station. It was almost empty now. A digital clock showed 00:06. Cleaners were mopping the floor as the last of the passengers headed off to other destinations. Unsure of what to do next, he followed them out of the bus station.

He came out on to a street. It could have been any street. He had no idea where he was. The city surrounded him, mazelike.

He followed the passengers up the road to the Victoria tube station, and there he found a kiosk that could sell him a map. He'd always been good with maps. Orienteering was one of the many outdoor pursuits he'd tried and discarded when he was younger.

He didn't like London. But after the Clock Tower and the Oubliette, he wasn't scared of it. It was just a challenge.

By the time he figured out where he was supposed to be going, the tube station had closed, so he walked over to a nearby bus rank and asked passers-by for directions. One of them pointed him to another bus stop on the other side of the road, where he could catch a night bus. It would take him close to where he needed to go. He found the stop and consulted the timetable. The bus wouldn't be here for another ten minutes.

There was a payphone nearby. He should call his parents, he decided. They would be in bed, but that didn't matter. He felt awful about the way he'd run out on them. He knew they'd never understand, but at least ... well, at least he should let them know that he was alright. Especially Mum. The thought of her crying over her missing son gave him a pang of sorrow.

He dropped in some change and dialled the number from memory. His parents' house was just about the only number he knew off by heart.

It rang for a long time. He was about to hang up when the handset was lifted with a crackle.

"Hello?" came a weary voice.

"Mum?"

"Oh, Seth!" she said, her voice full of relief. "I knew it would be you. No one else would call at this time! Where are you?"

"Don't worry, Mum," he said. He couldn't help a big grin on his face. Just hearing her voice eased his mind. "I'm okay. Everything's okay."

"Why did you run off like that?" she asked. Her voice was getting tearful already. "Why did you leave us again?"

"It's ... it's complicated," he said, his grin fading. "I wish I could explain, I really do, but ... just ... I just wanted to let you know that I'm okay. That's all. I'll come back as soon as I can."

She was crying now. Seth bit his lip in frustration. He wanted to tell her everything, but he knew her too well. It wouldn't go in. She wouldn't get it.

"There's something really important I have to do. It's more important than school, or anything like that. It's. . ." He ran out of words. "It's important."

"Then let us help you!" Mum said. "Do you need money? Is that it?"

"Please, Mum," he said. This was getting more and more difficult. "You'll understand one day."

"Just tell me where you are!" she begged. "I'll get in the car right now and come get you."

Seth felt a cold sensation flood through him. His throat went tight. He swallowed.

"You'll drive over and pick me up?" he asked, his voice weak.

"Yes!" she cried. "Yes! Wherever you are! Just tell me where you are and I'll be there."

Seth squeezed his eyes shut and gritted his teeth. "Mum?"

"Yes, dear?"

"You never learned how to drive."

There was silence on the other end of the line. A long, drawn-out silence. The kind when you know that someone is there, but you can't even hear them breathing.

"Nice try," Seth snarled.

He heard a chuckle. A horrible little chuckle that became a loud, cruel cackle, and finally a deafening screech. Seth slammed the phone back in the cradle and backed away, heart thumping in his chest.

Are they at my house? Do they have my parents? Or is it just some kind of trick? Are they just trying to lure me home?

He was trembling. He wanted to go home, right now. He wanted to make sure his parents were alright.

But that was exactly what they wanted him to do.

The bus pulled up to the stop. Numb, dazed, he climbed aboard.

Mum. Dad. I love you. I'm sorry.

The bus pulled away,

and took him onward

into

the

night.

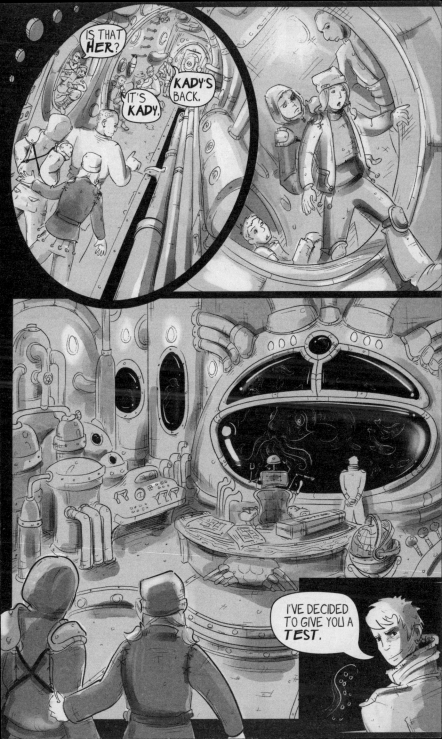

MALICE
THE TERMINUS.
WE'RE GOING TO TAKE OUT THE TERMINUS.
Grendel

As soon as the meeting was over, they were escorted by Parker to a tiny room, and locked inside.

"I'm sure you understand. It's best if everyone gets some sleep tonight," Jan said, as they were taken away. "I don't want them distracted by the excitement of having you back."

Kady went along with it. Jan was keeping her away from the other kids in case she bad-mouthed his plan, and he wanted to make sure she didn't try to escape. She knew too much now.

The room was bare except for a ratty bunk bed and a door into a minuscule toilet cubicle. Still, it was better than going back to that cell. Dylan had saved her once, mainly because the other kids were so surprised. But if she acted up too much, Jan would have no choice but to imprison her. Dylan might not be able to help her a second time. There were more on Jan's side than on hers.

"I don't like this at all," she said to Justin.

He was lounging on the top bunk, looking smug even with the bruises on his face. They'd both scrambled to claim top bunk the instant Parker closed the door on them, but Justin was faster. Now he was basking in his victory.

"What you gonna do?" he said. "We ain't got much choice. If we don't go along with the plan, Jan'll never let us stay. And if we don't stay with Havoc, Seth'll never find us."

"You don't care," Kady accused. She was leaning against the wall with her arms folded. "You *want* to go on the mission. You're just happy to get the chance to be a pain in the butt for Tall Jake."

Justin laced his fingers behind his head and lay back. "If you ain't being a pain in *someone's* butt, you ain't living right," he said philosophically.

"How's your face?"

"A little less handsome than it was this morning. And that ain't saying much."

Kady snorted a laugh. Justin could drive her mad at times, but his spirit was hard to break. Even after the beating he'd suffered, he was still joking. He was a good guy to have in your corner if things got tough.

"Look," he said, "you just gotta bide your time. In borstal, we always—"

"Borstal? What the hell is *borstal*?"

"Like a youth custody centre. Prison for kids."

"Oh, juvie hall. You were in juvie? Figures."

"Long story. Anyway, listen. In borstal, you'd get these kids. They were used to being top dog in their neighbourhood or whatever. They'd get to borstal and they reckoned the best way to get respect was to take top spot, right off the bat. But they got beat down, 'cause the guy at top, he was *established*. He had other kids to back him up."

"So what?"

"So the smart ones took it slow. They built up respect, built up a group around themselves, and waited for an opportunity. Sooner or later, the top dog would slip up. That was when they went in and took him down."

"Who says I want to take *anyone* down?" Kady cried. "Why does everyone think that I want to be the leader again?"

Justin smirked. "Oh, come on. I saw you in there. You think his plan is dumb. You had to bite your tongue to stop yourself arguing." He sat up and looked down at her. "You can't handle it when someone else is in charge."

"It's just . . . those kids we passed in the corridor, did they look like a well-trained army to you?" Kady said. "Or a band of experienced guerilla fighters? They're just a bunch of kids trying to survive."

"Sometimes you need to do more than survive," Justin said. He swung his legs over the edge of the bed and leaned forward, elbows on his knees. "You know why they stay in Havoc? It's 'cause it's all they've got. They *need* to fight back against Tall Jake, even if it's like a fly biting an elephant. Otherwise, it's like admitting they're scared and helpless." He rolled his jaw and winced. "Me, I'm the same. That's why I was looking for Havoc. I'd rather be in on Jan's plan, no matter how dangerous it is, than hiding in the tunnels under the Clock Tower, where Seth found me."

Kady thought about that. Maybe Justin was right. Maybe she *did* want to lead these kids again, if only to protect them. But first she had to get through the attack on the Terminus.

Nothing she could do would stop them going ahead with that. She could only hope that nobody got hurt.

At least she had one fact in her favour. Jan still didn't know that she'd lost her memory. And unless Scotty or Dylan talked, nobody else did either. As far as they were concerned, their formidable leader was back.

She just had to bide her time, and wait for her moment.

"I don't like it," she said again.

Justin lay back on his bunk and closed his eyes. "Well, suck it up. You'll get your chance sooner or later. Night."

Kady stood there thinking for a while.

"I wonder how Tatyana's doing?" she mused.

"She's asleep," said Justin. A moment later, he added: "So am I."

Kady took the hint. She lay down on the bottom bunk. It had been an exhausting day.

"I wonder how *Seth's* doing?" she said quietly.

Justin didn't reply. But she could tell he'd heard her. And he was wondering just the same.

Number 6

1

The house was dark.

Seth didn't have any idea of the time. Past one o'clock, surely. The street was asleep. At least, he hoped so. He wasn't certain that the people who lived at number 6 *ever* slept.

He hid around the corner of an arched brick alley. This was a secret place, a row of narrow mews houses, tucked away out of sight of the main road. The city was hushed here, flat and dead in the streetlights.

This was the street that Kady had found, when she followed Icarus Scratch from the comic shop. There was number 6, the house where she was almost caught by Miss Benjamin. Crouching on the landing, she'd heard the voice of Tall Jake below. Kady had told him the whole story after she'd rescued him and Justin from the pit in the Oubliette. It seemed so long ago now.

Seth took a deep breath. He didn't want to go in there. He wanted to be able to do what Alicia had done, to turn his back on it and go home. But he couldn't. He didn't even know if he had a home to go back to. He didn't even know if his parents were alright.

He forced those thoughts away. *Concentrate*, he told himself. *Concentrate on Kady*.

Just thinking about her made things clearer in his mind. He wanted to save and protect *everyone* – Mum and Dad, Alicia, Justin, Kady – but that was impossible. He couldn't be everywhere. So he'd save *her*. He'd protect *her*. If he could just do that, then it would be enough.

There would be a ticket inside that house. If there was one anywhere, it'd be in there. He just knew it.

He slipped across the street and tried the barred iron gate at the side of the house. At first he thought it was locked, but a quick examination revealed a small bolt at ground level. He reached through the bars and pulled it up, and the gate swung open. It obviously wasn't built for high security.

He sneaked down the covered alley and into the paved back yard. There was a clay trough full of decaying plants against one wall. It was overlooked by several other houses, but there was no sign of life.

He peered in through the windows of number 6, but the curtains were drawn. He went to the back door and tried it, but of course it was locked.

How did Kady get in? he thought. Then he remembered that she'd said she'd climbed an iron drainpipe to get in through an open window on the first floor. He found the drainpipe immediately, but the window at the top was closed. When Kady had been here, it was the end of summer. Now it was too cold to leave windows open.

He was wondering whether he should climb up and try the window when he heard a soft meow from behind him. He turned around. There, in the clay trough among the shrivelled plants, was a black tomcat. It stared at him, then pawed at the dirt and looked back him, intently.

The sight triggered a memory. Hadn't Kady said she'd had help from a cat to get inside? Hadn't Seth himself been led to the Shard by her cat Marlowe? In fact, hadn't Marlowe also warned Kady of approaching danger by spelling out "RUN" in pens on her desk?

Seth peered at the cat. The cat peered back.

"Are you Andersen?" Seth whispered.

The cat mewled. Seth was no wiser. In fact, he felt a bit stupid for expecting a yes or no answer from a cat. It didn't stop him trying again, though.

"Do you work for the Queen of Cats?"

The cat mewled again. Then it began to scrabble in the dirt once more.

Seth moved slowly closer. "Hey, kitty," he said, soothingly. "Are you trying to help me out?"

The cat paid him no attention, just carried on digging. He reached out to stroke it, to show he was friendly. But the instant that his hand touched its back—

—*a city of temples; a broken arch; a tower; a boulevard; a domed building; a plaza; a column; a canal; a bridge*—

Seth pulled his hand away, shocked. The pictures had

come like a barrage, pounding into his mind. The cat recoiled from his touch. It arched its back and hissed at him. Then it was gone, racing down the side-alley and away.

Seth blinked, unsure what had just happened. It felt like ... like ... well, he didn't know. As if something had pulled those pictures out of the cat's mind and thrust them into his. The cat didn't seem too pleased about it, that was for sure.

He wondered what it meant. Had he seen something he wasn't supposed to see? Was this all part of the strange gift that the Lack had given him in return for destroying the Mort-Beast in the Oubliette?

I have need of a champion, she'd said. *I choose you.*

A champion? To do what?

Too many questions, too many questions. He had a task to do. Drawn by curiosity, he looked in the clay trough. Where the cat had been digging, there was a glint of dull metal. He pulled out a key.

"Looks like you *do* work for the Queen of Cats," he said to himself.

But what did that mean? Seth had come to understand that the Queen of Cats was one of the Six, but he didn't even really know who the Six were, except that Tall Jake was one, and so were the Queen of Cats, the Lack and the Shard. They'd ruled Malice together once, until Tall Jake had ambushed them and taken the world from them.

Could he really trust them?

He dusted off the key. Now wasn't the time. He slid the key in the back door and turned it.

The lock clicked. The door opened. He was in.

2

The kitchen area was long and narrow and covered in dust and dirt. The linoleum floor had come up at the edges. There were crumbs and muck under the cupboards. Unwashed pans of beans congealed on the grubby stove top. The worktop was covered with open Pot Noodles and Coke cans.

Seth wrinkled his nose. The same feeling of dread came over him that he'd experienced at Philip Gormley's place, and later at the factory. He'd expected that and was prepared for it. But he wasn't prepared for the smell of rancid food and the tinny taste in the air. There was something else, too ... a musky, animal scent. A cockroach scuttled into hiding as he pushed open the door.

He listened for sounds that the house was occupied. Nothing.

He left the door open and the key in the lock. Beyond the kitchen there was a short hallway. On the right was an alcove. It was supposed to be for hanging coats, but the pegs were empty. Seth took that as a good sign.

He moved into a foyer. The front door was set opposite a stairway, with a tatty pea-green carpet mouldering on the steps. Beyond was a doorway that led into a dim living room. Yellow light from outside seeped around the drawn curtains.

There was a creak from upstairs.

Seth froze. He looked up the stairs. At the top, he could only see the end of the landing.

Was it just a night noise? The sound of the floorboards cooling?

As if in answer, there was more creaking. This time it was more purposeful and definite. The sound of someone – or some*thing* – moving around up there. But it didn't sound like footsteps. The rhythm was wrong. It was like. . .

Seth suddenly remembered. Kady had spoken of a *fourth* occupant in the house besides Scratch, Miss Benjamin and Tall Jake. Something that was locked in one of the upstairs rooms. Something she'd only spied through the keyhole. Something with a slitted eye, that had been staring back at her.

Get out, he told himself. *Just get out now.*

But he wouldn't let himself run. Not yet. He was here now. He should at least check out the downstairs area.

Besides, he told himself, *that thing upstairs might still be locked in its room.*

He didn't believe it, but it made him feel better.

The creaks stopped. Whatever that creature was, it was no longer moving. He crept onward.

The living room was a mess. A battered sofa had been jammed against one wall. Magazines and old newspapers lay about everywhere. Dirty plates were stacked in corners.

Fully half the room had been turned into a kind of makeshift office. Two tables – the kind you got in school canteens – had been pushed together for desk space. There were plastic chairs placed nearby. On one table was a cheap-looking computer, currently turned off. Next to it was a combined phone/fax machine, its READY light shining green. On the other were piles of paperwork and files bursting with documents.

Seth looked around helplessly, not knowing where to begin. He didn't dare turn the computer on in case it beeped. Besides, he needed Kady to find anything useful in there – he knew next to nothing about computers. He went over to the table full of papers and began looking through them. He had to peer closely in the dim glow from beyond the curtains. He didn't want to use his torch in case someone saw the light.

Delivery receipts. Purchase orders for packing boxes. Notices for rent overdue. Solicitors' letters. All in the name of Icarus Scratch.

Seth shuffled through the documents and was amazed. They were really running a *business* here. The process of creating, printing and distributing a comic wasn't a simple one.

But he still didn't know *why*. It couldn't be for profit. As far as he knew, Malice wasn't even sold for money. The comic found its way to those kids who investigated hard enough, through a shady system of recommendations, or through the shop in London. Maybe there were other ways Seth didn't know of. In any case, it was costing Scratch a lot of money to put out the comic, and he was getting nothing back.

Again: *why*? Why did Tall Jake want to steal kids away at all? Was it only for his own sick amusement? Why was Scratch involved in all this? What was he getting out of it?

Seth remembered Kady telling him about the conversation she'd overheard in this house, between Tall Jake, Miss Benjamin and Icarus Scratch. They were probably standing in this very room at the time. Tall Jake had wanted to increase the circulation of the comic, but Scratch had refused.

Keep it a rumour, Scratch had said. *A rumour is more powerful.*

What did that *mean*?

There was a series of creaks from upstairs. Something four-legged, on the move. Seth held his breath. The creaks stopped again.

I hope that thing is still locked in its room. I really do.

He picked up an envelope that was lying on the desk. It was addressed to this house, and it had been opened and was empty. Seth turned it over. On the back was a sticker with a return address:

> **The Printworks**
> **Matham Industrial Estate**
> **Stevenage**
> **Herts**

Seth's eyes widened. This must be the address of the printers who manufactured the comic! He stuffed the envelope in his pocket. Even if he didn't quite know what to do about it, it was an important clue. If he could trace the origins of the comic, he might be able to get to the heart of the mystery.

He looked down at the desk, and saw a train ticket. It had been covered by the envelope. His heart leaped and he snatched it up. But his joy lasted only an instant.

The ticket was black. It was just the same as a white ticket, but in negative. White ink on black paper.

This is no good. A black ticket only works inside Malice. I still need a white ticket to get there.

He took it anyway. He'd flicked through all the documents now, and he still hadn't found what he needed: a way to Malice.

There must be something else! he thought.

There was a loud electronic ring next to him, shocking in the silence. He jumped a mile. The phone. It rang twice, two shrill warbles, and then cut off.

The silence ached. His pulse thumped in his ears.

There was a slow creak from upstairs.

It's just the phone, it's just the phone. Seth addressed his thoughts to the unseen thing above him. *You don't need to come down and check it out. See? It's over now.*

But it wasn't. Suddenly the fax beeped and chattered. There was a piercing whine as it began to print. The ink cartridge thumped back and forth.

Seth began to panic. After the hush, the noise seemed

deafening. If the creature upstairs was loose, then surely it would come and investigate the racket?

Time to go.

Then he saw what was printing out. A page from the Malice comic itself. Scrawled on the top of the first page was a note:

New artwork from Grendel. It will go in the next issue, I assume? DB

Below it was a page of comic art. Right there, on the first panel, was Kady.

He recognized her, even in comic form. She had the same loose blonde pigtails and beanie hat she'd been wearing when he saw her last. She looked like she was inside some kind of submarine or something. There was Justin, too! His face was battered and bruised and he looked awful.

He felt a surge of pure joy at the sight of them. They were alive! They were okay!

Then the floorboards creaked overhead, and his joy drained away. The creature was moving again. Slowly, but it was moving. Sauntering towards the top of the stairs.

Seth was trapped. He wanted to run, but he needed to know where Kady was. He needed to know what had happened to them. But he was very aware that there were no exits from this room, except the one he'd come through. That meant he had to go past the stairs to get out.

If whatever was upstairs came down, he would be trapped.

He glared at the fax machine, willing it to print faster. The paper continued its steady crawl outwards. The first page fell on to the desk. Seth snatched it up and skimmed it. There were no clues there that could help him, except that his friends were in some kind of underwater laboratory.

His senses shrieked at him. *Run! Run, before the thing upstairs gets you!*

Another page was coming out of the fax. What if *that* page told him where Kady was? What if it turned out she was in danger? He needed to know!

The creaking stopped. Maybe it had reached the door of the room that it was locked inside? Maybe it couldn't go any further?

Come on! Come on! He wanted to scream at the fax machine. The page was showing a conversation with a blond boy Seth didn't recognize. They were talking about an operation they were planning. Could it be that they'd found Havoc? Every second was giving him precious information!

The creaking began again. No question this time. It was moving down the landing. It wasn't locked up at all. It was roaming around up there.

Every muscle in Seth's body was tensed to flee. *Go! Go! Go!*

But still he wouldn't. He had to know if Kady was safe.

The creaking upstairs faded a little. Moving away. Into another room, perhaps?

Now's your chance!

Seth's teeth were gritted with the effort of resisting his instincts. Another page dropped out of the fax. He gathered it up while it started working on a third. He skimmed it.

The creaking got louder. Coming down the landing.

Seth's scalp crawled.

It was at the end of the landing now. Right at the top of the stairs.

Seth stared desperately at the fax. It was still grinding through the third page. In the middle of a page was a speech bubble.

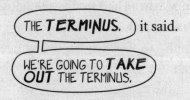

THE *TERMINUS.* it said.

WE'RE GOING TO *TAKE OUT* THE TERMINUS.

The topmost stair creaked.

Seth ripped the half-printed page out of the fax and bolted for the doorway. He flew past the bottom of the stairs. Out of the corner of his eye, he saw it: fang and bone and horn, fur and metal, leaping off the stairs towards him, claws outstretched.

His reactions saved him. At full pelt, he dropped to his knees and slid along the carpet, passing underneath it as it leaped. The beast landed on the floor of the foyer and skidded into the wall.

Seth spared it only a glimpse. It was the same beast that had chased him from Hathern – the same horrifying mockery of a lion. That was what Kady had seen locked up in here, that August night.

He raced down the hallway. The beast was quick. In the blink of an eye, it was back on its feet and after him. But he had a few paces' head start, and over such a distance, it was enough. He ran through the kitchen, and pulled the back door closed just as the monster came crashing in after him. He turned the key in the lock. The beast threw itself into the other side of the door, making the windows of the house shake.

But the door held.

Seth retreated, breathing hard. He stared at the house, then at the crumpled-up fax papers in his hand.

He wasn't sticking around to see what happened next. He ran.

3

"*Alicia. It's Seth. I suppose you've got your phone off; I mean, it is something like two o'clock in the morning after all. God, I hate answerphones. . .*

"*Listen, I found out something tonight. My friends are alive. But they're in big trouble. I saw them in the comic. But if I can read the comic, Tall Jake can read the comic. My friends didn't know that Grendel was . . . well, he was watching them, seeing them somehow. And he drew them while they were* making these plans. But now everybody knows what they're going to do! Alicia, they're walking into a trap!

"I can't afford any more delay. I have to go to Malice, right now. I'm heading to the train yard.

"I gave you Icarus Scratch's car number plate. I also found an address. It's where they print the Malice comic. The address is: The Printworks, Matham Industrial Estate, Stevenage, Herts.

"Now listen, I'm telling you this because, one way or another, I probably won't be coming back. I'll either be in Malice or . . . well, I don't want to think what else I might be. So someone needs to know. Someone needs to do something about it. And you're the only one I can tell.

"I know this is asking a lot. I wish I didn't have to. But even if you don't want to do anything about it yourself, you have to get this information to someone who will. Don't ask in that chat room, 'cause they'll know we're on to them then. I don't know what, but . . . you have to do something with it. This comic has to be stopped.

"I gotta go, Alicia. My bus is pulling in. Please don't ignore this message. There's too much at stake."

The Train Yard

1

Seth stood behind a wire fence at the top of a gravel bank which was overgrown with weeds and tough bushes. To his right was a road. Before him, the ground sloped down to a wide, stony cutting, at right angles to the road. Tracks ran along the bottom, splitting into a complicated tangle before they disappeared into three arches, under the road and into the hillside. Disused carriages sat on the tracks, waiting to be repaired or taken apart.

I wonder what's down there?

Dawn was still hours away, and in the darkness nothing moved. Seth didn't feel the slightest bit tired, even though he'd only slept for a couple of hours on the coach. There had been too many scares tonight. He was keyed up and alert.

He didn't want to brave the train yard. What if he came across the thing that had supposedly eaten those kids? What if he got to Malice and ended up in a place even worse than the Deadhouse? What if the rumours were wrong, and there was nothing here but forgotten trains?

What if? What if? he thought to himself in disgust. *You don't have time for what ifs.*

He shifted his backpack to sit more comfortably on his shoulders. He could feel the weight of the Shard inside.

"Whatever you are, Shard, you'd better be worth it," he said grimly.

He waited until there were no cars on the road and then clambered over the wire fence. Gingerly, he made his way down the gravel bank, but halfway there he felt the ground shifting under his feet. He skidded, slipped, and slid down the rest of the bank, scraping himself painfully on the way. Finally he crashed into some bushes at the bottom with a noisy rustle. A pair of crows, disturbed from their roost in a nearby tree, exploded from hiding in a flurry of wings. Their angry caws echoed away into the silence.

Seth didn't move for a moment. He listened, wondering if his clumsy approach had alerted anyone. All he could hear was the *swoosh* of cars on the road overhead. A now-familiar sense of oppression settled on him, a sense of wrongness in the air. He felt his stomach sink.

There's something here, alright, he thought. The rumours could be true, then. This might be a place like the factory in Birmingham, where the world of Malice was leaking into the real world. It should have made him pleased, but it just made him more wary. There was no telling what might have come through.

He picked himself out of the bushes. At ground level, the train carriages blocked his view of the yard. Shadows clustered thickly beneath them. There were a hundred places where something might be hiding.

Seth took out his torch. He didn't turn it on, because he didn't want anyone to know where he was. He could see well enough in the wash of light from the road overhead. It just made him feel better to have something in his hand to use as a club.

Of course, if there was something here like the creature he'd encountered at the house in Kensington, then a torch wouldn't be much use at all.

He crept into the yard, stepping over train tracks, ears straining for a sound. Everything was still. The carriages were coupled together in rows of two or three, forming aisles and barriers. The tracks disappeared into the black mouths of the archway tunnels.

The tunnels. Seth didn't want to go in there. Not until there was no other choice. He resolved to check out the yard first.

He peered around the end of a row of carriages. Nothing. Only the hush of the night. He moved to the next row of carriages, treading softly.

Then he heard something. A whimpering noise, like a hurt dog. Coming from behind the carriages he was approaching.

He went closer to investigate, clutching the torch tight. He slipped between two carriages, clambering over the couplings. Careful to keep himself hidden, he looked out.

A few metres away from him was a girl. She was sitting on the step of a carriage door, wrapping a rag around her shin. In the shadow, for a moment, she might have been Kady: she had long blonde hair and wore a woollen hat against the cold. But no, this girl was unhealthily thin, all skin and bone, buried inside a dirty orange jacket. The whimpering was coming from her. She was crying. He watched as she tied the rag around her leg. She flinched as she pulled it tight.

What's she doing out here? he thought. He was unnerved by her presence and the feeling of dread that hung over this place. By her appearance, she looked like she was homeless, even though she was only Seth's age. But Seth didn't trust in appearances since encountering Miss Benjamin.

He watched her as she lifted herself off the step and tried to put her weight on her leg. Her face screwed up in pain. She made it three steps before her leg gave out and she fell to one knee with a cry.

It was too much for Seth. He couldn't stand by and watch someone in trouble without trying to help. He wasn't that kind of person.

"Hey!" he said, quietly. She heard him, and looked up, startled. When she saw him hiding in the gap between two carriages, she scrambled to her feet and backed off, panic in her eyes.

"Hey! I'm not going to do anything!" he said, trying to reassure her.

She stopped backing off and stared at him suspiciously.

"How'd you get hurt?" he whispered.

"I got bit," she snapped. "Why are you whispering?"

He made a lowering motion with his hand, telling her to keep her voice down. "Where'd you get bitten?"

"On my leg, stupid," she sneered. Now that she'd got over her fright, she was a thorny customer.

"No, I mean, where in the train yard?"

She waved vaguely back towards the tunnels. "I think it was a dog. Didn't see it in the dark."

Seth looked. He remembered the story of the kids who'd been eaten here. Had they gone into the tunnels?

"You should go to hospital," he said.

"I don't do hospitals."

Seth came out of hiding. "You stay back!" she warned.

He held up his arms, the torch in one hand. "Okay," he said. She hopped back to the metal step of the carriage and sat on it, keeping an eye on him. "What are you doing here?" he asked.

"Why's that your business?"

"Just asking," said Seth.

She sighed. "Too cold to sleep," she said. "You keep on the move at night. Keeps you warm. I'll sleep in the day." She shrugged. "I was just poking around."

"It's dangerous here."

"Yeah, I know that *now*," she said, rolling her eyes.

Seth wondered at this girl. He'd read somewhere that a hundred thousand kids a year were reported missing in England. A hundred thousand like her. All the kids taken away to Malice would be a drop in the ocean. Who would notice?

"You need to get somewhere safe," Seth advised.

"Well, I ain't going anywhere on this leg," she said. "Don't you worry about me."

He had to get going. Kady needed him. But it felt wrong, leaving her like this. Who knew what else was in the train yard with them?

"Is it bad?" he asked, indicating her bandaged leg.

She shrugged. "I dunno. Hurts."

"Can I have a look?"

"If you like."

She watched him carefully as he put the torch aside and knelt down in front of her to undo the rag around her shin. She smelled of stale sweat and dirt. Seth wasn't sure what he could do about the bite, but at least he could see if it was something that needed hospital treatment. He wouldn't feel right if he didn't try to make her go. She probably needed a tetanus shot or something.

He undid the rag. Beneath was smooth, pale, unbroken skin.

"Where's the—?" he began.

Then she sprang on him.

2

Seth was taken totally off guard. He saw only a flash of mad yellow eyes and crooked fangs where there hadn't been fangs before, but it was enough to give him an instant to react. Enough so the bite that had been meant for the base of his throat sank into his shoulder instead.

The agony was colossal. He yelled at the top of his voice and shoved the girl away from him, hard enough to send her slamming back into the side of the carriage. She bounced off and fell in a heap as he staggered away, clutching his shoulder. Pain, so intense he could hardly breathe. He could feel hot, wet blood soaking into his T-shirt under his coat.

The girl was getting slowly to her feet. But she was hardly a girl any more. She was changing before his eyes. As if something on the inside was pushing out through the skin, shedding its disguise. Her hair was growing out rapidly and dropping off in clumps. Chunks of her scalp came out with it, revealing moist grey skin underneath. Her nails were getting longer, turning into filthy claws. Her face was changing, features twisting into a new and horrible formation.

"*This is* my *train yard, meat!*" the ghoulish thing said, in a voice that bubbled and gurgled like someone drowning in tar.

Seth ran. The ghoul was blocking his escape, so he fled in the other direction, towards the arches. There was a hiss from behind him, and she lurched off in pursuit. She ran hunched, with a limp. That injured leg really was lame. She was still changing into her true form, leaving bits of sloughed-off skin and hair behind.

Seth ducked between a pair of carriages and scrambled over the couplings. His shoulder thumped and stung. He was muttering under his breath, calling himself all kinds of names through his gritted teeth. *Stupid, stupid!* He should never have tried to help that girl. It was too risky. But he just had to play at being Sir Knight, didn't he?

He emerged on the other side to find himself hemmed in. Before him was another row of carriages. To his left was a pile of gravel and junk that blocked his way. To his right, the carriages disappeared into a tunnel.

He stared into the darkness. His torch was gone; he'd put it down just before the girl had bitten him. He didn't want to go in there, but his instincts told him that was where he had to go. If he wanted a way into Malice, he would find it in the deepest, most secret part of the train yard. Just like in the factory. That was where the crossing points existed: in the forgotten, in between places of the world.

He realized suddenly that he couldn't hear his pursuer any more. He looked around frantically. She could be anywhere. She could be crawling under the carriages, reaching out to grab his ankle. She could be circling round to cut him off. She could be clambering on top of a carriage to pounce on him.

Breathing hard, he backed away towards the tunnel.

There was no sign. That was even worse than if he could see her. He wanted to get out as fast as possible, back to the road and the cars and the safety of the streetlights.

But if he did, he would only have to come back tomorrow night. And by then it might be too late for Kady.

Kady. He thought of her. It was what gave him the strength to run towards the black mouth of the tunnel.

He passed under the arch. A few dozen paces in, the carriages came to an end. Faint light from behind him illuminated tracks that ran on into darkness. They were choked with weeds, scattered with small stones and rubble. He looked back, and saw nothing but an empty train yard. All he heard was the stirring of a sour breeze, and the sound of a truck rumbling overhead.

Maybe she's gone, he thought. *Maybe she's just going to leave me alone.*

He put his hand to his shoulder. How bad was it? How deeply had he been bitten? It felt terrible, but that didn't mean anything. Small cuts could feel huge. Was he bleeding a lot, or a little?

No time, no time. He hurried on. The light dwindled behind him. He made his way to the side of the tunnel, and ran his hand along the rough wall. He would need to navigate by touch, when his eyes became useless.

Very soon, there was no light to see by. He slowed down, so as not to trip over. It would be easy to step on a rock and fall.

His heart was fluttering against his ribs. He was

remembering the Oubliette, and the awful, crushing weight of the dark. It took all his courage to keep going forward.

He looked back towards the mouth of the tunnel. The arch, and the train yard beyond, was the only thing left to see in a world of blindness.

In the archway, he saw something move. A silhouette. Something scrawny and ragged, something hunched over and naked, with straggly bits of hair and long, sharp nails. It looked this way and that, and then craned its head forward, into the tunnel.

"*I know you're in here, meat! I have your blood on my tongue!*" The gargling voice drifted up the tunnel. "*I can taste you!*"

The ghoul came on, into the tunnel.

Terror clutched at Seth. He stumbled along as fast as he could. His fingertips dragged along the stone. A rock turned treacherously under his foot with a loud scrape. A wet cackle came back. It sounded frighteningly close, but that could have been a trick of the echo.

Could it see in the dark? Was it catching him up? Would there be an end to the tunnel?

Seth pushed away from the wall. If the ghoul was as blind as he was, then it had less chance of finding him in the middle of the tunnel. It might walk by him and never know. He was freezing cold (blood loss? Or straight-out fear?). He wanted to curl up and hide. He expected at any moment to feel the ground disappear under his feet, to fall headlong into a hole.

His shoe found the edge of a rail. The tracks! He could follow the tracks! He stepped over the rail and found a sleeper. He felt for the next one, and stepped to it. The next was the same distance, of course: it was a little easier. And the next, and the next. Quickly, he had a rhythm. He couldn't see, but he could feel how long his strides were. Sometimes he had to stop and adjust, when he felt the edge of the sleeper through his soles, but overall the movement was much faster than stumbling along the wall.

He didn't dare look back. He didn't dare find out if the ghoul was right at his shoulder.

Then, in the distance, he saw light.

His eyes fixed on it desperately. Light! Electric light! Somehow . . . he didn't know how, but somehow. . . Light!

He increased his pace, stepping recklessly from sleeper to sleeper. The end of the tunnel was brightening, and soon he could make out the outlines of the tracks at his feet. He broke into a run, throwing caution to the wind, racing up the tunnel. Once he stumbled as his missed his footing, and he almost fell, but nothing would slow him down now. The terror of the creature behind him and the welcoming promise of light propelled him onward.

His panting breath was loud in his ears. His shoulder throbbed. The tunnel bent to the left, the light brightened, and suddenly he saw a platform ahead of him. A train platform! There was a station here! He rushed up to the platform, clambered on to it, and ran into the comfort of the light.

The platform was run-down and abandoned. Dank bricks were greened with mould. Electric lights buzzed and crackled. There was a passageway leading off the platform, a way out, but it was secured by a folding gate. Seth ran up to it and tried to pull it open, but for all the rattling and screeching of the metal, it did no good.

He backed away from the gate. Next to it was a patch of lighter-coloured stone, where a sign had once been fixed. The sign was gone now, and someone had painted a crude replacement. Two words:

GRISTLE MILL

Gristle Mill? He'd never heard of it. Was it an old tube stop? He'd heard that there were many old tube stations in London, closed down and lost to memory. It certainly fitted the London tradition of strange station names, like Mudchute, Hatch End, Gallions Reach and Blackfriars.

He spun around, feeling trapped. Beyond the end of the grimy platform, the hungry dark waited. Out there somewhere was the ghoul. Here in the light, Seth couldn't see out, but his pursuer could see in. He searched around for a weapon, suddenly wishing that he'd picked up a rock when he was down on the tracks.

Where is she? Where did she go?

A sound came to his ears. A distant, rhythmic clacking noise. Getting louder.

That can't be what I think it is.

Warily, he went to the edge of the platform and looked into the tunnel. There was a light growing from the direction he'd come. The sound swelled until it was unmistakable.

A train was coming. Which was clearly impossible, because the only thing in that direction was broken-down carriages blocking the tracks, and an old train yard. There was nowhere for the train to come *from*. Unless. . .

Unless he was in Malice.

His hand went to his pocket. He had a black ticket! A black ticket, stolen from the house in Kensington. Now that he was inside Malice, he could use it. That meant he could catch this train to Kady!

His attention was fixed on the approaching light. So much so that he didn't see the ghoul until it was far too late.

She'd crept past in the dark and slipped up on to platform on the far side. Seth was looking back towards the train yard, not the other way. He only realized she was there when he heard her bare feet slapping on the platform tiles, an instant before she pounced on him.

Seth yelled as he was knocked to the ground. Suddenly, the creature was all over him, snarling and snapping, scratching at his arms and face with her dirty nails. He fought to keep her teeth away from his throat, trying to get a grip on her to push her off. She writhed and gargled in a frenzy, her fangs gnashing closer and closer with each lunge.

The sound of the train had swelled to fill the station.

Everything was chaos, noise and motion. Seth strained desperately, but the ghoul thrashed and flailed, scratching him everywhere, and he couldn't get her off him.

Then: a flash of memory. Kung fu classes. Yet another activity he'd started and given up because it wasn't exciting enough. Children in white *gi* suits watching the instructor demonstrate a move.

Use your opponent's weight against them.

Seth drove his knee into the ghoul's thin ribs. She squealed and bucked, enough for him to get a toe wedged against her bony hip. She bit at his face, and he rolled backwards, straightening his leg to launch his opponent away. The ghoul flew through the air, over the edge of the platform and on to the tracks. She scrambled to her feet, shrieked once—

Then there was only the rushing metal thunder of the train.

Seth lay on his back, panting. There were scratches on his cheek and chin which burned. He was a mass of pain.

But he was alive.

He picked himself up as the train came into the station and settled in a cloud of steam. If he'd needed any more proof that he'd really made it to Malice, the train provided it. It was all spikes and armour. Not like any you'd ever see rolling through the English countryside.

The doors hissed open and lifted away from the carriages. Standing in the doorway before him was the Conductor. Seth managed a wry smile.

"How is it you manage to be everywhere at once?" he asked. "Are there hundreds of you or something?"

"There's only one of me, sir," said the Conductor.

"And yet you're always there when anyone gets on a train," Seth said. He was feeling silly and giddy from his narrow escape. "Do you know Santa Claus? You have a lot in common. He visits every house in the world, all in one night."

"Remarkable," said the Conductor, in a voice that suggested it wasn't very remarkable at all.

Seth stepped on to the train. The Conductor's blank face turned to follow him. "Where to, sir?"

Seth handed over his ticket. "The Terminus," he said. Then he remembered his manners, and added: "Please."

The Conductor studied the ticket, then nodded. "Very good, sir. The Terminus it is."

The Terminus

1

The doors of the train carriage hissed open, and passengers leaked on to the platform. They came in all shapes and sizes: swarthy men with insectile eyes; obese blobs that had to squeeze to get out; scrawny groups of impish boys with sharp little teeth.

That was to name only a few. Inside the Terminus, there were thousands.

Kady gawked as she got off the train, her head tipped back to take in the pillared roof. It looked like a collision between a medieval palace and a 1930s jazz bar, with some of the dark Gothic grandeur of London's Houses of Parliament thrown in for good measure. Grand Central gone crazy. It was heavy and frowning and magnificent, and it made her feel small to be there.

"Could you not look quite so much like a tourist?" Justin said, at her shoulder.

Kady waved her hand to indicate the enormous hall. "Could you not be a little bit impressed?"

"It's just a building," Justin grunted. "Big whoop."

Kady let it drop. Justin wasn't the cultural type. She located the other members of Havoc, who were getting off different carriages. Tatyana slunk up to her and butted her leg with her head.

She tickled behind the tiger's ear. Tatyana clattered in pleasure. What a place the City was, where they could walk around with a clockwork sabretooth in tow and nobody would bat an eyelid. It was a comfort to have her there. Tatyana was her only protector in this wild and strange world. Well, unless you counted Justin, which she didn't.

They regrouped at the end of the platform, which was one of many. They could see at least six other trains in this hall alone. Kady had been told that there were other halls, too, with many more platforms. The Terminus was the transport hub for all of Malice. Its trains ran all over the City and outward to faraway destinations. There were so many people here, boarding, disembarking, changing trains or waiting for arrivals. The hall echoed with the ringing of voices.

How big is Malice? she found herself wondering. *As big as the United States? Bigger? How much is there?*

Even after all she'd seen, she still thought of this place as a handful of different zones – *domains*, Justin had called them – linked by a railway network. But she really had no idea of the true size of Malice. The City was the great metropolis, but she'd seen villages too. That meant there were other towns and settlements, with people living in them. And beyond that? Could she take a train all the way to the edge of Malice, and end up by the sea? She didn't know. She'd never seen a map, nor had anyone else she'd met.

Once they were all together, Jan muttered some quick instructions. "The maintenance door is on the other side of the hall," he said. "Follow me, and don't act nervous."

He cast a wary glance at Tatyana before heading off. Jan didn't like the idea of having the sabretooth along, but Tatyana wouldn't take no for an answer. She'd appeared that morning, as they walked through the wood to the train station. She followed them and ignored all attempts to put her off. Eventually Kady persuaded Jan that she should come. She would be a fearsome ally.

Jan reluctantly agreed. She was a fearsome ally, alright, but she was *Kady's* ally. He didn't like that. He was already mad at Scotty and Dylan for breaking Kady out of the brig, but they'd been part of the plan from the start, so he had to bring them along.

There were thirteen of them in all. Jan's three thugs had come too, and four kids Kady didn't know (or rather, didn't *remember*). The rest of Havoc had been left back at the Bathysphere. There was no need for everyone to be here. Jan had only brought the toughest and most level-headed.

Kady was relieved that at least *some* of Havoc were safe. She didn't like this plan one bit. Sure, if it worked, it would make a heck of an impression. But if it went wrong, the consequences could be terrible.

She kept her eye out for danger as they picked their way through the crowd on the platform. Regulators stood in pairs, overlooking the hall from high vantage points, their spear guns held ready. Others moved through the crowd, keeping an eye out for trouble.

Kady looked up at the ceiling and spotted a Reaper there, hanging motionless from a chain. A mechanical spider, armed with spear guns slung under its body: heavy-duty security. It was wrapped up in its own legs. Only its red lens-like eyes moved, scanning the crowd.

She shivered. Not for the first time, she thought how many people were in this hall, and how many might be hurt if a firefight began.

"They're not *people*," Jan had said, when she voiced her concerns. "What do you care about them? They're not even human!"

But Kady remembered Shaddly Bletch, and old Skarla from the Oubliette, and Nibscuttle. They'd all been kind to her. It didn't matter if one kept on losing body parts and one was mostly plant and the other had two heads. They may not have been human, but they were people to her.

They followed Jan across the hall to an out-of-the-way spot behind an enormous pillar. There they saw the maintenance door. It had three rotating dials set into it, like you might find on a safe. Parker snapped at them all to gather round, to block the maintenance door from sight. They pretended to look at a timetable and acted confused while Jan fiddled with the dials behind them.

A pair of Regulators passed by. One of them turned his head and stared at the group, but they walked on without stopping.

Jan returned with a triumphant grin, flashing white teeth. "Our information was good," he said. "The door's open."

He turned away, back towards the door, but Kady grabbed his arm. His eyes blazed as he glared at her.

"Jan," she said. She'd tried to keep her mouth shut, but in the end it was impossible. She couldn't let this go on without trying to reason with him. "It's not too late. This plan is *so* dangerous. If the slightest thing goes wrong. . ."

"Nothing is going wrong," he said coldly.

"What if it does? You don't even have an escape plan!" she said.

"We won't *need* an escape plan!" Jan said, through gritted teeth. "I knew you were going to be a problem, Kady. I should never have let you come. You just can't take it, can you? You're jealous! All that time you were leader of Havoc and what did you do? Nothing like this! This is going to be *spectacular*, Kady! Everyone in Malice will be talking about Havoc after this."

"And then what?" she asked. "Right now, we're a minor nuisance. After this, Tall Jake will make Havoc his number one priority. He'll hunt us down with everything he's got." She looked wildly around the group. "Are you all ready for that?"

They started to look nervous. Jan saw that they were

beginning to doubt him, and he snarled, "It's too late for talk, Kady. I'm sick of your negative attitude."

"I'm not negative about *good* plans," Kady pointed out, but he spoke over her.

"You obviously don't have the courage to be part of this, so you can stay here as lookout. Make sure no one comes in after us."

Kady opened her mouth to protest, but Jan held up his hand, one finger raised. "Shut up," he said firmly. He looked at Scotty. "You stay with her. Make sure she doesn't run off and warn the guards or something."

"Oh, come on!" Scotty said. "It's Kady!"

"She's not to be trusted!" Jan insisted. "And that tiger stays out here too. Everyone else, with me. Anyone who doesn't feel up to it can start packing their bags as soon as they get back to the Bathysphere. Havoc doesn't have time for cowards."

That settled it. Dylan patted Scotty on the shoulder as he walked past. Justin gave Kady an apologetic look. Kady glared at him. She knew he had to go, or get kicked out of Havoc, but it still felt like he was taking Jan's side. Besides, she suspected he would have gone anyway. Jan's plan excited him. The thought of causing so much chaos was too tempting to turn down.

Then they were gone, and the door closed behind them. Tatyana watched them leave without much interest, then lay down on the floor and went to sleep. Kady fumed. Scotty eyed her nervously.

"He might pull it off, you know," Scotty said. It was meant to reassure her, but it just made her more angry.

"He's playing with everyone's lives!" she said. "And for what? This is one big ego-trip for him!"

"It'd show everyone that there's someone fighting back against Tall Jake."

"There are better ways to do it," she said. "Less dangerous ways. He's got them convinced that they're some kind of guerilla army, but whichever way you cut it, Havoc is just two dozen kids. Sure, this is one daring plan, and if it works it'll bring the house down. But Jan just wants to show everyone how great he is. That's what this is about. A good leader doesn't risk the lives of his friends on a glory-hunt."

Scotty looked down at the floor and shrugged. "That's why we need you back, Kady."

Kady sat down against the pillar, and Scotty sat next to her. Looking for all the world like a pair of tired travellers and their mechanical pet. For a time, she was silent, thinking about what Scotty had said.

She didn't come here looking to be leader. She'd just been tagging along with Justin, really. When Seth left, Kady had nowhere to go, so she went with Justin. He was the one who wanted to find Havoc.

But now she'd learned that she used to lead this ragtag group. And that some people had admired and respected her for it.

She was becoming exactly what Jan feared she would be. Just by being here, she was becoming his rival. Sooner or later, she would be forced to challenge him for leadership. Because she didn't like him. He was an insecure bully, and he was playing a deadly game without respect for the consequences. He was going to get someone killed.

She was looking out into the crowd that swirled around the platforms, not really paying attention, when suddenly she caught sight of someone she recognized.

She sat up. It *couldn't* be.

She was on her feet and pushing into the crowd a moment later. Scotty was on his feet, shouting "Hey!" after her. Tatyana opened an eye, decided that the fuss wasn't worth waking up for, and closed it again.

"'Scuse me! 'Scuse me!" Kady said as she barged through the denizens of Malice. Big ones, small ones, fat and thin, scaly and feathered. Had she been wrong? Had it been a trick of the eye?

Then there he was, right in front of her, looking around as if lost. He was wearing a backpack and facing away from her, so she grabbed him by the shoulder and spun him round. The expression of surprise on his face was comical.

"*Seth!*" she squealed.

She flung her arms around him and he gave her a breathtaking hug. For long seconds they stayed like that, her head against his chest, crushed together. She could feel his heart bumping against his ribs. The sound of his life. She could hardly believe that he was really here.

"You came back," she said. "You found me."

"Promised you I would, didn't I? I've got the Shard, too."

She blinked back tears. "Sir Knight never breaks his promises," she said.

Then he broke off the hug, and became urgent. "Where's Justin?"

For the first time Kady noticed that his jacket was ripped at the shoulder, and the material was stained with blood.

"You're hurt!"

He waved away her concern. "Looks worse than it is. I checked it out on the train. It's messy, but it's not deep."

"What happened?"

"Something tried to eat me. The usual." He grinned. "Now where's Justin?"

Kady thumbed in the direction of the maintenance door. "He's gone on with Jan. They're heading for the control room."

Seth's face fell. "We have to stop them!" he said.

"Why? What's wrong?"

"They're walking into a trap!"

2

"We're going in after them," Kady said to Scotty. Scotty stared at her, bewildered. He looked over at Seth, who was on his knees in front of Tatyana, his arms around her neck in a hug. The sabretooth had leaped to her feet at the sight of him, and was nuzzling him enthusiastically.

163

"Who *is* that?"

"That's Seth," she said. "He's got the Shard."

Scotty's jaw dropped. "He does?"

Kady didn't have time to explain. "Listen. They know about Jan's plan. Seth saw it in the comic, so that means Tall Jake must have seen it too."

Scotty's eyes went wide in alarm. "Then why the hell are you talking to me? Get in there after 'em!"

"Aren't you coming?"

"Someone needs to watch the door," he said. "Otherwise you might come out right in front of a bunch of Regulators. Knock three times on the other side. I'll let you out when the coast's clear."

Kady patted him on the arm. "Alright. Good thinking." She looked over her shoulder. "Seth! Come on! We're going!"

Seth hurried over to her, Tatyana padding alongside. He nodded at Scotty in greeting. They scanned the nearby crowd, but there was no sign of any Regulators. Nobody was paying them any attention. Scotty opened the door and ushered them through.

Beyond was a spiral staircase. Cool, wet air came up from the bottom. They hurried down, and the door clicked closed behind them.

Tatyana was in the lead, Seth behind her, with Kady bringing up the rear. She was still dazed by their reunion, but the joy of seeing him was mixed with disappointment. She felt cheated. They had only had a few brief moments to hold each other before plunging off in pursuit of Justin and the others. She'd been looking forward to that moment for so long, hoping, waiting to see him again. But when it finally happened, it was nothing like she imagined it would be.

The stairs ended in a suspended metal walkway that stretched across a huge, echoing chamber. Above were dank brick arches, supported by enormous pillars that rose to either side. The floor of the chamber was flooded, a rectangular black lake. A train rumbled overhead and the lake began to shiver. The electric lamps hanging from the walkway rocked back and forth, and a million little wavelets glinted beneath.

They hurried along. There was no time to be cautious. They had to catch up with the others.

They could see something lying on the walkway, halfway across the cavern, and slowed as they approached it. It looked somewhat like a large brass crab, with a domed, shiny shell and little pincer arms hanging down. Small round lenses surrounded its body in a ring. They were dark.

"I think it's, like, a security drone or something," Kady said.

Tatyana growled and sniffed at it.

"Can she smell anything?" Seth asked. "Having a mechanical nose and all?"

Suddenly the drone moved, sliding a few centimetres across the floor to bump into Tatyana's muzzle. She yowled and backed off. The drone came with her, stuck to her nose.

Kady and Seth grabbed it and pulled it off her. It took some effort.

"Magnetized," said Kady. "They must have hit it with a frazzler."

"A *what*?"

"Electromagnetic grenades. Bad news for machines."

"Tatyana, you'd better be careful," Seth advised. The sabretooth flounced off ahead of them with an air of hurt pride.

"She doesn't like being called a machine," Kady whispered.

"But I didn't mean—" Seth began, and then gave up. "Girls are so *sensitive*," he complained.

The walkway ended in a gate, which was standing open. Through the gate they came to a corridor, leading left and right.

"Which way?" Seth asked.

"I don't know. Pick one!"

So Seth did, and a few dozen metres further on they saw another broken drone, and realized they were on the right track. Seth raced ahead while Tatyana stepped gingerly around the magnetized wreckage.

"Seth! Wait up!" said Kady, and chased after him.

The corridor turned and turned again, and ended in a doorway. The door was open, and beyond was a small antechamber with another door on the far side. That door was closed.

Kady caught him up as Seth slowed down. There was something amiss. All the other doors had been left open. Why not this one?

He stepped into the room. Kady saw a quick movement to his right. He turned his head just in time to see an iron bar swinging down towards him. Kady's hands went to her mouth. She shut her eyes –

– but the impact didn't come.

"Seth?"

She opened one eye. The iron bar hovered a few centimetres above his head. On the other end of it was Justin.

"Can you please get that thing out of my face?" Seth asked.

Justin laughed with glee, flung the iron bar aside and hugged his friend. Then Kady punched him in the arm.

"You idiot, you nearly smashed his brains out!"

Now she'd come in to the room, she could see the other boys, Jan and Dylan and Parker and the rest. They'd been hiding on either side of the doorway.

"We heard someone running after us," said Justin, scratching the back of his neck sheepishly. "So we thought, you know, whack 'em with an iron pipe." He shrugged. "Seemed like a smart idea at the time."

Seth didn't seem to care. He was grinning like a fool. "It's good to see you," he said. "Even if you do look like someone punched you silly. One too many wisecracks, eh?"

"Something like that." He eyed Seth's bloodied shoulder. "You're not looking too hot yourself, mate."

"Who *are* you?" Jan demanded of Seth. He looked angry.

"This is Seth," said Kady. "Everyone, listen up. He's got

something very important to tell you."

"I can do better than that," he said. "I'll show you." And he pulled out some sheets of fax paper. He handed them to Jan. Two and a half pages of artwork by Grendel. The last one – a splash page of the Terminus – had been ripped off halfway.

Jan stared at them. The others crowded round. He heard them murmur in amazement. There was Jan, and Justin and Kady, in the Bathysphere. They were talking about the plan.

"He could see us," Dylan said. "Grendel could see us, right inside the Bathysphere."

"If he can see the Bathysphere, he could be heading there right now!" Parker snarled.

"I dunno," said Dylan. "I mean, it looks like we're only seeing it from the inside. Maybe Tall Jake don't know what he's looking at. He don't know everything."

"Still," said Kady. "We should be careful when we head back there. Just in case."

"Yeah," Dylan agreed. "Keep on our toes, like."

Justin peered over Dylan's shoulder, then looked up at Kady. "Here, you don't look half bad in this, Kady," he said. "Much better than in real life."

"I think there's still some unbruised bits on the left side of your face," said Kady. "Want me to take care of 'em for you?"

"It's a trick," said Jan, quietly.

Everyone looked at him.

"It's a trick!" he said again. He scrunched up the fax

papers and held them up in his fist. "This! It's a trick!" He threw them on the floor.

"It's not a trick," said Seth, bewildered at his reaction. "Look, if *I* knew where to find you, then Tall Jake certainly does. You've got to get out of here right now!"

"The control room is just beyond that door!" Jan said, indicating the metal door on the other side of the antechamber. He was addressing the other boys in the room now. "My contact – the one who gave me the plans and the code to the door – *he* says it's not guarded. That means we just have to walk in there, throw a frazzler into the works and the whole system shuts down. Permanently." He pointed at Kady. "Nobody knows where she's been all this time! Nobody knows if she can even be trusted!" He pointed to Justin and Seth. "I don't even know who they are!"

Jan was getting more and more worked up. He couldn't handle the idea that he might be denied just at the moment of triumph.

"I dunno, man," said Dylan, in a deep voice. His eyes were on the crumpled papers that lay on the floor. "Seems like a lot of trouble to go to, just to stop us doin' this thing. If Kady was a traitor, they didn't need to make up no fake comic pages or nothin'. They could've caught us as soon as we stepped off the train."

"Yes!" said Jan. "They could have caught us straight off the train. But they didn't, because they don't know we're here! Or maybe they know but they haven't had time to get here yet. Whichever, let's get in there and do this! Every moment we waste arguing is—"

"You're walking into a trap!" Seth cried. "They'll be waiting for you in there!"

Jan's face was flushed with fury. "This is *my* operation and we *will* succeed!"

Kady could see that this was going to turn bad, fast. She pushed into the argument. "Listen, everybody. Remember why I left? I left to find the Shard. We'd heard it could be a weapon against Tall Jake, right?"

There were nods of assent from those who remembered her. She unzipped Seth's backpack, dug in, and pulled out the strange ornament. The ornament that had been sitting on her bookshelf for a year.

"Here it is," she said.

"That's it?" sneered Jan, unimpressed.

"How's it work?" Dylan asked.

"We'll figure that out," Kady said quickly. "The point is, it's here. I brought it to you like I said I would. Trapped inside this ornament is Tall Jake's greatest enemy. The only one who can defeat him."

There were whispers of wonder from the other boys. Jan fumed as he heard them.

"We've got something worth fighting for now," she said. "Wrecking stuff for the sake of it is no good at all. Taking out the train system isn't going to *hurt* Tall Jake. It's just going to get on his nerves. With the Shard, we can hurt him. We can *stop* him."

"You're not the leader here!" Jan cried. He appealed to

the group. "We've planned so long! We're so close! Nobody is turning back now!"

"Don't go through that door!" Kady urged them. "Tall Jake knows you're coming!"

"It's not your choice!" snarled Jan. "It's mine! And we're going!"

"I ain't," said Dylan.

Jan stared at him. There was a glint of something manic in the Swedish boy's eyes. "What?"

"I ain't goin'," Dylan said. "Kady says it's a trap, it's a trap. I ain't walking into no trap."

"Then you can leave," said Jan. "You can leave Havoc. See how well you do on your own."

Dylan shrugged. "Maybe you won't be leader no more when you get back." He walked over to stand with Kady, Seth and Justin. The others hovered uncertainly around Jan.

Jan glared at Kady, eyes blazing. "See what you're doing? You're tearing Havoc apart!"

"Maybe that's what needs to be done," she replied. She looked at the rest of the Havoc kids. "Whoever wants to get out of here right now, come with me."

There was a beat of silence. Then one of the kids, a boy she didn't know, stepped over from Jan's side to hers.

"You're out, too!" Jan snapped.

It didn't stop them. Three more kids crossed over, their heads down, not meeting his eyes. Soon there was only Jan and his cronies left. Even Parker wasn't looking all that confident.

Jan spat on the floor. "Cowards," he said. "Filthy cowards.

I'll deal with you when I get back. *We'll* be the heroes! Let's see how many kids follow you *then*!"

"Jan, don't. . ." Kady said, but it was useless. He stalked over to the metal door and pulled it open a crack. Then he motioned to the three boys who still followed him. They gathered around him.

"It's clear," he said. "Go!"

They slipped past him, through the door. Parker hesitated on the threshold. He looked back at Kady and opened his mouth as if to say something. As if he was thinking of changing his mind. Jan smacked him on the arm and told him to get going. Parker scurried through.

"Cowards," Jan said again, staring hatefully at Kady. Then he went after them, pulling the door shut behind him.

Kady breathed out. She felt drained by the confrontation. She put the Shard back into Seth's pack and zipped it up.

"Well, I guess we'd better—" she began, but she was cut off by a sudden, loud ringing, coming from all around.

"It's an alarm!" someone cried, and then from beyond the door they heard the sputtering, chattering sound of automatic spear guns. Spear guns, and screams. Kady felt her stomach knot, and she felt weak and sick.

"Oh God. . ." she said. "Oh God. . ."

"*Run!*" Justin cried, and they fled out of the antechamber. Back into the corridors, back across the flooded room, back up the spiral stairs towards the boarding hall.

And still the alarms kept ringing.

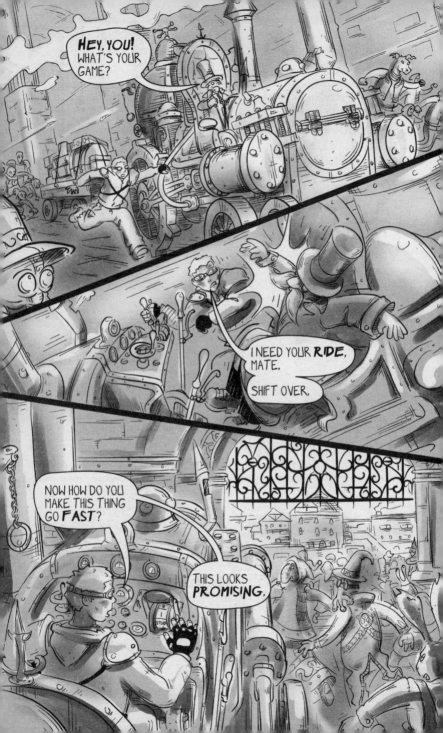

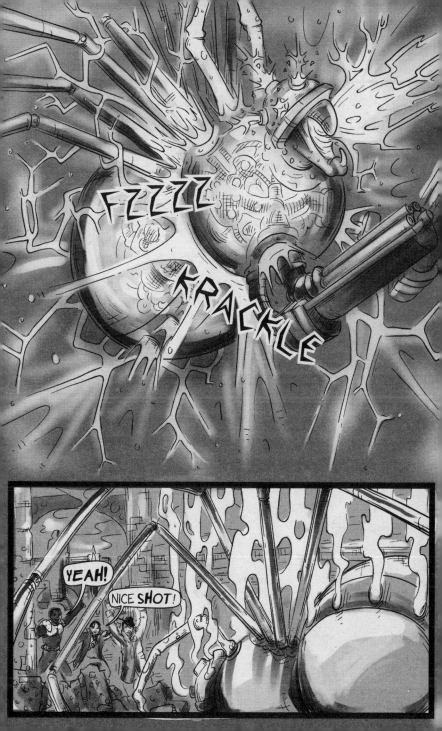

Perspectives

1

The next few days in the Bathysphere were slow and strange. Days for recovery and contemplation, to lick their wounds and mourn the dead.

Jan hadn't been well liked, nor had his cronies, but their absence was felt by the survivors of the massacre at the Terminus. Nobody in Havoc had died for a long time. Now they'd lost four at once, and they'd come close to losing many more. It sobered them. The game of tormenting Tall Jake didn't seem quite so much fun any more.

But Havoc lived on. That was the important thing. Havoc lived on, and Havoc was all they had left. Havoc was their family, their reason to exist. Without it, they would be lost and alone in this unfamiliar world.

Upon hearing Seth's story, some of the kids were uneasy about staying in the Bathysphere. They were worried that Tall Jake could see them. They posted extra guards, but Seth told them not to worry. If Tall Jake hadn't come by now, Seth didn't think he would. And if Grendel was watching them, he'd be able to sense it, like he had in the Deadhouse with Alicia. He'd sensed Grendel's eye on them in the Terminus, too, but he'd been too busy to do anything about it.

Some believed him, some didn't. Either way, they had nowhere else to go, so they stayed put.

Kady was the leader now. Nothing official was said, and she herself never claimed the title, but it was assumed. She spent time talking to all the kids, getting to know them. She learned how the Bathysphere worked. Scotty told her how he'd been stripping the place of valuable lab equipment and selling it in the City, in exchange for supplies to keep them all fed. Dylan told her stories of trading expeditions to keep good relations with other groups like them. He didn't say much most of the time, but he was the son of a market trader in the East End of London. He knew how to bargain. That was how they'd got hold of the frazzlers.

Kady did her best to settle into her new role, but she found it an uncomfortable fit. She'd been eager to get rid of Jan, because she felt he was endangering these kids; but now she was in his place, she was crowded with doubts. Her first impressions when she arrived in the Bathysphere were proved right: these weren't a group of warriors, but a bunch of frightened kids playing grown-up games. Deadly games. Whoever this Kady was that they all remembered, she seemed like a stranger. Kady was good at organizing people, yes. But to be *responsible* for them? That was a different matter entirely.

She wasn't sure she wanted this. But there was no one else willing to take up the role.

She found herself thinking more and more about her parents with each passing day. Whatever doubts and fears she was going through, they were dealing with worse. Their daughter was still missing. Her last sight of them had been when they caught her running away from home. She'd been angry and bitter when she left. Since then, they'd had no word. The agony of not knowing must have been terrible.

Mom. Dad. I'm sorry.

She started taking long walks, away from the lake and through the woods. Tatyana would go with her, a silent guardian. But there was nothing dangerous hiding in the trees. The woods were empty and dreary. Kady felt the same.

Her favourite route took her out of the woods, up a hill and along its stony ridge. From there, she could see for miles across the land. Malice was a world of deep greens and soft browns and pale greys: an autumn, watercolour world. The sun seemed smaller and fainter than the one she knew from California. Hills and valleys swooped and plunged. In the distance was a crumbled aqueduct of white stone, protruding halfway across a valley.

Somebody made this place, she thought. *How is that possible? How can a world in a comic book be real?*

One afternoon, as she was standing there, she heard footsteps coming up the ridge behind her. It was Seth. Tatyana padded off to greet him, and accompanied him back to her.

"How do you do it, Seth?" she asked, still looking out over the vista. "How do you go around feeling responsible for everybody all the time?"

"I dunno," said Seth. "I just do."

"I can't lead Havoc," she said. "What if I screw it up? What if I end up like Jan?"

"I saw what Jan's boys did to Justin," he replied. "You're not like Jan."

"But how would I know?" she said. "I mean, sometimes you can't see it. He thought he was doing the right thing. He did it for the wrong reasons, and he didn't account for the consequences, but in his head he was doing right by those kids."

Seth didn't answer for a while. He just stared out over the land. Finally, he spoke. "You just do the best you can, Kady. Sometimes it's not enough, but most of the time it is."

Kady gazed at him helplessly. "I should have tried harder to stop him," she said.

Seth didn't reply to that. He just put his arm round her, and she leaned into his shoulder.

"I'm really happy you're back, Seth."

"Me, too."

7

"Doesn't look like much," Dylan said.

The Shard sat in the centre of the table. Gathered

round it were Seth, Kady, Justin, Scotty and Dylan. They were in the Bathysphere's laboratory. Outside, it was night. The glowing marine animals of the lake flashed and flitted beyond the observation window.

"So how's it work?" Scotty asked.

"Your guess is as good as mine," Kady said. "Seth, didn't you do some mumbo-jumbo to wake it up?"

"I touched it, that's all!" Seth protested. "I don't know what I did."

"Remember back in Skarla's den, when she had that scrying orb thing, and Seth made it work?" Justin said. "I bet it was like that."

"Yes!" said Seth. "It's something to do with the power the Lack gave me."

Dylan and Scotty awaited an explanation.

"In the Oubliette . . . I kinda killed the Mort-Beast with the Lack's bow and arrow. And in return, she decided I was going to be her champion."

"Whatever *that* means," Kady added.

"Right," Seth continued. "But ever since then I've had weird things happening. I could sense the places where Malice had touched our world, like where Tall Jake had been, or the places where you could cross over. Other things, too. Like how I can tell when we're being watched."

"Try touching the Shard," Scotty suggested. "See if you can wake it up again."

"Better not," said Seth. "Last time it brought Tall Jake down on me. I think he can sense when it's awake."

"Oh well," said Justin. "We can use it to bash Tall Jake's head in, if nothing else."

"So what now, then?" Scotty said.

"When we met Skarla in the Oubliette, she said that once we had the Shard, the rest of the Six might join us," Kady said. "Maybe one of them knows what to do with it."

"Anyone know how to find 'em?" Dylan said.

There were blank looks around the table.

"Well, what do we know about the Six?" Kady asked, pacing around. "We know Tall Jake is one, and he's out. We have the Shard. So that leaves four."

"The Lack has already got involved," said Seth. "I get the feeling that if she was going to show herself, she would have done it when we killed the Mort-Beast. I don't think she wants to be found."

"They're all still scared of Tall Jake," said Scotty. "If he works out where they are, he'll destroy them, like he did with Crowfinger. At least, if you believe the stories."

"Let's say we do," said Kady. "That's two left, then. You mentioned another: the Cripplespite?"

"No idea about him," Scotty said. "Rumours are he disappeared and was never seen again. I've never heard anything different."

"Which leaves the Queen of Cats," Kady said. "And she's had her hand in this from the start."

"Her *paw*," Justin corrected.

"Whatever. The fact is, her cats have been helping us out all along."

"But we still don't know where to find her."

"We can look," she said. She turned to Scotty. "You said she used to rule from the Acropolis, right? Why don't we start there?"

Scotty shook his head. "Tall Jake wasted that place. It used to be this amazing city of temples, where cats were served and worshipped by people. But Tall Jake destroyed it, and put some kind of curse on the ruins. The way I hear it, the Acropolis is haunted. The living don't go there."

Seth frowned. *A city of temples. . .*

"This Acropolis," he said. "Would it have, like, columns and plazas and domes and arches and things like that? But all smashed up?"

Scotty shrugged. "I've never seen it, but sure, that sounds right."

"*I've* seen it," he said. "I saw it when I stroked one of her cats. It was the Lack's power again. It pulled those pictures out of the cat's mind and showed them to me. The cat wasn't too pleased by it, either. I think I saw something I shouldn't have."

They were all looking at him strangely.

"What if the Queen of Cats never went anywhere at all?" he asked. "What if she's still hiding in the Acropolis? The last place Tall Jake would look would be a place that he'd already demolished."

"Well, I guess it's possible. . ." Kady said doubtfully.

"It's more than possible!" Seth said. "I *saw* it. The Lack showed me the way through the Acropolis." He slapped the table excitedly. "I know how to find the Queen of Cats!"

TWO TRAILS

The Printworks

1

"*Please don't ignore this message. There's too much at stake.*"

Alicia took her mobile from her ear and put it back in her pocket. Her mum gave her one of those crinkly frowns she did.

"On your phone at breakfast? Didn't I bring you up better than that?" she asked in her bouncy Jamaican lilt.

"Just checking my messages," Alicia replied.

"Have some toast, hmm?"

"I'm okay, Mum. I'm not hungry."

"Well, eat anyway! I'm not having you going to school on an empty stomach."

"Oi, Mum, give us the butter!" Lemar called.

"No more phone at the breakfast table, eh?" Mum told Alicia. "Heaven forbid you grow up with manners like your brother."

"Yeah, heaven forbid Miss Goody-Two-Shoes should end up like the Big Bad Wolf. Can I have the butter now?"

Mum tutted loudly and passed the butter. "I don't know what's become of him," she said, shaking her head.

Alicia nibbled at the corner of her toast. Breakfast time at the Lanes' house. Dad was reading the paper, Lemar was being loud and annoying, Mum was clucking over everyone. Just like every other day.

Except everything was different now.

She'd barely slept these last five days. She went to school in a daze, sat in her classes and mechanically completed her tasks. Her friends worried about her, but she didn't know how to tell them what was wrong, so she avoided them. She listened to the message that Seth had left her, over and over. She knew it off by heart by now. Every pause, every stumble, every quiet crackle on the line.

She listened, and still she did nothing.

"I gave you Icarus Scratch's car number plate. I also found an address. It's where they print the Malice comic. The address is: The Printworks, Matham Industrial Estate, Stevenage, Herts."

She'd looked up the address on the Net. She'd put it into Google Earth and stared at a satellite photo of the location, seen from above. Just a bunch of low rectangular buildings and a few parked cars. Nothing special about it at all.

"Someone needs to do something about it. And you're the only one I can tell."

She wished she'd never got a lift with Lemar to Sally's house last Sunday. She wished she'd never met Seth. She wished she hadn't decided to help him.

Because now she knew about Malice, and she could never go back.

Every night she lay awake, terrified of going to sleep. Malice was real. Tall Jake was real. And she'd called on him. It didn't matter that it had been a dare, a bit of fun to get a scared giggle from her friends. One night, when she was alone, he would come for her. She'd end up in a place like the Deadhouse. Except this time, it wouldn't be half so easy to get out.

How could she carry on with her life, knowing that? What was the point of working for your GCSEs when, sooner or later, you were just going to disappear?

"Someone needs to do something about it."

Nobody could. Nobody except her.

"You look tired, Alicia. You still not sleeping well?" asked Mum, pouring tea from a pot. "Did you try drinking hot milk before bed?"

"I tried," she said. "It didn't do any good."

Mum made a sympathetic face. "It's just growing up, honey. All kinds of weird things happen. It'll pass."

Alicia managed to smile. "I'm sure it will."

"Just as long as it doesn't start to affect your studies," said Dad, from behind his paper.

Alicia felt a surge of anger. As if *that* was the most important thing in the world! The house could be burning down around them and Dad would still insist she did her homework before he let them out. Mum wasn't quite so bad, but she had to support Dad. They'd given up on

Lemar; Alicia was their last hope for a brilliant child. Except she didn't want to be a brilliant child. She wanted to draw.

Mum passed the cups of tea around. She was a tall, elegant, graceful woman, and everything she did was precise and smooth, even when she was distributing breakfast.

"Well, anyway, it's half term next week," she said. "A whole week off. You'll have plenty of time to rest."

Dad harrumphed and rustled his paper, which was Dad-ese for "Better not rest *too* much. There's homework to be done!"

"That reminds me," said Lemar. "Mum, I'm borrowing your car tomorrow, okay?"

"After what you did to your dad's?" she cried. "I don't think so!"

Lemar looked at Alicia expectantly. Alicia was slow to catch on, but then she remembered the deal that she'd made with him on the night of the crash.

"Oh, come on, Mum," she said. "It wasn't his fault. I was there, remember? There was no way he could have avoided that deer."

Mum pursed her lips disapprovingly. "And where would you be wanting to take my car?"

"London," he said. "Record shopping."

"What's wrong with the shops in Leicester?"

Lemar made a face. "Mum, they don't have *anything* in Leicester. London's got all the rare stuff."

"Isn't Stevenage on the way to London?" Alicia said suddenly.

"No!" said Lemar.

"Yes it is," sighed Dad from behind his paper. It was tiring to be right all the time. "You get off the M1 at Luton."

"What's in Stevenage?" Mum asked Alicia.

"A friend," Alicia replied, almost before she knew what she was saying. Then, because she had to cover up the lie, she added: "A friend of mine from school. Her family moved there a few months ago. I promised I'd go visit her when I could. Just for the day, I mean. I don't want to stay overnight or anything."

"Oh, no! Don't be thinking *I'm* taking you!" Lemar said.

"Young man, if you're borrowing my car, you can take your sister too," Mum said firmly. "You can get her on the way back."

Lemar threw up his hands in disgust. It was useless to argue when Mum took on that tone.

"Your brother will drop you off in the morning and pick you up in the afternoon," Mum told Alicia. "It'll do you good to take a trip, see your friend. You study so hard. Maybe you just need a little break."

Alicia nodded dazedly. It had all happened so fast. One minute she'd been despairing about the rest of her life, the next she was going to Stevenage. It was almost as if the decision had been made for her.

Something had to be done. She couldn't hide from Malice. All she could do was try to help stop Tall Jake and his terrible comic. So she was going to the printworks.

That night, she slept like a baby.

Lemar sulked the whole way there. He put on a CD of music she hated and played it at deafening volume just to annoy her. She didn't rise to it. She just looked out of the window.

When they got to the edge of Stevenage she started giving him directions off a printout from Routefinder. The industrial estate was easy to find, since it stood on its own in the middle of nowhere. When they got to the entrance, she told Lemar to stop and got out.

"You sure?" he said doubtfully. There was nothing around except for a cluster of long, ugly buildings walled with grey sheets of galvanized metal. A few cars were parked around the place, but no other signs of life were evident. The sky was heavy with cloud, and it looked ominously like rain.

"Her dad's got a meeting here. He's picking me up on his way out," Alicia said. "We're early."

Lemar looked uncertain. He was caught between being angry at her and worrying about his little sister. "I can wait," he said reluctantly.

"It's fine," she said. She held up her mobile. "Look, it's okay. I've got my phone. I'll just call her if there's a problem."

Lemar hesitated a moment more, then shrugged. "Alright. I'll phone you when I'm on my way back, yeah?" Then he gunned the engine and drove off.

Alicia watched him until he was out of sight. Suddenly, she felt very alone. She felt awful about lying to everyone. Now here she was, miles from anywhere, and she was stuck here all day.

She'd heard stories about terrible things happening to kids who lied to their parents and sneaked out to some party, or to meet someone they only knew over the internet. She'd always wondered how they could be stupid enough to get themselves into that situation in the first place. Now she knew.

A short road led into the industrial estate. There was a small car park off to one side, after which the road split to wind its way through the group of buildings. She followed it in. It was a Saturday, and the place was quiet. Most people wouldn't be at work, but there were a few cars in the car park, so *someone* was here.

She'd turned it all over in her head before they set off. What if she got there and nobody was there? What if the door was locked and she simply couldn't get in? Well, if that was the case, then she had a long day ahead of her. She'd brought a book, and her sketch pad, and her MP3 player in her bag. She would read, or draw, or listen to music until her brother came back.

But she hadn't counted on rain. "Great," she muttered, as she felt a cold drop on her nose.

She made her way into the estate. Covered forklift trucks and heaps of pallets lay idle. Plastic-coated wire fences bordered the lots. Weeds and scrub grass grew in untended corners. The boxy buildings had high, small windows. Some of them had hoardings on the side that proclaimed the name of the company which owned them: *Stormont Cabinets*; *Johnson's Timber*; *Imagination, Inc*. None of them were what she was looking for.

She investigated those buildings that had no hoardings on, and discovered they all had a small sign by the main door to identify them. As she wandered, she was spotted by two men in hard hats, carrying a long beam of newly cut wood between them. They asked her if she was lost.

"I'm fine," she said, and hurried on. She didn't want to mention the printworks. They didn't look like Tall Jake's sort, but you never knew.

The rain became a drizzle, and Alicia hugged her coat tighter, scampering from building to building with her head down.

She found the printworks near the back of the estate. It was a building like all the others, with a small sign outside. The faint whirr of machinery came from within. Printing presses, she guessed. Printing copies of Malice, perhaps.

She hesitated at the door, but the rain was getting heavier, and her thick hair was getting wet. She might have hovered outside for a long time, building up her courage, but the rain drove her onward.

It was only as she was stepping into the building that she realized she had no idea what to do or say if she was stopped. What would she say to the receptionist? What excuse did she have for being there? She'd been so concerned with getting here that she hadn't really worked out the details.

The door opened into a shabby reception area. It was like the waiting room for a doctor's surgery, except that nobody had hoovered in years. Only one of the striplights was working. The others had gone out, and nobody had replaced them.

She felt fear creep into her as she stood there. There was no heating on, and it was chilly. No ordinary office would be so neglected. This was a place that didn't expect to get any visitors.

No question about it. She was on the right track.

There were two doors leading out of the reception area. One had narrow glass sections set into it, to see through to the other side. Beyond was a long corridor. She listened at the other, and heard nothing but the crunch and whine of the machines. She pulled it open and peered through. Behind was a dim stairwell. She crept up it.

At the top, one storey up, was another door. She listened again. The machines were louder here. She peeked out. Beyond was a concrete walkway. It spanned the floor below, with another door at its far end. Seeing nobody on the walkway, she slipped carefully through and looked over the edge.

The sound of the printing press filled the room, loud enough to hurt her ears. There was a miniature factory floor beneath her. The press was the largest of the machines, but there were also several that Alicia couldn't identify, along with various computers and printers and photocopiers. Everything looked old and cheap – a second-hand production line.

Pages of comic art were sliding out of the press into a drop tray, where they were picked up by one of the workers who attended the various machines. There were six of them, men and women, all wearing ink-smudged orange boiler suits. They had a listless, dreary look about them. The women had lank, greasy hair and the men were unshaven and haggard. None of them spoke.

She crouched on the walkway and watched them. They carried the pages to a machine which punched staples into the pages and bound them together. Though she was too far away to see, she was in no doubt that she was watching copies of Malice being printed. In this dingy, cold, dim room, these strange, silent people were assembling the new issue. A new collection of terrible tales. When it was done, it would be distributed, by secret, underground ways, until it fell into the hands of the kids who thirsted for it. They would tell their friends, and their friends would dare each other to call on Tall Jake, just to show they weren't scared.

By the time they realized they *should* be scared, it was too late.

She heard a door open and footsteps approaching along the factory floor. As she hunkered down further, an enormous man strode into the room, carrying an artist's folder. He was wearing a long, grey coat, with matching waistcoat and trousers, and there was a fedora on top of his head that blocked her view of his face.

As he walked beneath her, she noticed that his hat and shoulders were wet. That meant he'd just arrived, because the rain was heavier now. She could hear it drumming on the roof. She felt a little surge of pride at the deduction. Being observant was what being an artist was all about.

The man walked over to a desk, opened the folder and pulled out several large sheets of card. They were covered with black and white panels and illustrations. Pages of art for the comic. They would be reduced in size when they were printed on to the page. Alicia craned closer, trying to catch a glimpse, but even at this size they were too far away.

"New artwork from Grendel," the man called. "You hear me, you pestilent bunch? I want this in the next issue!" His voice was high and he had a slight lisp: not at all the voice she would have expected from someone so large.

Nobody had paid any attention to him until that point. Now one of the workers came shuffling over and began to examine the pages.

"Make sure you get them in the right order this time, you moronic little scab," the man instructed. The worker merely nodded, as if he hadn't heard the insult. He picked up the sheets and carried them over to a battered scanner.

The man in the fedora surveyed the room. "Pathetic, all of you," he said. "I'm heading back to Crouch Hollow now.

Not that anyone cares." He waited for a response, but he was ignored. "Yes, Mr Scratch!" he said, talking to himself in a falsetto voice. "Thank you for bringing us some new artwork, Mr Scratch!" When nobody answered, he reverted to his usual tone. "Odious mongrels!" he snarled, and stamped off.

Alicia's heart was in her mouth. So that was Icarus Scratch! She recognized the name – Seth had given her the number plate of his car. He was heading to some place called Crouch Hollow. By the sound of it, that was where Grendel was, and even *she* knew that Grendel was the artist behind Malice.

She found herself seized by an idea. If Scratch was here, that meant his car was here. And if his car was here. . .

She had no time to debate it in her head. If she didn't act now, the chance would be gone. The trail would end here. She hadn't learned enough to stop the comic yet.

She hurried to the door which led back into the stairwell, pulled it open, and almost screamed as she found herself face-to-face with one of the workers.

Her hand flew to her mouth. She was caught!

He was a thin, unhealthy-looking man in his thirties, with thatchy stubble and hair that looked like he'd just got out of bed. He was wearing the same boiler suit as the rest of them.

There was no trace of surprise on his face. He gazed at her blankly with watery grey eyes. Alicia, terrified, didn't dare to move.

Then the man's gaze shifted away, and he walked past her, without saying a word.

Alicia couldn't believe it. She stared at his back as he ambled slowly along the walkway. He'd just ignored her. As if it was perfectly normal to find a stranger wandering around inside the building.

She remembered that she'd never heard any of them speak. Not even when they were being abused by Scratch. What was *wrong* with these people?

Then she saw the long, puckered scar on the back of his head. It ran along the base of the skull and up, disappearing into his hairline. She knew then why these people were so blank and docile. They were like the man she'd seen with the cage on his head. They'd come from the Deadhouse. They'd been *operated* on.

Suddenly she couldn't stand being here a moment longer. She fled, down the stairs, back to reception and out of the building.

3

The rain was falling hard outside. She put her head down and ran, her feet splashing on the tarmac road as she fled towards the entrance to the industrial estate. As she went, she fumbled in her pocket and pulled out the bus information leaflet that Seth had given her back in Birmingham. On it was written the number plate of Scratch's car. She memorized it, then stuffed it back in her pocket so the rain wouldn't make the ink run.

The car park only had a few cars in it. One of them was a beaten-up silver Citroën estate. The number plate matched.

She looked back up the road, towards the printworks. No sign of Scratch yet. Quickly, she raced up to the car, wiped the rain off the windscreen and looked inside. Maybe there was a clue left on the dashboard, or on the seat ... something that might tell her where Crouch Hollow was. She saw sweets wrappers, discarded crisp packets and open Coke cans, but nothing that would help her.

Move it, Alicia! Get out of here! What if he catches you?

But she couldn't go yet. She couldn't let him drive away without finding out more. She hurried round to the back seat. Maybe there was something there.

There wasn't. Only a shabby tartan wool blanket thrown behind the passenger seat, big enough to cover a horse.

There must be something! A picture, an address, anything like that!

That was when she noticed the doors were unlocked.

A thought occurred to her. One so reckless and stupid that she couldn't believe it had come from her own head.

You can't be thinking about getting in the car.

But she was. She tried the door – just to see – and it came open. She was amazed. Scratch was either lazy, absent-minded, or didn't care if his car got stolen (possibly all three).

"What are you doing, Alicia?" she asked herself, with a note of despair in her voice.

She looked up the road, and saw Scratch emerging from the doorway of the printworks. No more time to deliberate. It was now or never.

She pulled open the door, jumped inside and closed it behind her. Almost immediately, she began to panic.

This is criminal! You're a criminal! You've broken into someone's car! Not to mention what he'll do to you if he catches you! What's Dad going to say?

It was too late to run. If she tried to get out now, he'd surely see her. And where would she go? She was miles from any help.

Alicia had never been a risk taker. She never took an exam without thoroughly preparing herself, and she never did anything that might make her teachers or parents mad. She'd never really failed at anything important, mostly because she never tried things she thought she might fail. But Daddy's little golden girl had really got herself into trouble now.

There was only one thing to do: hide. She burrowed down behind the passenger seat, then pulled the old blanket over her so that she was buried beneath. The blanket stank of animal musk, foul and sharp. She suddenly wondered if the last thing using this blanket had been the monster that she saw that night near Hathern, when Lemar had accidentally hit a "deer".

She didn't want to think about that. She made herself as

small as she could and lay there. She could imagine Scratch getting closer and closer, striding across the car park. What if he'd seen her get in? Could she expect the door to be flung open, to be seized by strong hands?

Suddenly, she remembered her mobile phone. She dug it out of her bag, switched it off, and shoved it back. Then she heard footsteps, and went still, like a frightened rabbit.

A door opened; she couldn't tell which one. Alicia squeezed her eyes shut and held her breath.

Don't let him see me! Please don't let him see me!

A weight landed across her back, and she nearly shrieked. But it was only something light. Something light that rustled . . .

His coat. He'd thrown his coat on top of her.

The door closed and another opened, followed by a creak as Scratch eased his bulk into the driver's seat, huffing. He murmured curses about the weather as he pulled the door shut. She heard the hiss of a Coke can and then some thirsty gulping.

Curled up in the stinking dark of the blanket, she trembled and wished desperately that she was anywhere but here.

Scratch stuffed the can into the inside pocket of the door and fired the engine. "Back to Crouch Hollow," he sighed to himself. He released the handbrake, backed out of his parking spot, and they were on their way.

Crouch Hollow

1

It might have been an hour they travelled, or it might have been four. Alicia was locked in her private little nightmare, motionless, not daring to move. It seemed impossible that Scratch wouldn't notice her, crouched behind the passenger seat, only a foot or two away from him. Even if he didn't, he surely would when the journey ended. He would pick up the coat that lay on top of her, and she would be discovered.

Until then, she hid. Her body ached and there was a sparkling numb feeling in her thighs, but she didn't move a muscle. She took shallow, quiet breaths, trying not to take in too much of the musky stench. She prayed, wildly and desperately.

With her eyes closed, she had only her ears to tell her what was going on around her. She listened to the engine as the car sped up and slowed. She heard when the road surface changed and went from bumpy to smooth. Soon they were making a steady pace, and she realized they were on a motorway. Every minute that passed took her a mile further away from safety.

What would happen if Lemar called, and her phone was off? What if she couldn't get home by tonight? How would her parents feel if she went missing?

She couldn't worry about them now. She could only stay still – very, very still – and hope.

Icarus Scratch talked to himself. He flicked through radio stations restlessly, commenting on this song and that one, never settling. He discussed the bad driving of other road users. Occasionally he sang in a high, reedy monotone.

After a time, unable to find anything he liked, he switched off the radio and drove in silence. It wasn't long before he began talking to himself again, and this time what he said was so extraordinary that Alicia found herself listening to every word.

"I should have strangled him when I had the chance," he murmured. "I wish I'd never laid eyes on that wretched place."

Who does he mean? What place? Is he talking about Crouch Hollow?

"Just my luck, I suppose. Poor, poor Icarus. Nothing ever goes right for him. Nothing comes without a struggle. Nothing's ever simple." He paused, interrupting the flow of bitter self-pity. Then he blurted: "Who ever knew dear Daddy owned a place like that? Who ever knew the withered old rotbag would will it to me when he died? Sounds wonderful, doesn't it? I could have sold it off, made a million! But no! Things don't work out that way for Icarus Scratch, do they?

I bet he planned it, that twisted, incontinent so-and-so. I bet he *knew* Grendel was there, up in the attic, waiting for poor Icarus to stumble across him.

"I should have strangled him and sold the house. At least I'd be rich then. At least I'd be rich!"

There was silence for a time. Then he said: "This had all better be worth it. Because that's *my* money paying for that stupid shop and that stupid printworks and that stupid comic, and I'm not seeing a penny back! Not a penny! We're making a comic and *giving* it away! And it's poor Icarus humping back and forth with those accursed scribbles, poor Icarus who has to stand day after day in that awful shop, poor Icarus who keeps the wolf from the door! Well, it had better all be worth it. Tall Jake had better keep his promises and give me what's mine. Because we Scratches have long memories, yes we do. You don't want Icarus Scratch coming after you!"

He huffed angrily, but the outburst seemed to calm him down a little. Shortly afterward, he said, "I suppose it's not all bad. At least the staff is cheap," and burst out in a high giggle. Then he turned the radio on and found some jazz he liked, and he didn't talk much after that.

2

The rain kept coming. Eventually they pulled off the motorway and on to bumpy, uneven roads. Alicia felt the car turn often, and it sped up and slowed down more frequently. She decided that they were in the countryside, driving down winding lanes. It was important to observe all she could. The cool, clinical process of deduction kept her from total panic.

Then, quite suddenly, the car swung to the right and stopped. Before she knew what was happening, there was a loud rustle and movement around her, and her heart leaped in terror. The coat was gone from her back. But nobody pulled away the blanket to reveal her.

Scratch was grunting and creaking in the front seat, struggling to put on the coat while still inside the car. He must have reached over and picked it up, without really looking. Alicia could hardly believe her luck. She began to think that maybe, just maybe, the stowaway might go undetected.

But what then?

Scratch got out of the car and slammed the door behind him. Alicia heard footsteps and muffled voices. She steeled her nerve and poked her head out of the blanket.

After so long in the dark, even the dull light of a rainy day made her blink. She listened to the voices, to assure herself that Scratch wasn't standing nearby. They were too far away to make out any words through the sound of the rain. Very slowly, she raised her head and looked out of the window.

The car was parked on a drive in front of a big wrought-iron gate, which was set in a high wall of red brick. It was like the entrance to a stately home, except that the gate was patchy with rust and vines had crept through the metalwork. To the left of the gate was a small, run-down cottage – a gatekeeper's lodge. Trees concealed the drive from the road, and there was a wood beyond the wall.

By the door of the lodge, she saw Scratch and another man, blurred by the rain. She guessed the other man was the gatekeeper. He was wearing a mac with the hood pulled up. But it was Icarus Scratch who fascinated her. His pudgy white face, without eyebrows or lashes. He looked like a shop-window dummy or a doll.

Then the gatekeeper turned his head, and she saw the face beneath the hood. Or rather, the *faces*.

The gatekeeper's face kept changing. At one moment, it would look perfectly normal: a little ugly, with a long face and a hook nose. But then the rain would wash down the window, and just for an instant, she would glimpse something *other* underneath. Through the distorting lens of the water, she saw something monstrous. A wizened, wrinkled, fanged face, with goatlike eyes and leathery skin.

Scratch gestured at the wall and the trees beyond, and suddenly they both came walking towards the car. Alicia ducked down in fright and buried herself in the blanket again.

The door opened and Scratch got in, still talking to the gatekeeper.

"I want you to be especially vigilant, you hear? Someone got into our house in Kensington, and who knows what information they gathered. I don't want anyone finding Crouch Hollow."

"Don't trouble yourself," the gatekeeper assured him in a pinched, nasal voice. "There's things in that wood that'll pull you limb from limb in half a tick. Anyone tries to get over this wall, they'll be food. Only way in and out is up the drive, and I'll be watching."

"See that you are," said Scratch, and closed the door. There was a clanking and scraping as the gates were opened, and then Scratch drove slowly through.

Alicia stayed huddled and motionless. Her eyes were squeezed shut, but the image of the gatekeeper's face was burned on her mind. Not for the first time, nor the last, she wished she'd never got into this.

The car travelled on for a minute or two before Scratch killed the engine, opened the door and got out. Alicia listened as the door slammed, and then she heard shoes crunching away across gravel. After that, there was silence, except for the rain.

She didn't move for some time. Worn out by fear. She could hardly believe she'd made it the whole way without being noticed. She didn't want to get out of the car. Whatever was outside might be even worse.

But she'd only got through the first part. She couldn't give up yet. She would have to be brave again.

When she was certain that Scratch had gone, she took off the blanket and looked out of the window. The car was parked in front of a huge red-brick building. It looked like it had once been a hospital or something like that. Now, the windows were grimy and creepers grew on the walls. The bricks were covered in patches of lichen and damp, and the window sills were crumbling. There was a shattered roof slate on the driveway.

In front of the building was a vast lawn that had grown wild. Grasses and weeds were waist-high. The lawn ended at the edge of the wood, where the trees were shaking and hissing under the assault from the skies.

Alicia eased herself up on to the back seat of the car and checked the area. There was no sign of life anywhere.

She got out of the car and scampered over to the porch, out of the rain. The front door opened with the slightest of creaks. Gathering her courage, she stepped inside.

3

Alicia found herself in a large semicircular room which she guessed was once a reception area. Bits of paper stirred on dusty shelves behind a counter. It was cold and dark and smelled of mould. Water dripped from the ceiling and pooled in corners.

There were several doors leading away from the reception area. A trail of wet footprints and drips led through one of them. That was the way Scratch had gone. It seemed stupid to go following after him, but then again, the whole reason she'd gone to the printworks was to find out what was happening in the secret world of the comic. So follow him she did.

The door was plated in metal. On the other side was a corridor, with plaster peeling off the wall and dirty floors. Halfway up, the corridor was divided by bars, like a prison. There was a door set into the bars. It stood open now, but once it had been locked, to keep whatever was on the other side from getting into the reception area.

What sort of place was this?

Just beyond the bars, there were several cells on either side. The cell doors had circular portholes in them, to allow people in the corridor to look in. The cells were fitted with fixed beds, but no mattresses, and the grimy walls were scratched with graffiti. They were not occupied.

Alicia could hear faint voices coming from up ahead. They echoed in the empty spaces of the building. She crept closer. If she could hear where they were, then at least they couldn't jump out at her.

She passed by a small room that looked like a nurses' station. Beyond, the corridor turned a corner. She peered round and saw that the corridor ended in a half-open door, leading into a common area of some kind. The common room was dim and shadowy, the daylight choked by filthy windows. As she looked, a bulky figure crossed her line of vision.

Icarus Scratch. He was in there, talking to someone. She stayed where she was and listened.

"I *know* it was them! Those vicious little malcontents. Seth Harper and Kady Blake!"

"It might have been him, but it can't have been *her*." A woman's voice now, with a clipped, snooty tone. She couldn't see the owner. "She's been in Malice the whole time. Stirring up trouble."

"If only I'd recognized her sooner, that first time I saw

her in the shop! I *knew* I'd seen her before, in the comic. It's so hard to tell when you've never seen someone in real life. . ." He snorted and paced around the room. "How could I have forgotten her? She was the leader of Havoc!"

"And will be again, if her performance in the Terminus was anything to go by."

Scratch muttered something foul under his breath.

"At least we know they're both in Malice now," said the woman. "They won't bother us here for a while."

"But what if there are *more* of them? Seth got away from the Stalker somehow, when we almost caught him in Hathern. He couldn't have done that without help, Miss Benjamin."

The Stalker? Is that what that terrible thing is called? And who's Miss Benjamin? Oh, I wish I'd talked to Seth about all of this when I had the chance. But I just didn't ask, because I didn't want to know.

"He had help when I caught him using the chat room," Miss Benjamin agreed.

Alicia's eyes widened. So this Miss Benjamin was actually Mim from the IRC chat room. The one who had threatened to kill Seth.

She remembered Philip's response when they asked who Mim was. "*She's always around, being annoying. She keeps trying to make friends with people, trying to get them to meet up with her in real life so they can swap notes on Malice. She's pretty desperate. Nobody likes her much.*"

If only they knew. She wondered what became of the kids who *did* meet up with her in real life.

"If they broke into the house, they could find the printworks," Icarus Scratch was saying. "And that could lead them here. If they learn enough, they might get adults involved, and then we'll have all kinds of problems."

- They have the Shard. That concerns me deeply. -

A shiver ran down Alicia's spine. That voice! It was like the breath of the grave.

"The Shard is in Malice, Tall Jake," Scratch said. "That's your department, not mine. My concern is the comic."

Alicia's knees went weak. *Tall Jake? Tall Jake is in that room?*

"If the adults find out what we're doing, there'll be no more comic," Scratch continued. "No more comic means no more rumours. No more rumours means no more brats believe in you. And you want them to believe, don't you? You *need* them to believe."

"What can the adults do?" Miss Benjamin asked. "How can they stop us now? You're being preposterous."

"Do *you* want to explain how we got our staff at the printworks? A mob of brain-dead zombies who've been altered by the Meat-Men in the Deadhouse to work twenty-four hours a day, without the need for sleep or food? I'm quite sure we're breaking some labour laws there!"

"Your world and its foolish laws," sneered Miss Benjamin. "Your leaders have no strength."

Scratch ignored that. "Rumours work both ways, Miss Benjamin. If the parents get a whiff of scandal, if they think their precious darlings are being corrupted by a comic, they'll find a way to shut us down. That's how this country works. The British thrive on outrage. They're never happier than when they're foaming at the mouth."

"What a ridiculous notion!"

"It's a fact. You'd know that if you came from here. But you don't, which is exactly why you need me."

— You have my confidence, Scratch. Your methods have worked well thus far. Already so many children believe in Malice that it has begun to leak into this world. And my power grows with each new believer. —

A tall, thin shadow passed across the room, behind the half-open door. Alicia gasped. She glimpsed him for only the barest instant, with his tricorn hat like a highwayman and his long coat, its collar hiding his face. Just the sight of him was like a hammer to the senses. He was a dent in reality. A thing that shouldn't exist.

— It is only a matter of time before I am strong enough to bridge the gap between here and Malice, to bring through my army of Regulators. When I open my Deadhouse to spill into this world, when all their ogres and demons are made flesh . . . they will all believe in me then. —

"And I will have *my* reward," Scratch reminded him. "You'll give me the British Isles?"

— As we agreed. You may rule them as you see fit. —

Scratch giggled like a girl. "I think the first thing I'll do is round up everyone who went to my old school. I'll pluck every hair from their bodies and make them walk naked through the streets with everyone laughing at them. Then we'll see who's bullying who!"

"Your petty dreams of revenge are so tiresome," Miss Benjamin sighed.

A sudden movement, as Tall Jake lunged across the room. There was a strangled squeak from Miss Benjamin.

- You will not mock him, - said Tall Jake darkly. - When he found me, I was little more than a ghost. The faint dream of the idiot god in the attic. But we struck a pact, he and I. He would find me believers, and I would make him ruler of this land. If not for him, there would be no comic. If not for him, I would not have had the strength to fashion you from mud and blood and dust. You owe him your very life! -

"Forgive . . . me. . ." Miss Benjamin choked.

"You're forgiven," said Scratch airily. "Tall Jake, please don't kill her. This place is messy enough without corpses lying around."

There was a thump, and the sound of Miss Benjamin gasping air.

Alicia slipped away. Her shredded nerves couldn't take any more. She wanted to get some distance between her and the terrifying spectre that lurked on the other side of the door.

Besides, she had somewhere to go now. This was the second time she'd heard mention of the attic. She was pretty sure there would be something worth finding up there.

222

The Artists

1

Alicia turned the key and opened the door slowly. She found herself at the foot of a long, narrow wooden staircase. The dark lay thick on the steps. She couldn't see to the top.

The attic. It had to be the attic.

Crouch Hollow was a big place, but it was virtually deserted. She'd heard no other voices as she crept around the top floor of the building. Apart from the people downstairs, it seemed that the only living things here were spiders and mice. All that remained were awful reminders of the past.

If this place had been a hospital, it wasn't like any hospital Alicia recognized. There were cells and bars everywhere. She'd seen a table with restraining straps. A grimy autopsy room, with drains still flaky with old blood. An old Victorian machine that looked like a cabinet with gauges and dials, attached by wires to a metal cap. They used that to administer jolts of electricity to a patient's brain.

The atmosphere in this place was heavy with suffering.

Alicia felt like she could still hear the screams of the tormented patients, if she listened hard enough.

She reached inside the doorway and felt for a light switch. An old brass thing. She flicked it on.

The shadows fled. Literally. Instead of being annihilated by the brightness, the darkness *retreated* from it, like a swarm of cockroaches scuttling to cover. And the noise! A racket of clicking and tapping, like a million tiny claws.

Or like the rats in Philip Gormley's attic.

Alicia caught her breath. The shadows had pressed themselves into the corners now, hiding in the creases of the stairway. There was a door at the top. A single bulb hung on a wire, sputtering unsteadily.

She really didn't want to go up those stairs. For a while, she just stood there, unable to make herself move. She was trapped in Crouch Hollow, and downstairs was Tall Jake himself. Her only hope of escape was to hide in Scratch's car again and hope she went unnoticed when he left. But she didn't think she'd be so lucky a second time.

The only way is to keep going forward. Seth had said that to her when they said their goodbyes at the train station in Birmingham. At the time, she hadn't understood him. But she understood him now. Just like him, she'd committed herself, and there was no way back.

It'll be alright, she told herself. *It's just like when you were a little girl. Fear of the dark. It's not far to the top.*

She took a deep breath, and put her foot on the first step.

Nothing happened. There was a soft, restless clicking from all around her, but nothing happened.

She took another step, and another. The shadows stayed pressed in their corners.

One more step. One more. One more after that.

Just keep going. Don't turn around now. You're nearly there.

Every instinct she had urged her to turn and run, to plunge down the stairs and out into the safety of the corridor.

Another step. Another. Another.

The door behind her slammed shut.

Oh, no.

The clicking grew in volume. A terrible, predatory, hungry sound. She looked around the stairwell in horror and saw that the dark was spreading from the cracks and hollows, welling up like ink.

Panic seized her. She ran down the stairs. The oozing darkness sucked at her boots, trying to slow her. She grabbed the handle of the door and turned it, but the door stayed shut. She threw her shoulder into it. The door held fast. Immovable.

This isn't happening! This isn't happening!

The tapping, rustling dark was swelling to consume the stairway. It spread along the ceiling and crept down the wire towards the bulb. It began to spread across the glass, swallowing the light.

Alicia screamed. She couldn't help it. With nowhere

else to go, she ran up the stairs towards the door at the top. She was only halfway when the bulb went out with a loud *ping*.

The darkness was total. She ran blindly, desperately, but without the light she missed her footing and fell hard on to the stairs. Her bag went flying from her grip. Her fingers came down on to something, something *moving*, like a thick carpet of tiny mites. She pulled away with a shriek, but they were on her hand now, swarming. She scraped at herself frantically, but instead of coming off her they spread to her other hand.

She became hysterical. There didn't seem to be enough air in her lungs to get out all the terror and panic inside her. Flailing clumsily, she crawled up the stairs towards the door. The clicking things were making their way up to her elbows now. They were on her feet, pouring into her boots. They were in her hair, busy like insects. Coming towards her face. The noise in her ears was deafening.

Alicia had never known what it was like to be close to madness. Not until now.

One wild arm slammed into the door at the top of the stairs. She pawed for the handle, and found it. There was movement beneath her palm: the handle was coated in the repulsive things that lived in the dark. She gripped hard and turned it, but her hand slipped on the metal. It was as slick as ice.

She pounded at the door, howling. All reason had left her now. She felt something come flooding over her cheeks and lips. She gagged and choked. Her mouth was filled with a million little mites, racing about, pouring over her tongue and into her throat. The dark was inside her, filling her lungs. She was drowning in it.

She was going to die.

Then she was falling forward, as the door she was pounding on was pulled open. Beyond was light, dim light but light all the same. Her eyes couldn't seem to focus. A hulking shape reached in and grabbed her by the arm, then yanked her through with painful force. Her glasses slipped from her nose and skittered across the wooden floor.

She fell to her hands and knees. The door slammed shut behind her. She tried to take a breath, but nothing would come. Then there was a surge in her guts, and she threw up. What came out wasn't vomit but darkness. Darkness like tar, heaving up out of her and splattering on the floor.

The sight of it was too much. Another kind of darkness took her, and she fell unconscious.

2

Alicia woke in an unfamiliar place. There was a dusty, sour scent in her nostrils and a vile taste in her mouth. There was softness underneath her. She was entangled in rough woollen blankets.

She blinked and looked around. Without her glasses, anything further than a metre away was a blur, but she could tell she was in a bed. Well, maybe calling it a *bed* was a bit generous. It was just an old mattress that lay on the floor, without a sheet.

The mattress was in the corner of a room, in the angle where the sloping roof came down to meet the floorboards. It was screened off from the rest of the room by a row of easels and canvases, all leaning together. A makeshift little den. Untidy heaps of art supplies surrounded her: pots and tubes of paint, jars of dirty water with brushes in them, pens and crayons and piles of rolled-up sketches. It smelled of sweat and paint and mouldy things.

Still, it was better than the nightmare she'd woken up from. The thought of that clammy, clinging darkness . . . it was more than she could bear.

It's over now, she told herself. *Wherever you are, whatever happened, it's over.*

She lay there for a while, just breathing. Several places ached where she'd banged them, and her shoulder hurt from being pulled so violently to safety.

Safety, she thought. *Someone saved me. But who, and why?*

She could hear a scratching noise coming from the room beyond the screen. The sound of a pen darting across paper. There was a grunt, like an animal.

Gingerly she pushed aside the blankets. Frightened as she was, she made herself stay logical. If she was in danger, why had they bothered to save her? Why put her to bed with such care? Whoever was on the other side of that screen probably meant her no harm, she decided. But it was the *probably* part she was worried about.

She tried to find her glasses, but they weren't anywhere nearby. She remembered them falling off, just before she blacked out. With no other option, she got quietly to her feet, picked her way through the junk, and looked around the edge of the screen.

She was in the attic. It was a big room, with a sloping roof that peaked in the middle. Skylights ran along its length. It sounded like it had stopped raining, and by the gloom Alicia judged it to be evening.

Beneath one of the skylights there was something moving. At this distance, it was little more than a smudge, but Alicia could make out enough to tell that it was a man. A huge man, like a boulder. He was sitting on a stool in front of a canvas. Drawing.

That's him, she thought. *It must be. It's Grendel.*

A chill ran through her. She was suddenly aware that she was deep in forbidden territory here. Of all the secrets of Malice, this was the most closely guarded of all. The identity of Grendel had been the subject of furious debate among the Malice faithful ever since she'd first heard of the comic. Now she was in the same room as the mysterious creator of Malice. She wondered if anyone outside Tall Jake's inner circle had ever seen him.

Alicia looked around the rest of the attic. There were balls of crumpled paper everywhere, stained rags, plates of decaying food. Across the room, she could make out the brown rectangle of a wooden door. It seemed to be the only way out, but she knew what lay beyond. The stairway, and the dark. Nothing would persuade her to go through that door again.

Grendel grunted suddenly, snorting like a pig. Alicia jumped. He still didn't seem to have noticed her.

Unable to think of what to do next, she said, "Hello?"

At least, she tried to say it, but her throat was too dry and all that came out was air. She swallowed and tried again.

"Hello?"

Grendel snorted and carried on drawing. He was paying her no attention at all.

Puzzled by this reaction, Alicia went closer. He didn't seem like a threat, and she wasn't sure why he'd saved her from certain death only to ignore her.

As she walked warily over to him, he started to come into focus. He was seated with his back to her. She saw that he had massive shoulders and a great big belly. He was leaning close to the canvas. He seemed to be concentrating furiously, like a giant trying to thread a needle. His pen nib danced and scratched.

She hesitated. Grendel was misshapen. His back was humped unevenly and he sat awkwardly, as if his spine wasn't quite right. His arms were like tree trunks and he looked monstrously powerful.

"Hello?" she said again. Then: "Are you okay?"

He didn't reply at all, or make any motion to chase her off. She plucked up courage and went to stand by his shoulder. As she got closer, her eye was drawn by what was on the canvas.

Malice. He was drawing Malice. He was inking panels with frantic speed. There was no pencil sketching or preparation at all. Alicia had to sketch everything before she drew it, to make sure she got the perspective and proportions right, but Grendel was just putting it right down on to the paper.

A boy with long brown hair was climbing a cliff. His expression was terrified. A monster was climbing up the cliff after him. It was something like a cross between a preying mantis and a scorpion, except that it was the size of a tiger. Alicia's eyes skimmed across the panels as the boy grabbed a handhold, the handhold crumbled, the boy fell. . .

She looked away. This wasn't just a story. Somewhere, right now, that boy was plummeting to his doom. She didn't want to see the next panel.

Grendel had his face about a foot away from the canvas. The shiny, steel-tipped pen scratched around right in front of his nose. His head was tiny, hunched down between his shoulders, with a little thatch of black hair on top. His skull wasn't round but lumpy, and it bulged on one side.

She felt a sudden pang of sympathy. He was cruelly deformed. She wouldn't wish that on anyone.

Still he paid her no attention. It was like he was in a trance.

"Hey," she said quietly, touching his shoulder.

He reacted immediately, turning his face to her with a

sudden snarl. The sight of him was a jolt. His whole face sloped to the side. One tiny eye drooped under a great folded brow, while the other was large and glaring. His jaw was set wrong, so that his teeth didn't fit together. He had a cleft palate, a crevasse in his face between his upper lip and his nose, so that he looked like he was permanently sneering.

He stared at her, angry at the interruption. But despite his great size, Alicia wasn't frightened. There was something about him that told her he wasn't a monster, whatever his appearance. Her eyes welled with tears at the sight of him.

"You poor thing," she whispered.

Grendel's anger faded and he frowned at her, puzzled.

"I'm Alicia," she said.

Grendel studied her a moment longer. His mismatched eyes roamed her face. Then he grunted and went back to his work.

Alicia searched the attic until she found her glasses. Miraculously, they'd survived undamaged, and she slipped them back on to her nose. Now that she had her sight back, she saw that the attic was bigger than she'd first thought. There were canvases and sketches everywhere.

She looked at some of them. Buildings, landscapes, people and monsters, all of them from Malice. Some were hastily scribbled, some were carefully painted. They were done in charcoal, in ink, in watercolours or pencils. Everything in a muddle. A mind spilled on to paper: Grendel's cluttered imagination forcing its way out.

Against one wall was a huge canvas, eight feet wide and five high. It was a landscape in watercolour, a mournful valley with all kinds of strange buildings in it. Next to it was a portrait of a frightening figure. A tall man in a coat, wearing a tricorn hat, his collar covering his face. Sinister eyes glittered in the shadow of his hat. It was painted life-size, and looked real enough that the figure might step out of the painting and grab her. She shivered and turned away.

She wished she had her mobile with her. She could call for help then. But she'd lost her handbag on the stairs. The thought of attempting to retrieve it was more than she could deal with at the moment.

She began to feel restless. The attic was secure, with only one way in or out. She was safe, for the moment. But Grendel was still ignoring her. He was lost in his work. She would have to wait till he was finished to try and get any sense out of him.

With nothing else to do, she picked up some paper and a pencil, and she drew. She sat cross-legged on the floor and sketched Grendel as he worked. At first it was just an idle way to pass the time, but after a while she began to concentrate. It was a challenge to get his proportions to look right. She became obsessed.

The discipline of art calmed her. The rules of light and shadow, lines and angles. It made sense of the terrible shock she'd had on the stairwell. Here in the world of her picture, she was in control.

At some stage, she became aware that she could no

longer hear Grendel's pen strokes. She looked up from the paper and saw that he'd turned on his stool and was staring at her, with a curious look on his twisted face.

She brandished the sketch. "Look," she said. "What do you think? I don't think I got your hands right, hands are really hard, but . . . well. . ."

He took the sketch from her and stared at it, then at her. He didn't seem to know what to make of it.

"It's you!" she said, pointing at him.

Grendel's mouth curved into a crooked grin. Then he opened his mouth and honked like a seal. Laughing with delight. Alicia was surprised enough to laugh too.

They heard the handle of the door rattling at the bottom of the stairs.

3

Grendel's expression changed from happiness to alarm in an instant. He seized Alicia roughly by the arm and pulled her over to where a pile of easels were covered by a sheet of dirty cloth. He raised the cloth and gestured frantically. Alicia got the idea. She scrambled underneath, between the legs of the easels.

Footsteps were coming up the stairs. *My bag!* Alicia thought. *My bag is still on the stairs!*

Grendel dropped the cloth, concealing Alicia beneath. He lumbered back across the room just as the door opened and Miss Benjamin came in.

"You left the door unlocked again, Scratch!" she was saying over her shoulder. "Why can't you remember to lock anything?"

She held the door open as Scratch huffed up the stairs. "My mind is occupied with higher things," he replied as he passed her. Then he saw Grendel, who was standing guiltily in front of the easel. "You've been wandering about!" he cried. He strode across the room and slapped Grendel around the back of the head. "Get back to drawing! I don't feed and clothe you just so you can idle about, you repulsive grotesque!"

Alicia, from her hiding place, could see under the hem of the cloth as Grendel cowered and sat on his stool. Scratch came and stood by him, studying the canvas he was working on.

"Who's this?" he demanded. "Some boy falling off a cliff? Why does he matter? Don't you know that Havoc has the Shard now? Show us the Shard! Show us more of their hideout! Show it to us from the *outside*, so we can *find* it!"

Grendel stared at him fearfully. He didn't understand what was expected of him. He grunted and pointed at the canvas, as if to say: *There! Look! I'm drawing!*

"Moron!" Scratch exclaimed, and threw his hands up in exasperation.

Alicia was horrified by what she was seeing. Nobody deserved to be treated like that! Then she remembered her bag. Surely they'd seen it on the stairs? Unless . . . unless it had *gone*. Unless it had been consumed by the hungry things in the dark.

If not for Grendel, that could have been her.

"Do you think he chooses what he sees?" asked Miss Benjamin, walking over to look at the canvas. "Is he capable of that? Or does he merely flick from one point of interest to another, like an animal?"

"God only knows," said Scratch. "Pathetic creature! In all this time – ever since I inherited this ramshackle old asylum and found him up here, drawing in the attic – he's never spoken a word. All he does is draw. Nothing else, except when he eats and when I have to take him to see to his vile bodily needs. I don't know who he is. I don't know how he got here. A former patient, perhaps."

"And yet you cared for him, Scratch. How touching."

"I thought I could make some money from him," he sniffed. "Sell his drawings, perhaps. Instead he's cost me almost everything I have."

"Stop complaining. You'll get your reward."

"I'd better."

Miss Benjamin studied Grendel, who had returned to his work. He seemed to have lapsed into a trance again.

"He created Malice. He created my master, who created me," she mused. "He imagined it, and it became real." She looked at Scratch. "Do you suppose he really is a god?"

"I think he's a freak."

Miss Benjamin turned away from the canvas. Her eye

fell on something lying on the floor. She bent down and picked it up. A sheet of paper.

Alicia's picture.

She felt a thrill of dread as Miss Benjamin raised it to her pointed nose and sniffed it. Her face took on a wicked, hungry look.

"What's that?" asked Scratch, peering over her shoulder. "He's doing self-portraits now?"

"I think not," said Miss Benjamin. She dropped to her hands and knees and sniffed at the ground, like a bloodhound after a scent.

"What is *wrong* with you, you ridiculous woman?" Scratch demanded.

Miss Benjamin was sniffing along the floor. Closer, closer . . . then she raised her head and looked directly at the spot where Alicia hid. Right into her eyes. She grinned horribly.

"I think we have a visitor," she said. She lunged towards Alicia, grabbed her by the wrist and dragged her,

SHRIEKING,

into the open.

The Acropolis

1

"I've had just about enough of this!"

Justin threw down his machete into the dirt. The others stopped hacking their way through the thick undergrowth and looked back at him.

Kady wiped sweat from her dirty cheeks. "What's the matter?" she teased. "Don't you like the great outdoors?"

"I'd like it better with a roof on it," Justin panted. "My clothes are damp, I'm cold, I'm knackered, and my feet are ninety per cent blisters." He swept his arm around to indicate the rainforest that surrounded them. The leaves still glistened from the last downpour, and there were dark clouds overhead. "There *has* to be an easier way than this."

Seth wished there was, but if so, nobody knew about it. There was no easy way to the Acropolis. Craggle Spur, the nearest train station, was at the foot of a forbidding mountain range, which was covered in dense rainforest. *Cold* rainforest. Seth didn't know such things existed.

At least if it had been a jungle, the rain would have been warm.

Stumps, their guide, appeared from the undergrowth to find out why they weren't following. He was a strange little man they'd hired in the village near Craggle Spur. He was short and squat, with a long brown beard and a shaggy pelt of fur all over his body. With his yellow eyes and sharp teeth, he looked like a cross between a dwarf and a wolf. Since his name was an unpronounceable snarl, Justin dubbed him Stumps, and it stuck.

"What is problem?" he barked.

"Justin thinks there must be an easier way," said Kady.

Stumps glared at Justin. "Lazy," he said. "Lazy lazy. Nearly there."

"We've been *nearly there* for the last three days!"

"Nearly there," Stumps insisted, and scampered ahead again.

Justin shouldered his pack, picked up his machete and shook his head. "I hate that guy," he muttered, and slogged onward.

Seth, for his part, was enjoying the journey. He could tell Kady was too. She was a veteran of camping expeditions with her mother, although the terrain in Yosemite was a little friendlier than this endless rainforest. Seth liked the feeling of exerting himself, making his muscles work. Best of all, he liked the feeling of being an explorer. Out here, they had only themselves to rely on. Any help was days away.

Back home, you were never out of mobile-phone range of an air ambulance. You really had to work hard to get yourself into trouble. Not like Livingstone, trekking through darkest Africa. Not like Scott and Amundsen, racing each other to the South Pole. Seth never felt more alive than when he was risking his neck. And he'd never felt more dead than when he'd been stuck in Hathern, watching stupid people doing stupid things on stupid TV shows. Even if he could find an adventure back home, he couldn't afford it. But here in Malice . . . here, he felt like what he did *mattered*.

I'm so glad to be back, he thought. *This is where I belong. Not at home. Right here. And I don't ever have to leave again.*

That thought made him happy, and a big smile spread across his face.

Justin slapped a mosquito on his neck and swore. "What are *you* smiling about?" he demanded. "Sodding mozzies are eating me alive!"

"Look on the bright side," Seth said. "Last time you saw mosquitos, they were three feet long, clockwork, and trying to kill us."

Justin's eyes took on a distant look as he remembered their journey through the Timekeeper's deadly Menagerie in the Clock Tower. "Good times, good times," he said wistfully. "Nice and warm in that place. I don't remember what it's like to be warm and dry."

Thunder rolled across the sky, and the first droplets of a new downpour splashed on to their heads.

"Now you've made it rain!" Kady said irritably.

Justin rolled his eyes and looked at Tatyana. "Can you believe her? Everything's my fault!" Tatyana just grumbled to herself and plodded along with her head down.

2

"There," said Stumps, standing on the dizzying heights of a cliff and pointing down. "Acropolis."

Seth stared. Far below them, in a great forested mountain valley, was the city of temples. It sprawled across the valley floor, hidden from the world, white like a bone. Seth saw domes and aqueducts, pillars and boulevards. It must have been awesome once, but now the domes were shattered, the aqueducts crumbling, pillars broken and boulevards cracked. Not a thing moved that he could see. The Acropolis was deserted.

Justin wheezed his way up to the cliff edge and looked down. "Anyone else get the impression the Queen of Cats doesn't *want* to be found?" he said.

Kady was petting Tatyana. "Well, tough. We need her to help fight Tall Jake. She's gonna get found whether she likes it or not."

Seth was still gazing at the Acropolis, drinking in the sight of it. "Did you ever think you'd do anything like this?" he said. "A lost city. Look at it. We found a lost city."

"You know, it *is* pretty cool," Kady admitted, regarding the view with her hand on her hip.

Justin rolled his eyes. "Great. Stuck in the jungle with Indiana Jones and Tomb Raider. What's that make me?"

"You can be the sidekick," Kady replied. "Comic relief."

"I'll sidekick *you*," Justin growled.

Seth paid them no attention. "You know, back home, this would be crawling with tourists. No matter how hard it was to get to, there'd be someone in a Hawaiian shirt walking around taking photos." He took in a deep breath and sighed happily. "We just might be the only living beings here."

"Let's hope so," Justin said.

"What is down there, it do not live," said Stumps.

Their guide pointed out a way down into the valley, but he refused to go any further. "Bad ghosts," he said. "I wait. Set up camp."

"You'd *better* wait for us, Stumps," warned Justin. "Remember, you get the other half of your pay when we're safe back at Craggle Spur."

Stumps grunted. "I wait," he said. "But if you not back by tomorrow, you not coming back at all."

They unloaded their packs to lighten their loads, taking only what they needed for a couple of days. Stumps began setting up camp as they made ready to depart.

"One thing," he said, as they were leaving. "Ghosts come at night. Best you leave before sun go down. Otherwise, you hide. If you can."

242

3

The Acropolis was a strange place.

At first, it didn't seem so bad. Most of the buildings were still intact, and the city felt peaceful. Vines had made their way up the walls and weeds pushed through the flagstones, but the Acropolis still kept its majesty. It looked to Seth like ancient Rome, or Athens in the days when the Greeks were the greatest civilization in the world. But this was even grander. There were pillars everywhere, courtyards paved with flagstones, plazas with elaborate fountains that had long dried up.

Everywhere there were mosaics. Every plaza and boulevard was decorated in pictures made up of tiny chips of stone, and sometimes with gems. They depicted scenes of worship, of great meetings, of battles. Men knelt before cats, offering gifts. The cats were not the small, domestic kind, but fierce-looking things that resembled leopards and cheetahs and panthers, except that they had strange markings. They fought with one another. They led armies into battle. There were mosaics that showed meetings between two obviously important cats, with human servants in attendance. Each one told a story, but most of them Seth didn't understand.

"The history of the city," said Kady, as they passed another. "This must have been an amazing place, once."

But as they made their way into the Acropolis, they

became increasingly uneasy. There was a feeling of *oddness* in the air. Kady commented that she couldn't hear any birds, not a single one, and after that the silence was no longer peaceful but creepy. Their voices echoed down the empty streets, and made them uncomfortable. They talked less and less.

"I feel weird," Kady announced at one point. "Does anyone else feel weird?"

"Yeah," said Seth. "I'm getting it too."

"It's like . . . we walk down a street, and I can see how long the street is, and it feels like it'll take us a minute to get to the end. But suddenly we're at the end of the street, and I realize it was much shorter than I thought. My perspective is all off."

"That's right," said Seth. He'd been noticing the same thing, but didn't know how to put it. "It's like you're looking into a fish tank."

"This place makes me seasick," Justin complained. "You sure this is healthy?"

"No."

"Oh. Okay," said Justin. He scratched his ear under his hoodie. "Are we just walking around for fun, or are we looking for something?"

Seth shaded his eyes and checked the sun's position. "We're looking for a huge arch, broken in the middle. It rises above the other buildings. I saw it from above, when we were on the cliff, but it's not so easy to find from the ground."

"And you saw that in your mystical vision?"

Seth gave him a long stare. "Yes," he said flatly. "My mystical vision."

Justin grinned. "Just saying, is all. You got directions from a cat."

Tatyana growled.

"Oh, come on, Luggage. I didn't mean you. I'm sure you're great at directions."

The clockwork sabretooth slunk away angrily to investigate a nearby alley.

Seth tipped his head back and surveyed the rooftops. "We should get some height. See what's what."

"I'll go," said Kady. "You guys climb like elephants." Off she went, scaling the side of a pillar, using the tough vines as handholds. The boys watched her as she clambered fearlessly upward.

"Thanks for taking care of her while I was gone," said Seth.

"I said I would, didn't I? Besides, she don't need much taking care of, to tell you the truth."

"I suppose not," said Seth. "Still. Thanks."

"Y'welcome."

They watched her as she climbed to the top of the pillar, apparently unconcerned about the drop.

"Y'know, it'd be ironic if she fell off now, right? After what we just said."

Seth gave him a look.

"Just saying." Justin shrugged.

"Hey," Kady called suddenly. "Hey, I see it!" She pointed theatrically, like a sailor in a crow's nest. "Thataway, boys!"

Justin nudged his friend. "She's quite something, ain't she?"

"Yeah," said Seth, distantly. "She's something, alright."

4

The day wore on as they followed Seth's directions into the Acropolis. The sun climbed to its zenith behind a hazy veil of cloud, and then began to decline.

From the broken arch, they headed towards a tall tower that Seth had seen in his vision. They climbed the stairs on the inside, and once they were above the city they spotted a long, wide boulevard with pillars on either side and fountains running down the middle.

"That way," said Seth, and they went.

After the boulevard they found another spot that Seth recognized. This time it was a domed building with a statue of a lion-like animal rearing on top. Seth studied the statue, frowning.

"Seems like it wasn't just a bunch of random images you pulled out of Andersen's head," Kady mused. "This was his route home. The route to the Queen of Cats."

"Remember I told you about that thing that chased me out of Hathern? That I saw later in the house in Kensington?"

"Course I do. I think it was the same thing that chased *me* out of Hathern a while back."

Seth squinted up at the statue. "It looked kinda like *that*. I mean, all messed up and everything, with spikes and armour and some kind of metal mask, but. . ." He trailed off.

"Maybe you're right," said Kady. "Maybe Tall Jake got hold of one of the Queen of Cats' subjects, took it to the Deadhouse, and let his Meat-Men work on it." She looked over at him. "You think that's what happened?"

"I don't think I wanna know," said Seth. He shook his head. "This place is getting to me."

Kady put a hand on his arm. "It's getting to all of us," she said.

Seth couldn't deny that he was getting jumpier the longer he stayed here. The quiet was getting deafening. Tiny noises alarmed him. He had the unsettling feeling that they were being watched. Sometimes he thought he caught a quick movement on the edge of his vision, but when he looked, there was nothing. Then there were the sounds: tiny sounds, amplified by silence. A little fall of pebbles from a rooftop; a rustling in the grass; distant, low laughter, almost too faint to hear.

Imagination? The wind? Or something else?

"Scotty warned us about this, remember?" said Kady. "Tall Jake nuked the Acropolis with sorcery. There's bound to be some weirdness left over. Like radiation or something."

"But look at this place!" Seth said. "It's hardly damaged.

All this decay is because it was deserted. He didn't *destroy* it. It's like everyone just disappeared."

"My dad – Greg, I mean, not my biological dad – he went to Hiroshima for a tech conference once. You know, where America dropped the first H-bomb? They've got a museum there, all about what happened. In it, they've got the steps from this building that was standing in the blast; I think it's the library or whatever. They actually cut them out and put them in the museum. And if you look, you can see the shadow of the man who was sitting there when the bomb went off. Burned into the stone." She blinked as her eyes became suddenly wet. "People, turned into shadows, just like that."

Seth put his hand on her shoulder. "Let's go, huh? The sooner we get out of here, the better."

Justin had taken to leaving marks as they walked, so they could find their way back again. At each corner, he scratched an arrow into the wall with a sharp stone. None of them needed reminding of Stumps' warning. None of them wanted to be here after dark.

Tatyana seemed as uneasy as the rest of them. Normally it was a comfort to have such a powerful companion at their side, but it wasn't bandits or raiders they were dealing with here. They didn't know *what* they were dealing with. Maybe the ghosts were just rumours. Maybe not. Either way, they didn't want to find out.

According to the cat's route, their next destination after the dome was a large plaza. They couldn't see it from the rooftops, so they had to scout the surrounding streets. Nobody wanted to split up, so they travelled together. Presently, they came across a particularly large mosaic that took up one whole side of a building. It was a massive piece, depicting city folk and cats running in terror. Looming over the city, his arms outstretched, was Tall Jake. His face was half-hidden by the high collar of his coat, but the mosaic was so detailed that they could see the scarring on one side of his face, where he'd been wounded by the Shard during their last battle.

The sight reminded Seth of the weight in his pack. The ornament containing the Shard. What if the Queen of Cats didn't know what to do with it? What if all of this was a waste of time?

But Seth didn't pay much attention to what ifs. He preferred action to worrying. *Let's just find her first, huh?*

"Is this what happened when the city was destroyed?" Kady asked, studying the mosaic.

"Must be," said Seth. "I guess these are the last moments of the city. After this, all the cats and their worshippers disappeared. It's been deserted ever since."

Tatyana gave a low growl. Seth looked down at her. She was glaring at the mosaic, her teeth bared in a snarl.

"What's up with her?" Seth asked.

Justin stared at them in amazement. "I can't believe the *cat* got it before you did." He gestured at the scene in front of them. "You think they stopped to knock up a quick art project while they were running for their lives?"

Seth was still puzzled. "What do you mean?"

Justin patted the sabretooth on her back. "I think what Fleabag is trying to say is: if this place is so deserted, and those are the last moments of the city, then *who made that mosaic?*"

5

They found the plaza, and another landmark after that, but the next proved very hard to find. It was a dried-up canal, an old waterway through the city. Because it was set lower than street level, they couldn't locate it from above. They searched and searched, but it was hidden in a district of mazy streets, and they kept on getting lost. The sun was going down, and tempers were fraying.

"We've *been* this way!" Kady cried.

"We haven't," Seth insisted.

"I recognize that mosaic," she said, pointing.

"But we haven't been down this street. I swear I've never seen those decorated columns."

"And I'd have marked it with an arrow if we'd been here before," added Justin.

"Maybe there are two identical mosaics?" Seth suggested.

"Oh, sure," Kady scoffed. "Have you seen two alike since we got here?"

Seth had to admit that he hadn't. But he was certain they hadn't been down this street, either.

Justin checked the sun. "Look, I hate to say it, but I think a tactical retreat would be good about now."

"No!" Seth cried. "There's two more landmarks we have to find. The last two in the vision. The canal leads to a bridge. We go under the bridge and we're there!"

"We could search for hours and not find that canal," said Kady, who liked Justin's idea. "It could be anywhere around here, and this is a big place."

"Listen, mate," Justin reasoned. "We're all knackered and it's a long trek back. Let's go meet Stumps, start again early. We can follow the arrows to this spot. It'll be much quicker, since we don't have to search for the landmarks. We'll be here by mid-morning, then we've got all day to find the canal and the bridge. No hurry, eh?"

Seth's jaw was set in frustration. After tramping around all day, he felt cheated. They were so close. He knew that Justin and Kady were only being sensible, but he was hurt by their lack of faith all the same. They didn't trust him to lead them to the Queen of Cats before sunset. They didn't want to risk it.

"I'm pretty tired, Seth," said Kady, her voice softening. "And I don't want to be stuck here at night."

Seth shrugged. "Okay," he said, with childish resentment in his voice. "If that's what you both want."

"Right, then," said Justin, clapping his hands together. "We're agreed. Unless the cat has anything to add to the debate?" He looked expectantly at Tatyana, who stared back at him blandly, as if to say: *I know you're making*

251

fun of me, but don't forget I have fangs the size of your forearm.

They began to retrace their steps, using Justin's arrows. Seth found that, despite his disappointment, his heart lifted at the thought of getting out of here. The feeling of being watched had got stronger as the day headed towards sunset. The thought of a campfire, food and sleep was a welcome one.

They'd not gone far before Justin stopped at a corner. "Um," he said.

"What?"

Justin studied the wall. "This ain't right."

Kady frowned. "Where's the arrow mark?"

"What do you think I'm lookin' for, genius?"

"You sure you put one here?"

"I've been putting one on every corner for hours!" he snapped. "Yes, I put one here." He seemed angry, though Seth suspected he was angry with himself rather than Kady. Maybe he'd made a mistake. He could easily believe it. Being in a place like this messed with your head.

"Doesn't matter, anyway," said Justin. "We just came up this road a few minutes ago. I remember it."

"He's right. I remember it, too," said Kady.

"So do I," said Seth. He pointed. "That way."

"There'll be an arrow on the next corner," Justin assured them.

There wasn't.

Justin slapped his hand against the wall in frustration. "I put one here!"

"It's this way!" Kady said, indicating a street that led off to the left. "I remember that mosaic. The one with all the people at the market."

"Wait, though," said Seth, looking to the right. "It wasn't that street, it was *this* one. I remember there were vines all over that building. Look, there they are."

"It wasn't! The mosaic! I remember it!"

"Well, I remember the vines!"

"One bunch of vines looks just like another!" Kady cried.

Justin indicated Tatyana. "What about her? Doesn't *she* know the route back? Aren't cats good at that stuff or something?"

Tatyana just groomed her paw with a mechanical tongue.

"She's not a homing pigeon, Justin," Kady said. "Cats get lost just like everyone else."

"Well, which way? Left or right?" Seth asked. He wished Alicia was here at this moment. She would have remembered the way out. "Justin, you get the casting vote, I suppose."

Justin looked left and right, but it was obvious he didn't remember either street. In the end he said, "Left." Kady beamed in triumph. Justin looked at Seth apologetically. "One bunch of vines looks just like another," he said, with a shrug.

Within half an hour, they were completely lost. Nobody recognized any of the streets or the mosaics, and there was still no sign of Justin's arrows. They were hot and tired from hurrying, and they were getting scared. The sun was dipping fast. Time was running out.

"Look, we can forget about picking up the trail," Kady said eventually. "The arrows are gone, or we lost them somehow, but either way we'll never retrace our steps."

"Alright," said Justin. "Let's pick a direction and stick to it. We'll walk to the edge of the city."

Kady climbed a column so she could see out across the rooftops.

"That way!" she said. "It doesn't look too far!"

Kady was mistaken. When she climbed up another column half an hour later, to get her bearings, it seemed that they were no closer to the edge of the city. But it still looked like the most direct route out, so they kept going. It was another hour before Kady admitted that her eyes had probably been tricked. The warping effect of the magical fallout had made the distance seem much less than it was.

Seth looked up at the sky. The sun was falling towards the horizon. Shadows were getting longer, and the light took on the candle-glow texture of dusk.

"We should find somewhere to hole up," said Seth. "Night's coming."

The Devils in the Walls

1

"We can't go out there, Seth!" Kady protested. "*They're* out there!"

Seth wasn't listening. He had his shoulder under Justin's stone arm for support, and was helping him down the corridor towards the entrance of the building. Justin stumbled and tripped next to him, barely able to keep his head up. Kady and Tatyana followed.

Outside, they could hear the sinister rumbling of the devils in the walls, the sound of the mosaic-creatures moving about the city.

"He needs help!" Seth said.

"Just wait till dawn!" Kady said. "They don't come out during the day."

"Can't you see that stuff is spreading up his arm? By dawn he'll be a mosaic himself!"

"But—"

"Will you shut up for five minutes?" he snapped. Kady was shocked into silence.

It wasn't really Kady he was angry with. It was his fault that Justin was like this. He'd brought them to this place. If Justin died, it would be on his head.

He'd lost one good friend to Malice already. He wouldn't lose another.

He pushed open the door, and they went out into the moonlit streets of the Acropolis.

The grinding sounds were louder out here, like the rolling of great boulders or the noise of distant landslides. So *this* was what happened to the people of the Acropolis. *This* was Tall Jake's punishment for worshipping the Queen of Cats. These creatures had come out of the walls one night and stolen them all away.

Well, now he knew why they kept getting lost. The mosaics had been moving around. No doubt they'd been erasing Justin's arrows as fast as he made them. They'd wanted to keep the intruders here till nightfall. Once it was dark, they could come out of the walls again.

On the doorstep of the building, he paused and looked both ways up the moonlit boulevard. Everywhere, there was the sense of movement in the shadows.

He was still shivering from the encounter with the mosaic-creatures. The Lack's power had left him freezing cold and exhausted. He was overwhelmed with a terrible sense of emptiness and desolation. The touch of the Lack was like being exposed to the endless cold and loneliness of deep space.

He had no idea how he'd unleashed it. It just came out of

him. He had to hope that the mosaic-creatures were scared of him now. Scared enough to give them passage through the Acropolis. Because, if he was honest, he didn't think he would be able to pull that trick twice.

Justin's stone arm was a huge weight across his shoulders. Justin's breathing was ragged and laboured, and he could barely pick his feet up. Seth didn't know how far they'd get with both of them in such bad shape.

But he didn't want to think about failure. He wanted to be doing something. He couldn't just sit back and watch his friend turn to stone.

He headed out into the streets, Justin with him. Kady stuck close, her eyes fearful. Tatyana loped alongside, growling quietly.

"Where are we going?" Kady demanded.

"We're going to find the canal," said Seth. "We're going to get Justin to the Queen of Cats. Maybe she can help him."

Now Kady understood how desperate his plan was. "The canal could be anywhere!" she cried. "We must have walked an hour away from the last landmark, and we can't even navigate in the dark. You'll never find it!"

"We're gonna try," said Seth.

"You can't drag him across the whole of the Acropolis in his state! You're killing him!"

"I'm *saving* him!" Seth snarled, and there was such fierceness in his expression that Kady backed off. "I'm going to *save* him."

Kady gave him a worried look. Seth knew that look. It said: *You're crazy. You're not acting sane.* And maybe that was true, but he didn't care. He didn't care about anything but saving his friend's life. No matter that it was a one in a million chance to find the canal in the dark. One in a million was still a chance.

"Hey, you two..." Justin croaked. "No need to fight over me. Plenty ... plenty of Justin to go round." He grinned weakly.

Even now, Justin was joking. You just couldn't break his spirit.

"You hear me, whatever you are!" Seth shouted into the night. "You stay away from us! Anyone tries to stop us, you'll end up like your friends did. You hear me?"

There was an angry rumbling from all around, loud enough to shake the ground. Tatyana crouched and bared her fangs. But there was no attack. The mosaic-creatures were wary enough to leave them be for the moment.

"Take his other arm," he said to Kady, and she slipped under Justin's shoulder. "Let's go."

Seth set a cruel pace. Justin stumbled and staggered along between them as they carried him through the deserted boulevards and plazas. Tatyana darted here and there, snapping at shadows, guarding them as best she could. The mosaics stayed just out of sight, swift glimpses of movement in the night, making that awful sound like the grinding of stone teeth.

Just keep moving, Seth thought. His back and legs ached

from carrying the weight of Justin's arm, but he firmed his jaw and kept on going. *Just keep moving.*

Justin was becoming heavier and heavier, as he took less and less weight on his own feet. Even with Kady and Seth helping him, he couldn't put one foot in front of the other. His head lolled and his eyes kept fluttering closed.

"Justin!" Seth snapped. "Stay with me! Keep going!"

Justin couldn't. The last of his strength had gone out of him. They dragged him halfway up the next street, but the going was slow and Kady wasn't strong enough to do it for long.

"Mate. . ." Justin murmured. "Mate, stop it. I'm done for. Put me down."

"No!" Seth cried. "No, I—"

"Put him down," said Kady. Her eyes were filled with tears.

Seth sagged, defeated. There was something in her weary tone that got through to him at last. It was hopeless. He understood that now. There was nothing he could do.

He eased Justin down and sat him against a pillar. Justin's head rolled. He was fighting the urge to give in to unconsciousness, but it was a battle he couldn't win. Seth could see how the stone chips had spread up to his shoulder now, to meet those spreading down his neck from his face. He was slowly drying out, cracking, turning to stone.

Seth felt a fury like he'd never felt before. He was so helpless! Right then he could have wept with frustration. But tears didn't come easily to him. He kept it all inside instead.

"I'm so sorry," he whispered. "I'm so sorry."

"What for?" Justin breathed.

"I brought you here," he said. "It's because of me that you're—"

Justin half-laughed, half-coughed. "Don't ... don't flatter yourself, mate. I do what I like. I'm here ... 'cause I wanna be." He took a ragged breath. "You know ... what I had at home? Brother who's a murderer ... a dad who kicked seven shades of Sunday out of me every ... every chance he got. No education ... looking forward to a lifetime of ... scraping a living." He gave Seth a broken smile. "We had some adventures, didn't we?"

Seth took up his good hand and held it in his own. Justin's grip was pathetically weak. *This can't be happening. This can't be happening. I won't let you die.*

"Now don't get mushy on me," Justin murmured. "I ain't much one for goodbyes."

Kady was sobbing in the background. Tatyana came up to Justin and nuzzled him.

"Wow. Things ... things must be bad," Justin wheezed. "Even the tin moggy ... wants to make nice."

His eyes flickered and closed, he let out a long sigh, and then his chin fell forward on to his chest.

2

Seth just stared. A numb feeling was spreading through him, worse even than the touch of the Lack. There was disbelief on his face. He was waiting for Justin to open his eyes, to shake it off, to grin at the joke he'd played. But it wasn't any joke. There would be no more flippant comebacks from Justin. No more complaining.

Seth was so stunned by the thought that he didn't pay any attention to the noise coming from up the street. It was only when Kady cried out that he tore his gaze away from the still face of his friend.

"What?" he snapped.

"Marlowe!" she said. "It's Marlowe! It's my cat!"

It *was* him. Kady's cat, from her parents' house. A silver tabby tom, sitting there in the middle of the street in the moonlight, meowing at them. As Seth looked up, he ran away a few steps, then stopped and looked expectantly over his shoulder.

Kady wiped her eyes with the back of her hand. "He wants us to follow!" she said.

Follow him where? Seth thought. Suddenly it dawned on him. The Queen of Cats! He would guide them to the Queen of Cats! And that meant . . .

"Justin!" he shouted. He knelt down in front of his friend and shook him. "Justin! He can take us to the Queen of Cats! Don't give up yet!"

But Justin wouldn't wake. Seth felt his throat. A fluttering pulse under his fingertips.

"He's not dead!" Seth said. "He's not dead yet! Justin! Wake up! Wake . . . *up!*" He slapped Justin hard across the side of his face that wasn't yet stone.

Justin didn't move for a moment. Then his face screwed up slowly in pain. "Ow," he said.

"Help me get him up!" Seth told Kady. She ran to help, and together they got him to his feet. "Put him on my back!"

"He's too heav—"

"*I don't care!*"

He knelt down and Kady struggled to tip Justin on to Seth's back. With his stone arm he was a crushing weight. Seth linked his arms under Justin's legs, and with a grunt he got to his feet, Justin riding piggyback.

"That's . . . a bit more . . . like it," Justin gasped.

"Hang on," Seth said. "You're not dead yet."

"Think I'd . . . *prefer* it at this stage."

"I mean it, Justin. I'll kill you if you die on me."

They went after the cat, hurrying as fast as they could. Marlowe would run on a little way, stop to check that they were still following, and then allow them to catch up before racing off again. In such a way, he led them through the Acropolis.

The rumbling of the mosaic-creatures and the restless movement of the dark was still all around them, but Seth had no time for that now. He was concentrating. One foot in front of the other. After the first effort of lifting Justin, he quickly got used to the weight and decided it was bearable. Soon, his muscles began to complain, and his legs started to ache, and the strength began to drain out of him.

But he wouldn't stop. He didn't care about the consequences. He didn't care if it crippled him. You could push your body as far as you liked as long as you didn't care.

So he gritted his teeth, and he carried his friend.

The journey might have been long, or it might have just seemed that way. Seth didn't think any further ahead than the next street. *I just have to make it to that corner*, he would tell himself. When he got there, and saw that there was another street ahead of them, he would tell himself: *I just have to make it to* that *corner*. And so on, over and over.

"You still here?" he asked.

"Just about," said Justin. "You?"

"I think you gave me a hernia."

"What are friends for?"

But Seth's heart lifted, because Justin's voice sounded a little stronger. He redoubled his efforts. Even though the pain in his legs and back was enough to make him want to scream, he increased his speed.

I . . . will not . . . give up!

Suddenly, before them, there was a stone trench cutting across the street, deep and wide enough for a small river. The canal! A set of steps led down from street level, and sitting on the wall near the steps was a familiar black cat. Andersen. Seth could have sworn the cat took on an expression of disdain when he laid eyes on the boy who had stolen his memories.

Seth took the steps down to the canal slowly, careful not

to topple over. Andersen watched them pass, then darted down after them when they were safely at the bottom.

The rumbling of the mosaic-creatures was muted here. With the two cats leading the way and Tatyana guarding him, Seth staggered onward. The muscles of his legs protested at their treatment. His lower back was aflame and the bones of his spine felt like they were being ground together. He was so exhausted that he barely knew where he was. Only the pain kept him from falling over.

One foot in front of the other. Just one step. Just one more.

Ahead, there was a bridge that he recognized, and a tunnel leading under it.

I just have to make it to that tunnel.

He kept going, step after step. Once they got to the tunnel the canal sloped gently down into the darkness. It wasn't much of a hill, but in Seth's condition it was heartbreaking. With the weight on his back it shifted all the effort to his shins and thighs, and he had to brake all the way down.

I just have to make it to the bottom of this hill.

He walked in a trance. Kady was saying something, but he couldn't tell what. He guessed by her tone that she was encouraging him. It was almost pitch dark, and he followed the green lamps of Tatyana's eyes.

At some point, light grew ahead of them. The ground became level. It was so much easier to walk on level ground that Seth wanted to smile, but he was too tired even for that.

The way ahead was blocked by a huge, round sewer gate. Red weeds and vines wrapped through the bars. The cats ran ahead and slipped through the gate, and it opened with a screech before their slower companions got there. Seth was grateful he didn't have to stop. He wouldn't have been able to start again.

They trudged onward. Maybe twenty metres, maybe a hundred. There was the end of the tunnel, coming closer with each step.

I just have to make it to the end.

He did. And there, on the other side of the tunnel, was the temple of the Queen of Cats.

3

The tunnel opened out into an enormous underground hall, shaped like an old Greek amphitheatre but much more grand. It was built in a semicircle, with great stone steps rising up and back. Water ran along the steps in little channels, spilling down the levels until it came to the circular pool in the middle of the hall. Enormous, exotic trees surrounded the pool. They grew right out of the stone floor, without sunlight or soil. In their branches were shining white globes. More light came from fire pits: two trenches of glowing coals that filled the chamber with a sweltering heat and tinted everything red.

Then there were the cats. Cats, everywhere, of all kinds,

lazing across the steps, drinking from the pool, loafing in the branches of the trees. Most of them were breeds the visitors didn't recognize. Some were bigger than lions, though none were smaller than a house cat. There were slender cats the size of cheetahs, with red and yellow fur like flame, and spiky manes. There were ghostly white, hairless, flitting cats that darted through the branches like squirrels. Some were like chameleons, who could only be seen when they moved, and turned invisible when they stopped still. Some were massive and fanged, like the huge cats of prehistoric times. The kind Tatyana was modelled on.

Lying before the pool like a black sphinx was the queen of them all.

She was enormous, perhaps three metres high at the shoulder when she stood. She was like a panther, but sleeker, strangely slender and feminine. Her eyes were utterly black, even darker than her fur. All around her hung precious metals, like beautiful armour. Gold, silver, rubies. Earrings, anklets, a neck piece that looked like it belonged on an Aztec god. She'd been worshipped in the past, and it seemed she'd never forgotten that.

Seth barely took any of this in. He staggered onward, too weary to feel triumph or fear. He sank to his knees and Kady helped him as he tipped Justin off his back and on to the floor of the chamber. Still on his knees, because he couldn't get up, he gazed blearily at the Queen of Cats.

"Help him," he said. "Please."

Justin lay on the floor, his eyes closed, barely breathing.

275

The Queen of Cats stirred. She shifted her gaze to Kady, expectantly.

It took Kady a moment to catch on. She knelt alongside Seth.

"Please," she said.

The Queen of Cats rose slowly with a jangle of precious metals. She loped over to them. Her huge head lowered and she sniffed at Justin. Then, with one paw, she scooped him gently towards her, and began to lick him, holding him like a cub.

Seth looked on in amazement as her rough red tongue scraped over his friend's unconscious body. At first he thought she was going to eat him; but as he watched, he saw that with each stroke of the tongue, flakes of stone were falling away from Justin's skin. Little chips pattered on the floor as they dropped from Justin's arm and face.

When she was done, she laid him carefully down. His arm and the side of his face were pink and raw, and he was soaked in saliva, but the stone had all gone. Kady rushed to him and cradled his head in her arms.

"Justin! Are you okay? Justin!"

Justin's eyes opened a little. His nose wrinkled.

"Why do I smell like tuna?" he asked.

Kady burst out laughing. A smile spread across Seth's face. The warm swell of relief was too much for him. He fainted.

Three of Six

1

Seth awoke to the sound of rain, and the smell of wet earth and leaves. The air was chilly on his skin. Hoots and cheeps echoed in the distance. Everything ached.

He opened his eyes and found himself lying on a bedspread under a rock overhang. Outside was the rainforest. He was wrapped in damp blankets on a makeshift stretcher of tree branches and tarpaulin.

Tatyana slept at his feet. Sitting with their backs to him, looking out at the downpour, were Justin and Kady, talking in low voices. Kady laughed at some joke he made and shoved him playfully. Then she looked back at Seth, and her face lit up. "Seth!" she cried. "You're awake!" Tatyana bolted upright and pounced on him, butting him affectionately in the face.

"Okay, okay, I'm awake," he groaned, fending off Tatyana's mechanical assault. The others hurried over to him. "Feel like I've been trampled by a hippo, though." He looked at Justin. "You need to drop a few pounds."

"So do you," Justin grinned. "See that stretcher you're lazing about on? We've been hauling your sorry butt through the forest all night."

Seth sat up. Justin hunkered down next to him and held out his hand to shake. "Owe you one, mate. You saved my life."

Seth took his hand and pulled him into a hug. Justin stiffened awkwardly for a moment, then relaxed and hugged him back. When he was released, his face had gone red.

"Aw, look at him! He's blushing!" Kady teased.

Justin coughed into his fist. "Just not comfortable with all these male-on-male displays of affection, that's all. Go on: your turn."

Kady hugged Seth too, throwing her arms round his neck. Seth held her tight, burying his face in her neck. Suddenly, he was desperate to hold her and not let her go.

She drew away, perhaps surprised by the strength of his hug, and gave him a strange look. "Why are we out here?" Seth asked, before she could say anything.

"We had to hoof it from the Acropolis," said Kady. "The cats too. It wasn't safe any more."

"I had some tarp and twine in my bag, so we knocked up a stretcher for you with some branches off those big trees in the temple," Justin said. "The cats wouldn't carry you on their backs. It's beneath them, apparently."

"We're not too popular with them right now," Kady said. Tatyana butted her leg. "Well, except that one."

"What did we do?" Seth was bewildered at this new turn of events.

"We gave away their hiding place," said Kady. "Apparently, Grendel was watching us last night. The Queen of Cats told us. That means Tall Jake knows we were in the Acropolis looking for her. He'll send his forces to tear that place apart in the hope of hunting her down. They're probably there already."

"Grendel was watching? I didn't . . . I didn't sense it. I mean, the whole place already felt so strange."

"Probably all that leftover magic in the air," said Kady. "You'd think those mosaic-monsters might have told Tall Jake about the Queen of Cats long before we arrived, though."

Justin shrugged. "Why would they? They're monsters. Who says they can speak at all? Tall Jake's probably never been back to the Acropolis since he junked the place."

"So the Queen of Cats had to abandon her temple?" Seth asked.

"Right," said Kady.

"And that was our fault?"

"Right."

"Oh."

"She wanted to see you as soon as you awoke."

"Don't I get breakfast first?"

"I'm worried we're gonna *be* breakfast," Justin said.

"You don't want to keep her waiting," said Kady. "She's kind of pompous. A *queen*, don't you know? She's all 'kneel before me.'"

"It don't sit right with me," Justin complained. "I don't like kneeling to anyone."

"Well, you'll do it, since we need her, and she saved your life just as much as Seth did," Kady told him sternly.

Seth tried to sit up and was rewarded with a back spasm that took his breath away. "Well, if I have to kneel to anyone, I don't think I'm getting back up again," he said.

2

The Queen of Cats and her retinue were gathered in a cave on the mountainside, sheltered from the rain, with vines and creepers hanging over the entrance. Even in these circumstances, the Queen had managed a touch of glamour: glittering seams of shiny metal lined the inside of the cave, shining in the weak afternoon light. The Queen sat in a regal pose, surrounded by dozens of cats of all sizes and types. She was guarded by silver tiger-like beasts the size of horses.

Kady, Seth, Justin and Tatyana picked their way through the busy cave towards her. The gloom was alive with lazy stirring. Cats groomed themselves, yawned, padded this way and that. Seth spotted Andersen and Marlowe tracking them through the cave. Suddenly, he knew how a cat's prey must feel. There was a sense of casual danger about this place, as if the cats might tear their visitors apart at any moment, if only they could be bothered.

The Queen of Cats regarded them coldly as they came

towards her. The guards backed off and made room. As they approached, Seth saw the ornament that held the Shard lying next to one of her great paws.

"You gave it to her?" Seth asked Kady.

"She took it." Kady shrugged. "I couldn't exactly stop her."

Tatyana lay on the floor before the Queen, submissive. Kady and Justin knelt, Justin wearing a reluctant grimace. Seth lowered himself to one knee with a struggle. He was stiff as a board and his thighs were in agony.

A voice rolled around their heads. It was soft, like a purr, but it carried a tone of bored disdain. The words seemed to come directly into their minds without passing through their ears.

The end has begun, said the Queen of Cats. *And you have begun it.*

When nobody else spoke, Seth said: "We didn't mean to lead Tall Jake to you. Your cats, Andersen and Marlowe, have been helping us. We thought—"

Yes, I was gracious enough to send my soldiers to help you. The one you call Andersen, in particular, is a most trusted subject. He has walked in many realms and passed through many stories. The Queen's gaze grew sharp. *It did not mean I wished to be found.*

"Then why send your cats to guide us through the Acropolis?" Seth asked. He wondered if he should be more polite, but he didn't know how to behave in front of a queen.

By then the game was up, said the Queen. *And you did have the Shard. It is safer with me than with you.*

"But Marlowe helped me *before*. He led me to the Shard, back in Hathern."

He waited until Tall Jake and his minions were convinced that you were no threat. That your memory had been erased. Then he led you to the Shard. You were supposed to bring it back to Malice quietly. But the Shard responded to the Lack's power in you, and woke up. Tall Jake sensed his ancient enemy awakening and came after you. After that, he knew you carried the Shard, and he was on your trail. I wanted what you carried, but it was too dangerous to make direct contact with you, in case you led Tall Jake to me. Which is exactly what you did.

Seth winced. "Sorry," he said. He rubbed his hand through his hair. "Do you know how to use it?" he asked. "The Shard?"

A scornful chuckle. If you mean, do I know how to release the Shard from his prison, then yes. Nobody uses the Shard. He is an uncontrollable force.

"Then will you? Release him, I mean?"

When the time is right, said the Queen of Cats. *The Shard is hungry for revenge, and he is not known for his reasonable attitude. He will go after Tall Jake immediately. I will not let him out until we are all ready.*

"And when will that be?"

When our forces have gathered and we face Tall Jake on the field of battle.

Justin looked up sharply, one eyebrow raised. "You what?" he asked, rather inappropriately. The Queen's guards growled at him. He cleared his throat, gave them a nervous glance, and corrected himself. "I mean: you what, *Your Majesty*."

Kady rolled her eyes. "I can't take you anywhere," she whispered angrily.

The Queen of Cats shifted herself and settled. The floor of the cave was less comfortable than she was used to.

Crowfinger is dead and the Cripplespite is gone, she said. *But with my army of cats, the Lack's dark worshippers, the Shard, and whatever small forces you can muster, we have a chance to take back this realm. It is not a cat's way to work with others, but you have left me little choice. Separately, we will fall. Together, we may not.*

"The Lack?" said Seth. "How will you find her?"

Oh, she's listening, said the Queen of Cats. She raised her head suspiciously. *Aren't you, my dear?*

Seth felt the temperature plunge. The hairs on the back of his neck stood on end. The gloom thickened, a shadow passed through the cavern, and out of the darkness stepped the Lack.

He recognized her from the statue in her shrine at the bottom of the Oubliette. Her skin was silver, and gave out a cold light, like distant stars. Her pupils were the white of bitter frost. Her thick hair was black, and gathered behind a headdress. She wore the clothes of a huntress, and carried with her an elegant bow. Seth knew that bow.

He'd used it to destroy the Mort-Beast.

I AM LISTENING, she said, in a voice like wind through icicles.

The Queen of Cats regarded her sternly. *You have caused me great inconvenience*, she accused.

SOMEONE HAD TO FORCE YOUR HAND. YOU WOULD NEVER HAVE ACTED OTHERWISE.

So you used these children?

The Lack smiled faintly, as if at a private joke. A NUDGE HERE AND THERE, NO MORE. THEY ARE REMARKABLY RESOURCEFUL. She walked over to Seth and looked down at him. ESPECIALLY THIS ONE. MY CHAMPION.

She put her hand on his shoulder, and a numb chill spread from it throughout his body. When she took it away, the chill faded; but so had the aches and pains of last night's adventures.

STAND UP, ALL OF YOU, she said. I DO NOT NEED MY SUBJECTS TO KNEEL TO MAKE ME FEEL SUPERIOR.

The Queen of Cats growled low at the insult, and the atmosphere in the cave turned ugly. But nobody contradicted the Lack, so they got to their feet. Seth was amazed to find that his muscles didn't protest in the least.

"What did you do to me?" Seth asked the Lack.

I TOOK AWAY YOUR PAIN, said the Lack. THAT IS WHAT I AM, CHILD. I AM SADNESS AND EMPTINESS, THE LONELY VOID, THE ACHE OF

LOSS. I DRAW OUT YOUR PAIN, AND TAKE IT UPON MYSELF. THAT IS WHAT I OFFER MY FOLLOWERS. HEALING.

The Queen of Cats snorted. *Be careful, my guests. First she'll take your pain, then she'll take the rest of you.*

The Lack gave them that faint smile again, as if to say: *believe what you want.*

Seth shook his head. "No, I didn't mean that. I meant, what did you do to me *before*? In your temple. Ever since, I've . . . I've had these *abilities.*"

THEY WERE NOT YOUR ABILITIES. THEY WERE MINE, she said. I HAVE BEEN HIDING. She put her hand on Seth's chest, over his heart. IN HERE.

Seth just stared at her, not understanding.

TALL JAKE IS POWERFUL, AND I HAVE BEEN GREATLY WEAKENED BY MY LAST BATTLE WITH HIM. I WAS REDUCED TO HIDING IN MY BROKEN TEMPLE, TRAPPED INSIDE MY STATUE, KEPT THERE BY THE MORT-BEAST. UNTIL MY CHAMPION CAME ALONG.

She looked into Seth's eyes. She was beautiful, like a sculpture, and he felt the power of her gaze and was drawn to it. He wanted to please her. But there was something terrifyingly inhuman about her too, and it frightened him.

I HID INSIDE YOU, AND LET YOU CARRY ME OUT OF MY PRISON. I HAVE BEEN WITH YOU EVER SINCE. IT WAS TOO DANGEROUS TO COME OUT IN THE OPEN, BUT TALL JAKE

WOULD NOT FIND ME IF I WAS CONCEALED
INSIDE ANOTHER BODY.

"It's been you? The ... the things I've sensed, the
way I pulled Justin from the mosaic, all of that?" He felt
suddenly angry. "It was you who showed me what was
in Andersen's head, wasn't it? The route through the
Acropolis. You wanted me to lead Tall Jake to the Queen
of Cats!"

I HAVE BEEN WATCHING OVER YOU, SETH.
KEEPING YOU SAFE.

"You didn't keep me very safe when that ghoul in the
train yard tried to bite my head off!"

The Lack tipped her head slightly, regarding him as if
he was an infant throwing a rather amusing tantrum. He
felt suddenly ashamed.

IN YOUR WORLD, OUR POWERS ARE WEAK.
WE HAVE FEW BELIEVERS. THERE WAS LITTLE
I COULD DO.

"I don't get it," said Kady. "What do believers have to do
with anything?"

BELIEF IS A REMARKABLE THING, she said. IT
CAN MAKE THE IMAGINARY REAL.

"Explain," Justin said with a puzzled frown. "In words
of three syllables or less."

VERY WELL, said the Lack. THOUGH THE QUEEN
MAY WANT TO CLOSE HER EARS. SHE PREFERS
TO BELIEVE THE ILLUSION RATHER THAN THE
REALITY. SHE THINKS MALICE HAS ALWAYS

286

BEEN HERE, AND THAT YOUR WORLD IS MERELY
ANOTHER THAT LIES ALONGSIDE OURS. A
PARALLEL WORLD. BUT SHE IS WRONG.

You have nothing to say that I have not heard before,
the Queen said stiffly. And they were lies then, too.

The Lack tossed her head and laughed. I SEE YOUR
MIND IS NOT TO BE CHANGED. WELL, THEN.
LISTEN, AND YOU MAY LEARN SOMETHING
NONETHELESS.

She turned to the others. Seth felt his blood cool as he
met her gaze.

OUR WORLD BEGAN WITH GRENDEL. HIM,
AND ONLY HIM. I DO NOT KNOW WHERE HE
CAME FROM. I DO NOT KNOW EXACTLY WHAT
HE IS. I DO NOT KNOW IF YOU WOULD CALL
HIM A GOD OR A FOOL. BUT HE POSSESSES
THE MOST EXTRAORDINARY MIND. A MIND
THAT COULD BUILD A WORLD, AND CRAFT
EVERY INCH OF IT IN EXQUISITE DETAIL. HE
PAINTED AND SKETCHED AND DREW, TUNING
AND TESTING. EVENTUALLY HE HAD IMAGINED
IT SO PERFECTLY, HE BELIEVED IT SO MUCH,
THAT THE WORLD INSIDE HIS HEAD BECAME
REAL. IT TOOK ON A LIFE OF ITS OWN, AND
PASSED BEYOND HIS CONTROL.

The Queen of Cats snorted and laid her head on her
paws. Lies, she said simply. This world was born from the
womb of the First Cat.

YOU HAVE PROOF THAT THIS FIRST CAT EXISTS? asked the Lack.

I do not need proof. I have faith.

THEN WHY DO YOU BELIEVE THAT STORY AND NOT MINE, WHEN THERE IS NO PROOF OF EITHER?

Because my story is the right one.

AND WOULD YOU LAY DOWN YOUR LIFE FOR THE FIRST CAT? WOULD YOU KILL FOR HER, IF SHE ASKED YOU TO?

Of course. Without a second thought.

The Lack turned to her audience and indicated the Queen of Cats. YOU SEE HOW BELIEF CAN BE A DANGEROUS THING.

The Queen of Cats bared her fangs, but said no more.

"So what about Tall Jake? I mean, *he's* real, right?" Kady asked. "I heard him talking in the real world."

AFTER TALL JAKE DROVE OUT THE REST OF THE SIX AND TOOK OVER MALICE, HE BECAME OBSESSED WITH ONE IDEA: WHO CREATED HIM? HE RULED THIS REALM, BUT HE STILL FELT THAT HE WAS UNDER THE POWER OF ANOTHER. SO HE USED ALL HIS SORCERIES AND ARCANE KNOWLEDGE, AND HE FOUND A WAY TO MEET HIS MAKER. She raised a wry eyebrow. FROM WHAT MY SPIES TELL ME, HE WAS LESS THAN IMPRESSED.

"But how is that possible? An imaginary being appearing in the real world?"

POSSIBLE OR IMPOSSIBLE, IT HAPPENED, said the Lack. TALL JAKE APPEARED IN THE ATTIC OF CROUCH HOLLOW. HE STEPPED OUT OF HIS OWN PORTRAIT, SO I AM TOLD. AT THAT TIME, HE WAS LITTLE MORE THAN A SHADOW, A GHOST THAT LURKED IN THE ATTIC. UNTIL ICARUS SCRATCH FOUND HIM.

"Scratch," Seth muttered. "That lisping sack of lard. I'm gonna get that guy one day."

TALL JAKE NEEDED BELIEVERS. THE MORE PEOPLE THAT FEARED HIM, THE MORE HIS POWER GREW. ICARUS SCRATCH UNDERSTOOD HOW A RUMOUR, PROPERLY HANDLED, WOULD GAIN STRENGTH UNTIL IT BECAME TRUTH. SO THE TWO OF THEM STRUCK A BARGAIN. THEY TARGETED THE YOUNG, BECAUSE THEIR MINDS ARE MORE OPEN THAN ADULTS. CHILDREN WANT TO BELIEVE. AND SO THE COMIC BEGAN.

"But why is he taking kids away?" Seth demanded.

BECAUSE IF HE DID NOT, NOBODY WOULD BE INTERESTED. IF MALICE WAS JUST A COMIC, NOBODY WOULD CARE. BUT IT'S A *DANGEROUS* COMIC. IT'S A DARK SECRET. FORBIDDEN. SCRATCH KNEW KIDS WOULD READ IT IF THEY BELIEVED THOSE WERE REAL KIDS FIGHTING FOR SURVIVAL. IF NOT FOR THAT, IT WOULD BE ONLY ONE COMIC AMONG MANY, AND IT WOULD DISAPPEAR WITHOUT TRACE.

Seth was appalled. "You're saying that if we weren't so hungry to read about horrible things happening to other people, then Tall Jake wouldn't be taking kids away at all?"

The Lack's faint smile was back.

Seth couldn't believe what he was hearing. All those kids who had died just to feed the appetite of Malice's readers. He felt dizzy.

"The ritual..." he said, weakly.

AH, YES. ONE INGREDIENT FOR EACH OF THE SIX. A CROW FEATHER FOR CROWFINGER, A TWIG FOR THE CRIPPLESPITE, FUR FOR THE QUEEN OF CATS. The Queen of Cats snorted again and narrowed her eyes in displeasure. MINE IS THE TEAR, FOR LOSS AND SORROW. TALL JAKE TAKES A LOCK OF YOUR HAIR TO FIND YOU BY. AND LAST IS FIRE, FOR THE SHARD, THE GREAT DESTROYER.

"But why? What does it mean?"

NOTHING.

"Nothing?"

RITUAL IS PART OF BELIEF. IT GIVES IT ORDER AND SHAPE. IT MAKES IT SEEM GRAVE AND IMPORTANT, IT GIVES IT POWER. AS LONG AS YOU DO THE RITUAL, YOU DON'T HAVE TO THINK TOO HARD ABOUT WHAT LIES BEHIND IT. THE IMPORTANT THING IS THAT IT SEEMS TO MAKE SENSE.

Seth couldn't take any more. It was like some bad joke.

Scratch had played them all like an expert. He knew exactly what to do to make his audience sit up and beg. Just thinking about it made Seth furious.

"What happens if we don't stop him?" Kady asked.

SOON, HE WILL BE STRONG ENOUGH TO INVADE YOUR REALM WITH AN ARMY OF HIS FOLLOWERS. ALL THAT YOU LOVE WILL BE DESTROYED. There was an odd note of relish in her voice as she finished. Hunger for all that sorrow. She stared at Kady. YOUR MOTHER AND FATHER, TOO.

Kady went pale. Her gaze dropped to the floor. When she spoke, her voice was quiet and firm.

"What do you want us to do?"

Go back to your people, said the Queen of Cats. *Spread the word among those who oppose Tall Jake. There are many. Tell them a reckoning is at hand. Tell them if they do not join us now, there will never be another chance.*

"And you think Tall Jake will face us?" Seth asked. "On our terms?"

He will have to. We will attack the Deadhouse, the seat of his power. He cannot let the Deadhouse fall.

"And you'll contact us? When the time is right?" Kady asked.

I will send Andersen. He will tell you where to go.

"He doesn't speak!" Justin said. "How's he going to tell us? Mouse code?"

The Queen of Cats sighed and laid her head back on her paws. *Go away, you strange little creatures. You're tiring me. One of my subjects will lead you out of the rainforest.*

With that, they were dismissed. They picked their way through the cats and out of the cave, and headed back through the rain to the overhang.

"Mouse code," said Seth, shaking his head, and the boys burst out laughing while Kady rolled her eyes.

THE DEADHOUSE

Preparations

1

They were unusually quiet on the long journey back. Each of them was wrapped up in their thoughts. When they talked, it was usually about the battle to come. How would it be? How could they contribute? They weren't fighters. Kady said she wouldn't let Havoc get involved until they had some way of defending themselves against Tall Jake's Regulators and the creatures of the Deadhouse. Justin said he was just looking forward to kicking in some heads. Seth didn't say much at all.

He was thinking of what would happen afterwards. Kady seemed to have forgotten what she'd said that night in the Acropolis, but he hadn't. She said she was going home. No argument. No interest in how he felt about it. It was just like Kady, to plant her feet like that.

It hurt him deeply. Why couldn't she see how dull and boring he found life back home? Why didn't she feel crushed by the idea of getting up at the same time every morning, going to the same school or the same job, day after day? Here in Malice, you didn't have to worry about getting good grades so you could get a good job. Malice was a world stuffed with wonder and excitement and danger. There wasn't much of any of those left back home.

But she was leaving. He resented her for that. He resented her for making him choose between her and Malice.

They'd left the Shard with the Queen of Cats. Seth was glad to rid himself of the burden. They'd delivered a great weapon to Tall Jake's enemies, who knew how to use it. Whatever happened now, they'd at least done that much. They'd struck a blow.

But Seth knew it wasn't over yet. Not till Tall Jake was destroyed and those kids who read the comic were safe. Not till there were no more deaths like Luke's.

He thought about Alicia then. He wondered if she'd got the message that he'd left before he went to the train yard. He wondered if she'd done anything about it. Probably not, he decided. He'd liked her in the short time they'd spent together, but she was the type who followed the rules. She'd probably deleted the message as soon as she got it.

They plodded after their new guide – a jaguar – through the jungle. The walk was hard, and sometimes they had to hack their way through the undergrowth. Justin made jokes about what Stumps might be up to right now, whether he was still waiting for them at the camp or if he'd run off as soon as they left him. Either way, they'd saved themselves half his fee, which Justin was happy about.

Seth didn't feel happy. He felt a strange sense of loss.

Maybe it was Kady, maybe it was just the feeling that things were coming to an end. But he thought it was something else. He'd been carrying the Lack around inside him for months, and now she was gone. There would be no more sixth sense, no more startling bursts of strange energy. He felt like something had been taken away from him. Her cold, beautiful face hung in his memory like a portrait.

In some odd way, he missed her.

2

They were greeted with rapture back at the Bathysphere. Many had feared they were never coming back at all. Justin got a lot of mileage out of his brush with the mosaic-creatures, and enjoyed the attention it brought. Some of the girls had decided he'd become suddenly interesting now that he'd nearly died.

Once the excitement had faded, the reality set in. Most of them were looking forward to a showdown with Tall Jake, although some of them were secretly terrified. Kady made plans with Dylan and Scotty to get in touch with the other gangs and rebel groups that they knew of. Dylan thought they'd get behind the idea once Kady explained it to them, since most of them wanted revenge on Tall Jake for one thing or another. Everyone had a relative who'd been taken to the Deadhouse or a friend killed by Regulators. Everyone knew someone in a village that had been destroyed. Tall Jake had made a lot of enemies.

"But how are we supposed to fight?" Kady asked Dylan.

"Yeah, we can't go into battle just waving sticks around," Justin added.

"Come on," grinned Dylan. "I got something to show you."

Dylan, Kady and Justin went down into the depths of the Bathysphere, where Dylan opened a heavy submarine-style pressure door and showed them into the chamber beyond.

"My little treasure room, innit?" he said.

Kady stared. The dimly lit chamber was cluttered with all manner of things. There were strange ornaments, Regulator helmets, bits of armour that didn't look like they fitted on humans. There were little clockwork devices and steam cylinders and all kinds of machine parts. There were billycans and tins on the shelves, and small crates piled against the wall.

"Where did you get all this?" Justin cried, and ran into the room to poke around. The mechanic in him loved to tinker with junk.

"Swapped, stolen, bought or begged," said Dylan proudly. "I been dealing with the gangs round here for ages now, and there's tons of dealers in the city. You just got to bring them something they want, and you get something *you* want. Easy."

"So when the Regulators come to kill us, we're going to throw bits of trash at them?" Kady ventured.

"Hey! This is *not* trash!" Justin said, surfacing from behind a heap of gears and sprockets.

"Remember them frazzlers we used back in the Terminus?" said Dylan. "They ain't the only weapons we got. We knocked over a supply train a while back and robbed the hell out of it. Got a whole bunch of stuff."

"I remember!" said Justin. "You took down a section of the track. That was when they shut down the trains. I was in the Clock Tower at the time, with Seth."

Dylan shrugged. "Don't know about that. But I know we got *these*."

He took down something from the wall. It looked like a small medieval lance, but shorter and with the end cut off. It was made of dark and tarnished metal, and thick cables ran from it to a chunky pack with straps that was obviously meant to be worn on the back.

"What's that? A flamethower?" Justin guessed hopefully.

"Nah. Wish it was. These are power lances. Got about twelve of them in all, which is probably about as many people in this place as I'd trust on a battlefield. The rest should stay at home, I reckon."

"What do they do?" Justin asked. He slipped one of the packs on his back and picked up a lance. There was a grip inside the handle of the lance, and a trigger.

"They shoot a bolt of some kind of electricity. Knocks you out."

"For how long?"

"Well, one of the kids we took on the raid, he accidentally shot himself in the foot. Put him down for twenty-four hours or so."

"Why didn't we have these in the Terminus?" Kady asked.

Dylan gave her a look. "They ain't too subtle. You can't exactly hide 'em under your clothes."

"I can't believe you didn't tell me about this place," Kady muttered, looking around.

Dylan shrugged. "You were all makin' plans to go to the Acropolis. Didn't think about it."

There was a shriek of energy and a blinding light. Kady and Dylan jumped and shielded their eyes. When they dared to look, they saw a nearby pile of crates crackling with blue arcs of electricity. Justin was delicately putting the lance down.

"Oops," he said. "Well, they work, anyway."

3

Kady spent the next fortnight with Dylan, going from place to place, drumming up support among the local rebels. She returned occasionally, but only to sleep and check on preparations. Seth saw little of her. He hung out with Justin, feeling miserable.

It took him a long time to work out why. At first he thought he might be secretly scared of the battle to come. He *was* scared, he had to admit that; but that wasn't it. He thought that maybe he was depressed because of losing the Lack, and that sense of loss she'd left behind her; but that wasn't it either. He wondered if it was something to do with Kady, but even that wasn't the whole reason.

It was Justin who got it in the end. "Mate, you're feeling down because you don't want it to end. You want to keep going like you are. If we do beat Tall Jake, what then?"

They were sitting in a small laboratory in the Bathysphere. Justin was at a workbench while Seth sat on a window sill, looking out at the fishes in the lake. Justin had taken to borrowing broken things from Dylan's treasure room and trying to fix them up.

"What if we do beat him?" Seth asked. "Does that mean they stop making the comic? No more comic, no more readers. If kids stop reading the comic, if they stop *believing*, does that mean Malice disappears?"

"Well, I ain't the sharpest tool in the drawer, but the Lack said that Malice was around *before* there was a comic. It was Grendel who made it happen. Now if *Grendel* dies, well, I don't know what happens then. But you want my opinion, I don't think Malice is going anywhere. It's *here* now. It's real. You get me?"

Seth nodded. But he wasn't convinced. Now he'd found this place, he couldn't bear to lose it. He was scared of the end of things.

Scotty organized the lancers and drilled them. Nobody had any idea what to expect in the upcoming conflict, but Scotty wanted them prepared. As Dylan had said, there were only twelve members of Havoc who would be worth anything in a fight. Among them were Kady, Seth, Justin and Scotty himself. Tatyana would go as well, of course. The others were too young, too scared, or not strong enough to run around with the battery packs on their backs.

Seth drilled for hours each day, until his battery pack was depleted and he had to charge it again from the generator in the Bathysphere. It helped him keep his mind off things.

Kady came and went, but there was a wedge between them now, and she was occupied with other things. She didn't ask him to come along on her expeditions, and he didn't ask to go. They both sensed the divide, and were careful to stay away from it.

One day, Andersen arrived. There was a message in his collar. Scotty took it out and read it, looked at Seth, and nodded gravely.

It was time.

The Dark Before
the Dawn

1

It was several days later that Seth found himself sitting on a high ridge, looking across broken and blasted plains at the Deadhouse.

Dawn was turning the night sky blue, but the stars were still bright, and the moon gazed down on Malice with an empty, idiot face. A yellowish mist had come with the night, cloaking the plains in a thick, slow sea of murk that stank of rotten eggs. Sometimes, a breath of wind would stir the mist, and vague shadows of *things* could be seen moving within.

Under the cover of the mist, Tall Jake's army was assembling.

Rising over the mist was the Deadhouse itself. A great black sprawling building of iron and steel and pipes. A monstrous, dirty factory that seeped smoke from its many chimneys. It was built on many levels and made up of several buildings, connected by bridges and surrounded by an enormous metal wall. It glowed a deep, smouldering red from within. The light came from its many fires, shining out through the cracks in its dark shell. Its roof bristled with deadly cannons.

It looked like the forge of the Devil.

The ridge Seth sat on was near the foot of a range of crumbling hills. Somewhere behind him was an army. An army of cats, humans, and the strange followers of the Lack known as the Coven. They numbered in the thousands. Too many to sneak up on Tall Jake; his scouts had seen them coming. But would it be enough to defeat him? Seth stared at the Deadhouse, and wondered.

In the morning, they would attack. The thought of what was to come terrified him. He was afraid for himself, but he was more afraid for the others. What if Justin died? What if Kady did? He couldn't stand to lose either one of them.

Kady had said that he loved danger. Well, maybe he did. But maybe it was just that he never really thought, deep down, that it could touch him. He thought he could get through anything if he was brave and smart enough. Secretly, he thought he was invincible. Because that's what real heroes were like.

But this was war. Down there, he wouldn't be in control. Down there, he was just one of thousands, and it was a roll of the dice whether any of them lived or died.

He heard footsteps behind him, and turned to look over

his shoulder. It was Kady, with Tatyana padding alongside. She looked weary, but she managed a smile as he saw her.

"There you are," she said. "Couldn't sleep."

"Can anyone?"

"I guess not." She came and stood next to where he was sitting. Tatyana nuzzled him, wanting to be stroked. He scratched behind her ear and she purred noisily.

Kady gazed out over the plains, the sea of vile mist and the hellish Deadhouse at its centre. "What's out there?" she asked distantly. "Waiting for us, under the mist?"

"I don't want to know," Seth said.

They shared a silence for a time. Seth felt a pressure to speak, but he couldn't. Even though this might be his last chance, he couldn't. There were too many things he wanted to say to her, but he was never good with things like that. He could never find the words to express it properly. It always came out sounding wrong. Better to keep quiet.

"They want to see you," she said eventually.

"Who?"

"The Lack. The Queen of Cats."

Seth got to his feet. "Lead on."

Kady gave him one of her looks, the kind that said she knew something was wrong but she didn't know whether to ask about it. A look that said: *Tell me, Seth. What's going on?*

But he didn't.

They headed back up the hill to the camp. Coven sentries watched them approach, clicking and rattling to themselves. The Coven made Seth's skin crawl. He'd first seen them in the Oubliette, initially as statues and then as corpses in the Lack's temple. He still had no idea what they looked like under their alien, close-fitting armour. They had spindly limbs, knees set backwards like the hind legs of a horse, long skulls encased in smooth helmets of black metal. They carried pikes with a blade at both ends, and talked in a horrible ticking, clattering language, punctuated by shrill whines and shrieks.

Once past the sentries, they picked their way through the camp. Hundreds of tents had been pitched here, mainly for the human forces. They gathered round fires, cleaning and sharpening their weapons and talking in low voices about the battle ahead. Kady had done a great job spreading the word. Havoc was made up of kids, but most of Tall Jake's enemies were adults. Thousands of them had come flocking at the prospect of settling things. They were a ragtag army at best: mountain tribesmen, village militia, intellectuals from the City. But they all shared a common cause.

Kady had been careful to explain that they would be joining an army led by the Lack, the Queen of Cats and the Shard. The human forces were made up of many groups with many leaders, and they would never agree on one between themselves. But the Lack and the Queen of Cats had adopted Kady as their contact among the human forces. She'd become the unofficial leader, even if nobody admitted it. No adult wanted to be led by a kid.

Justin spotted them and caught them up as they made their way through the camp. "Mind if I tag along?" he said. "It gets kinda boring waiting to be chopped into bits by Tall Jake's zombie hordes."

"Yeah, I can imagine how boring that must be," said Kady, deadpan.

2

They found the Queen of Cats and the Lack inside an ancient circle of standing stones. The stones stood on a bare hilltop, weathered and leaning inward. Some of them were split and blackened by lightning. A half-dozen great cats prowled around outside, guarding their queen within.

They stopped at the edge of the circle. Kady turned to Seth and touched his arm. There was an odd, pleading look in her eyes.

"You don't have to do what they ask, Seth," she said.

"You know me," said Seth. "Sir Knight, right?" It came out sounding bitter. He knew it hurt her to throw her affectionate nickname back in her face. He looked away, regretting it. "I'll do what I have to."

He walked towards the stone circle. The others stayed where they were. The cats looked him over as he approached, but they let him pass.

The Queen of Cats was sitting sphinx-like. She wore fine armour now instead of jewels. The Lack was a beautiful statue, crisp as frostbite.

The Queen of Cats stared at him expectantly. He stared back.

You should be kneeling.

"Should I?" Seth replied. He felt pointlessly defiant. They could all be dead in a few hours. He wasn't going to kneel to her any more. She wasn't his queen. To be honest, he probably wouldn't have knelt to *his* queen, either.

The Queen of Cats turned her head away in disgust. The Lack favoured him with that wispy smile of hers. She approved. For some reason, that made him glad.

MY CHAMPION. YOU CLEANSED MY TEMPLE OF THE MORT-BEAST AND YOU DELIVERED US THE SHARD. NOW I HAVE ONE LAST REQUEST OF YOU.

Seth waited silently.

THE BATTLE TO COME WILL NOT BE ONE WE CAN BE SURE OF WINNING. TALL JAKE HAS ONE GREAT ADVANTAGE. WE ARE FACING HIM ON HIS TERRITORY. HE HAS THE DEADHOUSE. IT IS AN ALMOST IMPENETRABLE FORTRESS. IF THE TIDE TURNS IN OUR FAVOUR, HE WILL RETREAT INTO IT. ITS CANNONS WILL ENSURE THAT AN ASSAULT ON THE DEADHOUSE WALLS WILL BE . . . COSTLY.

"What do you plan to do?"

WE PLAN TO DESTROY IT WHILE HIS ATTENTION IS ELSEWHERE. BUT WE WILL NEED YOUR HELP.

308

Seth understood. "The route through the factory. You were with me in Birmingham, when me and Alicia got in by accident."

YES. A BACK WAY INTO THE DEADHOUSE. TALL JAKE KNOWS YOU GOT IN – HE HAS READ THE COMIC, NO DOUBT – BUT HE DOESN'T KNOW HOW.

She held out a small mechanical device, about the size of a lunchbox. Seth took it. It was an assortment of metal tubes, with a dial in the middle which was obviously a timer. There were two vials set among the tubes. One fizzed with a blinding white light. The other one was so dark that it felt like it was sucking Seth in as he stared at it.

THE UNIVERSE IS MADE UP OF MANY THINGS, said the Lack. SOME ARE NOT MEANT TO BE MIXED. WHEN THEY ARE. . . She blew into her hand and splayed her fingers, miming an explosion.

"You want me to take this inside the Deadhouse?"

The Lack nodded. WE CANNOT TRAVEL IN YOUR WORLD. WE WOULD BECOME FAINT AND ALMOST POWERLESS. NOR CAN WE SEND ONE OF OUR OWN, FOR IT REQUIRES GREAT POWER TO SEND SOMETHING INTO YOUR WORLD THAT DOES NOT BELONG THERE. ONLY CATS HAVE THE POWER TO CROSS WORLDS AND STORIES WITH EASE, AND THEN ONLY THE SMALLEST AND NIMBLEST CAN DO IT.

The Queen of Cats rumbled proudly in the background.

BUT IT IS SIMPLE TO SEND YOU, SETH, FOR
YOU ARE FROM THAT WORLD AND IT WANTS
YOU BACK. YOU MUST TAKE THAT DEVICE
THROUGH THE OLD FACTORY AND INTO THE
DEADHOUSE. IT WILL BE EMPTY NOW; ALL HIS
FORCES WILL BE OUTSIDE. YOU MUST PLACE
IT IN THE HEART OF THE BUILDING, IN THE
ENGINE ROOM, AND ESCAPE THE WAY YOU
CAME. IF WE CAN DESTROY THE DEADHOUSE,
TALL JAKE WILL BE MUCH WEAKENED. WITH
OUR COMBINED POWER, WE MAY OVERCOME
HIM THEN.

Seth stared at the device in his hands. His heart was sinking.

"You're asking me to go back to the real world?"

I AM ASKING YOU TO HELP US DEFEAT
TALL JAKE.

That wasn't all she was asking. Even if he did manage to do it, he would have to escape back through the factory, and he would come out in Birmingham. With no ticket back to Malice.

What if he couldn't even get into the Deadhouse? What if Tall Jake had somehow closed the route through the factory, or it didn't work twice or something? What if he ended up trapped in the real world? That thought scared him more than the battle did.

But even as he debated it, he knew there was no real choice. This wasn't about him. It was about Luke and Colm and all those kids who had died because of Tall Jake. It was about all those who had summoned him but hadn't yet been taken, like Alicia and Philip Gormley. It was about all those parents and friends and brothers and sisters who had their lives ruined when some kid disappeared without a trace. He was the only one who could do it. The only one who'd been there before.

Sometimes he hated having to do what was right. But that was just how he was.

"I need to say some goodbyes."

The Lack stared deep into his eyes. "I know how this hurts you, Seth. Remember who I am. I can take away your pain."

Just for a moment, Seth was tempted. He wanted to forget all about Luke. He wanted to stop worrying about his parents and what could be happening to them now. He wanted to stop feeling angry or confused whenever he thought about Kady.

But that would be giving up, and Seth wasn't the kind. Besides, there was something dangerous in her offer. He remembered what the Queen of Cats had said, back in that cave in the rainforest. *Be careful, my guests. First she'll take your pain, then she'll take the rest of you.*

"I'll hang on to my pain, thanks," he said. "It makes the happy bits seem better."

He walked out of the stone circle, to where his friends were waiting.

"So?" Justin asked.

"They want me to go into the Deadhouse. Blow it up."

"What did you say to them?" Kady asked. He got the sense that she'd already known about the plan, and was hoping he would refuse. At least she cared that much for him.

"I said yes," he told her.

Justin clapped his hands and rubbed them together. "Right, then. When do we leave?"

Seth shook his head. "This one's just on me. I can't ask you to come. It's too dangerous."

Justin snorted. "Who says I need to be asked?"

"We'll have to leave Malice. Go to our world. We might not get back again."

That gave Justin pause for a moment, but he soon brightened again. "You're the only person I know who wants to stay in Malice even more than me," he said. "If you think we can make it back, I'm in."

Seth was smiling in spite of himself. "Justin, I can't ask you—"

"Listen. I'm going with you," Justin said firmly, poking him in the chest. "Deal with it."

Seth's smile became a grin, and suddenly he gathered up Justin in a hug. Justin waved his arms and looked awkward. "Whoa! Little too much man-love going on lately, mate. You're getting me worried."

Seth couldn't help himself. He hadn't realized until that moment how much he didn't want to face the Deadhouse alone. Justin had been with him through the Clock Tower, the Oubliette and the Acropolis. Together, they could take on anything. Justin was the kind of friend he'd always wished for. Solid as a rock. Always on your side. There weren't many like him in the world.

Justin struggled out of his grip and he turned to Kady. She was gazing at him sadly.

"I can't go with you," she said. "They need me here."

"I know," he said. It felt like they were always saying goodbye nowadays, and he couldn't summon the strength to say something meaningful this time. "See you later, I suppose."

"Yeah," said Kady. "See ya."

Tatyana butted his head with her leg. He knelt down and rubbed his forehead against hers.

"You have to stay here and take care of Kady," he said. "Make sure she gets through the fight okay." The sabretooth dipped her head in agreement.

Then he got to his feet, and with one last backwards glance, he went with Justin back into the circle.

"Can you send both of us?" he asked the Lack.

YES.

"Won't we need weapons or something?" Justin asked. He was thinking of the power lances they'd been training with.

THEY ARE TOO DELICATE. THEY WILL NOT SURVIVE THE CROSSING.

Justin cursed under his breath. "Alright then. I guess we just try not to get caught, huh?"

"Will we remember?" asked Seth. "After you send us back? I mean, I don't want my memory wiped *again*."

I WILL TAKE CARE OF THAT, she said.

Seth and Justin looked at each other. Justin shrugged.

"Well," he said.

"We're ready," Seth told the Lack.

YES, she said. YOU ARE.

Before they could figure out what she meant by that, they were gone.

3

It was like waking up suddenly from an unexpected sleep. Seth sucked in a breath, his head came up sharply, and he was elsewhere.

It took him a moment to recognize the derelict factory in Birmingham. He was standing on scrub ground inside a fenced-off area. The air was different here: heavier, oilier, subtly polluted with car exhausts and chimneys. It was almost dawn, and the streetlights on the road nearby marched away towards the brighter glow of the city.

Justin was standing next to him, looking around with an expression of distaste on his face.

"Ugh," he said. "It's worse than I remembered."

"It's not the prettiest spot in England, to be fair," Seth said.

"You got *that* right," said Justin. He hawked and spat. "You look like you know this place."

"I was here before, with this girl. Alicia." He caught

himself. "I should call her, see if she's okay. You think we have time?"

"No," said Justin. "They're relying on us back in Malice. Let's get this done, eh?"

Seth nodded. He was right. "Isn't there anything you want to do while you're here, though? Make a phone call, send a message? I mean, if you could?"

Justin scuffed at the ground with his toe. "Mate, I just want to get out of here, quick as I can."

"I wish I could talk to my folks. Just to let them know I'm okay."

But he dared not call them. Not after last time. If Tall Jake had them, it was better if Seth didn't know. If he knew they were hostages, he would have to try and save them — and that was just what Tall Jake wanted.

Justin sensed his train of thought and patted him on the back. "Look on the bright side. How many times do you get to blow up the enemy fortress, outside of a computer game?"

Seth laughed. "Never was one for computer games," he said. "But I know what you mean."

"We'll be heroes!" Justin said.

"*Actual* heroes," said Seth. "Not the rubbish kind who end up advertising shaving cream and burger chains."

Justin picked up a length of broken iron piping from the ground and swung it experimentally. "That's the spirit," he said. "Beats thinking about getting eaten by zombies, anyway. Get yourself a weapon, eh?"

Seth scanned the scrub ground until he found a weapon of his own – a thick wooden chair leg that had come from God knew where. He handed it to Justin. "Hold on to that for me, will you? I have to carry this." He held up the Lack's device. The glow from the bright vial lit the underside of his face.

"Put it in your pack," Justin suggested.

"We'll need the light," he said. "It's dark where we're going."

"Joy," said Justin sarcastically. He shoved the chair leg into his belt. "Ready?"

"Ready," said Seth.

"Lead on."

To the Deadhouse

1

Kady felt sick.

The sun was rising over the dry and cracked plains. At the base of the hills, an army of thousands had gathered. Kady stood among them, with the boys and girls of Havoc around her. She was wearing a heavy battery pack, holding a power lance in her hands. The smell of nervous sweat was in the air, the animal musk of the cats, the sour odour of the Coven. She felt buried among the waiting crowd.

The Deadhouse was a filthy grey-black in the growing light. The foul yellow mist that surrounded it was burning off in the sun, thinning steadily. Restless silhouettes moved behind it. Occasionally they would catch a glimpse of something huge, like seeing the flank of a great ship slide past in a fog bank. Then it would be gone, leaving only a promise of the battle to come.

How had she ended up here? She just wanted to be at home, wrapped up in a blanket, drinking a mug of her mom's Fairtrade organic sugar-free calorie-free hot chocolate. She wanted to read a book in the bath. She wanted to waste hours wandering around the Net. She wanted to see her friends at school.

She had good parents and a great life back home. Things might have got a bit dull sometimes but hey, it was better than being here, waiting to run headlong into battle. She wasn't a warrior. She wasn't a leader. She was a modern girl. The most danger she came up against back home was burning her mouth on microwave pizza.

And where was Seth? Gone, on a mission of his own. The two of them, always in different worlds. It saddened her that it had to be this way. But she couldn't stay here and he couldn't stay there. Neither would be happy if they did. It wasn't fair. Life wasn't fair. And there was nothing either of them could do about it.

A stirring in the ranks interrupted her thoughts. She looked for the cause, and saw it. There, on the roof of the Deadhouse, a figure had appeared. Even at this distance, he drew the eye like a magnet. Towering, thin, wearing a high-collared coat and a tricorn hat.

Tall Jake.

Fearful whispers ran through the army. The mere sight of Tall Jake had unsettled them.

Then, a great bellow echoed across the battlefield. A sudden wind blasted through the army, blowing Kady's pigtails about. It swept down on to the plains and lifted away the foul mist.

Kady went pale.

Revealed beneath was Tall Jake's army. No, not an army: a *horde*. A terrible chaos of monstrosities from the Deadhouse. Flesh was fused to flesh in awful combinations. There were leering zombies with four arms which ended in meat cleavers. Fat, grotesque, blind men with lashing tentacles where their limbs should have been. Massive dogs that had no skin but were all glistening muscle and teeth. Mixed in among them were the black uniforms and helmets of the Regulators.

But that wasn't the worst of it. For among them stalked the giants. Kady had heard of these. She'd even seen one before, when she faced the Mort-Beast in the Oubliette. They were Tall Jake's proudest creations, the true monsters of the Deadhouse: the Juggernauts.

They were four, five, six metres tall. Big as dinosaurs. Their huge jaws gaped and their many eyes rolled. One of them had a stumpy body and two long, snaking necks that ended in different heads. Another was like a ball of eyes and mouths, its round body supported by crab legs. One resembled a preying mantis with a head like a decaying horse. They were abominations, as if someone had taken nature's construction kit, spilled it out and fixed everything back together in a jumble. They were experiments in bone and sinew. Tall Jake's living toys.

Kady almost turned and ran then. The army shuffled backwards, as if they were all thinking the same thing. They couldn't fight this!

But then the Queen of Cats roared, and it shook the

earth at their feet. They took strength in that. The Queen of Cats was mighty too, and they felt it in her voice. Her roar was taken up by the big cats at her command, and the land shivered with their fury. They were joined by the terrifying cry of the Coven, an awful shriek that sawed through the air. The strange black-armoured warriors thrust their pikes skyward.

The humans took heart, and they shouted too, yelling at the tops of their lungs, children and adults alike. Kady felt a great wave building underneath her, and there was nothing she could do to stop it. She raised her power lance and yelled as loud as she could, but she couldn't even hear her own voice over the pummelling cloud of sound.

The front ranks broke, and began to spill down the hill towards the Deadhouse. The rest of the army came after them like a landslide. Kady felt the surge around her, and she had to run, or be trampled. Swept up, she charged.

The battle had begun.

2

Machine oil and meat and the faint scent of burning. Clanks and cackles and distant screeches.

Seth was ready for the Deadhouse this time. He didn't remember the exact route through the tunnels under the factory, and he still didn't notice exactly when the stone walls turned to grimy metal. But this time, there was no surprise. He just stopped and said: "We're here."

They turned a corner, into the light of a buzzing electric bulb set inside a cage. Several iron vats were placed against one wall, with windows in them to peer inside. Seth didn't need to. He knew what was in them.

"That's *it*?" Justin asked, as Seth put the Lack's device into his backpack. "I didn't feel anything. I was expecting a kind of mystical light show, like off *Stargate* or something."

"*Stargate*?" Seth asked, bewildered.

"You really need to watch some TV sometime," Justin said. He put his hands on his hips and surveyed the corridor. "Well. Flying visit to the real world, then right back to Malice. Suits me."

"Keep on your toes," Seth advised. "This is a bad place." He held out his hand, and Justin gave him the crude wooden club he'd picked up outside the factory.

"Worse than the Oubliette?" Justin asked. "Doubt it. At least here I can *see* what's trying to bite my face off."

Seth slapped him on the shoulder. "Come on," he said. He felt better about being here now. Justin's banter always lifted his spirits.

Or maybe it was just that he was relieved to have made it back. He'd been afraid he would be stuck out in the real world, that the bridge to Malice would be closed. But everything had gone to plan so far.

Kady would say you're crazy, he thought. *You'd rather be in the Deadhouse than Birmingham.*

But that was the difference between them.

The Deadhouse was quieter than he remembered it.

321

The corridors were empty. Occasional dull booming noises came from above, and the sound of fire and machinery rumbled through the walls. They crept along and listened at every corner, but they didn't hear anything moving.

They're all outside, thought Seth. *And Kady's out there with them.*

"Those are cannons," Justin said, listening to the booming sounds coming from above. "Cannon fire."

Seth frowned. The battle had already started. "Let's move," he said.

"Move where? What are we looking for?" Justin asked, as they hurried down another grubby corridor. Rat bones lay among the dirt in the corners.

"The Lack said we have to find an engine room. The heart of the Deadhouse. That's where we put the bomb."

"Oh, right. We need to head down, then."

Seth stopped and stared at him. "How do you know that?"

"I can hear it. It's below us."

Seth listened, but he couldn't make out anything amid the mess of machine noises, the clanks and squeaks of the Deadhouse. "You sure?"

"Sure I'm sure. You just got to know how to *listen*, mate."

Seth grabbed him suddenly, pulled him into a doorway, and clamped his hand over his friend's mouth. A moment later, something came winging down the corridor. It was over a metre wide, swimming through the air like a manta ray, with a wide mouth of short, sharp teeth. It swept past the doorway where they hid and disappeared up the corridor.

Seth took his hand away from Justin's mouth. He breathed out.

"Didn't hear that one coming," Justin said.

"You just got to know how to *listen*." Seth grinned. Justin hit him.

The journey through the Deadhouse was a nerve-wracking experience. After their close encounter in the corridor, they realized that not *every* creature that lived here was outside on the battlefield. Shuffling zombies haunted the corridors, wearing straitjackets, their heads enclosed in cages. Some were barely aware of their surroundings; others looked like they might be violent. Seth and Justin took care to avoid them all.

At one point, they came across a vast, circular pit with metal walkways running around the edge. It was too dark to see to the bottom, but they could hear the wet breathing of something huge. They beat a hasty retreat when a long, slimy tentacle came coiling out of the pit and almost snatched Seth away.

All the time, the cannons boomed atop the Deadhouse. Seth tried not to think of the artillery falling on the army of the Queen of Cats. Kady and Tatyana were out there, and Scotty and Dylan. He gritted his teeth at the thought. Tall Jake had to be stopped. He wouldn't let himself fail.

Justin's ability to pick out different machine sounds was

uncanny, and it came in useful again. He heard the whirr and hum of a lift and guided them towards it. It turned out to be a cargo elevator stained with old blood and oily handprints. Justin ran a finger down the wall and examined the tip.

"This place *needs* blowing up," he muttered.

"You reckon this'll take us to the engine room?" Seth asked.

"One way to find out," said Justin. He took hold of a lever and pulled it. The doors slid shut with a shriek.

"Going down," said Justin. The elevator lurched and began to descend.

3

Kady's stomach was knotted, her throat closed tight, blood pounding in her head. Somehow she kept running forward. All around her was the thunder of feet and paws, the roar of the big cats, the yelling of their human allies. Over it all was the screeching of the Coven, like the shrill whine of microphone feedback.

She looked to her left and right and saw frightened, excited faces, teeth bared, eyes glittering with fever. The madness of the charge. She was gripping the handle of the power lance so hard that her knuckles hurt.

She'd never experienced any feeling so terrible.

The foul horde from the Deadhouse washed towards them like a spilled bucket of guts. Behind them, the cannons roared. Explosions threw broken bodies into the air. The ragged holes it tore in the rebel army were quickly swallowed up in the charge.

The cats had taken the lead as they raced across the plain. They were bigger, stronger and faster than the humans. The Regulators in the front ranks let fly with their spear guns. Cats fell, crashing to the dusty plain and rolling to a halt. There were so many targets, it was impossible to miss. The cats leaped over the fallen bodies of their companions and kept on coming.

Now the Regulators dropped back and the ogres pushed to the front, carrying huge clubs and wielding wicked-looking swords. They stood ready to resist the charge. The two sides collided in a bloody churn of bodies. Claws and teeth slashed. Ogres roared and swung their blades. Skin and fur were spattered red.

Kady was carried headlong into the crush. Bodies thrashed and fought all around her. Kady looked wildly about in panic. She didn't know where to go, what to do. Something that was all teeth and muscle reared up to her left. She pointed her lance at it, closed her eyes and squeezed the trigger. There was a loud shriek of discharged energy. When she opened her eyes, the monstrosity was lying in a heap, crackling with electricity.

Suddenly the Coven swept in and overtook her, and she was surrounded by beetly black shapes, swarming past. She was pushed this way and that as they raced by. She couldn't see anyone from Havoc, or even another human face. An explosion nearby showered her with dirt and made her cringe.

Oh God, oh God, get me out of this! Get me out of this!

She turned around and came face to awful face with a Deadhouse zombie whose hands had been replaced with maces. It gaped eagerly and lunged at her, eyes hungry. She raised her power lance but it swung out an arm and knocked it from her grip. The other arm swung round towards her head –

– and then Tatyana was there, a snarling avalanche of brass and clockwork. Her eyes shone red as she bore the zombie down under her weight. With one crushing swipe of her paw, the zombie lay still.

Kady rushed to her and flung her arms around the sabretooth's neck in relief. "Stay with me," she begged. "Please."

Tatyana dipped her head in agreement. Kady took up her power lance again, and together they plunged back into the battle.

4

The elevator doors squealed open in a gust of hot, stinking air. The sound was deafening: the clanking of pistons, the hiss of steam, the low bellow of fire. It was dark down here, but the deep red of the furnaces leaked out of the grates, casting demonic shadows that flickered and lunged. The arms of enormous engines pumped and swung overhead.

Everywhere was noise and movement, pounding at the senses.

Justin peered gingerly out of the elevator. "I think we went down a bit too far," he said. "This must be hell's boiler room."

"Looks right to me," said Seth. "Let's find a good place to stash the bomb."

They crept from the elevator and into the aisles that ran between the furnaces. Seth's nerves crackled with anticipation. The firelight tricked the imagination and made him see shapes in the shadows. With this amount of noise they would never hear anything sneaking up on them. He hefted his chair-leg club. It made him feel a bit better, even though he suspected it would prove useless. They just had to hope they remained unnoticed.

A blast of steam suddenly filled the aisle in front of him. He was a metre away, but even so, it was hot enough to scald him. He fell backwards into Justin, who caught him and turned them both away from the heat.

The steam continued venting for thirty seconds or more before it died down, leaving the corridor sopping wet.

"That has *got* to break some safety regulations," said Justin.

Seth's cheek and hand were still stinging from the heat. He stayed back while Justin went over to examine the iron valve that had spewed the steam.

"Come here, have a look at this," he said.

"Is it safe?"

"It is now."

Seth came over, and Justin showed him a pressure gauge on the side of the valve. Most of the gauge was coloured green, but there was a red section that signified danger. The pressure was very low, well into the green.

"When the pressure gets to red, they blow," he said. "Someone should probably be looking after these. Controlled venting, like. But they're probably all busy at the moment with the battle."

There was a loud clank from a nearby aisle: the sound of something metal falling to the floor.

"Not all of them," Seth said.

"That could have been anything," Justin reassured him. He tapped the gauge. "We should watch out for these."

They moved further into the engine room, checking gauges as they went. Seth wanted to get near the centre of the room before he planted the bomb, to make sure it did what it should. It wasn't enough to just damage the Deadhouse. They had to destroy it. They had one chance, and he wanted to do it right. But he didn't know how much longer his nerve would hold.

Then Justin grabbed his arm and pointed. Up ahead of them, a furnace grate threw its glow into the aisle. The shadow of the bars was clear in the firelight. As they watched, something moved across the face of the furnace: a distorted silhouette, something huge and lumbering.

"Forget finding a good spot. Let's dump that thing and peg it!" Justin urged.

Seth was inclined to agree. He crouched down next to a row of steam pipes and pulled the Lack's device out of his backpack. The light vial shone brightly; the dark vial ate the light. There was a timer dial set among the metal tubes that linked the vials, but Seth couldn't make head or tail of the numbers on it. To be safe, he twisted it until it wouldn't turn any more. When he released it, it began to tick. He dropped the device back in his pack to muffle the light. Then he stuffed the pack behind the steam pipes, where it wouldn't be seen.

As he did so, he felt an obstruction. There was something *else* behind the steam pipes. He reached in and pulled out a little box of black metal.

"What's that?" Justin asked, peering over his shoulder.

"No idea," said Seth, stuffing the pack back in. What on earth was a little metal box doing here? He flicked the catch and opened it, but just then Justin tapped his shoulder.

"Er, mate. Trouble."

Seth's heart sank at his tone of voice.

Standing in the middle of the aisle, looming in the red dark, was an ogre. The same massive, twisted brute that had chased them out of the Deadhouse on his last visit. Roughly human, but only just. Three metres high. Veins bulging on a thick neck. Tiny eyes glittering in the blackness. He held a thick metal club as long as Seth's leg.

Quivering lips skinned back over rotten teeth. The ogre growled, low and threatening.

Seth and Justin looked at the pathetic weapons in their hands. They looked at one another. Then they bolted.

They fled through the maze of aisles between the furnaces and the steam engines. Fiery grates flashed by; machines crashed and thumped. The noise confused and disoriented them. As they ran, Seth snatched up what was inside the little metal box and jammed it in his pocket, then tossed the box aside.

Shadow and fire, shadow and fire, and the hot reek of the engine room.

Suddenly the light was blocked. The ogre had got ahead of them and cut them off. Seth skidded to a halt and scrambled backwards. It swung its club at his head. He felt the whoosh of air as it missed his nose by a centimetre. Justin grabbed him and pulled him away. The ogre lunged after them, but it missed its footing and stumbled to one knee. Justin and Seth ran back the way they'd come.

"I got an idea!" Justin panted.

He slowed down as they approached one of the great iron valves on the sides of the steam engines.

"What are you doing? Keep going!" Seth cried.

Justin squinted at the pressure gauge, then shook his head. "No good," he said, and accelerated again.

They came to the next gauge, and Justin slowed again to squint at it. Seth looked fearfully over his shoulder. The ogre was pounding up the aisle, roaring angrily.

"No good," said Justin again, and ran on.

"Will you stop stopping?"

"Next one's lucky, I can feel it!" he replied.

They turned a corner, and there was another valve. Justin ran to it and grinned. "It's in the red!"

"What?"

"Never mind!" Justin cried. "Get out of the way!" And he whacked the valve with the iron bar he'd carried all the way from Birmingham.

Seth hurried over to stand next to Justin. The ogre's thumping footsteps were close enough to be heard over the racket coming from the engines.

Justin whacked the valve again, hard enough to dent the metal. "Come on!" he cried. "Come on!"

The ogre appeared around the corner. It laid eyes on them and lunged forward with a roar. At that moment, Justin whacked the valve again, and finally it gave way and exploded in a colossal blast of steam.

Seth fell away from the valve, his skin and eyes burning. Somehow he still had hold of Justin, and he pulled him away too. The two of them struggled back, shielding their faces, stumbling free of the scalding cloud, blinking back tears.

The ogre was caught right in the blast. It roared and staggered, a huge shadow thrashing in the red mist. Bellowing, it tried to find its way out, but only succeeded in crashing into a wall. For long, horrible seconds, it flung itself this way and that, but finally it sank to the ground.

When the blast ended, the ogre lay still, soaking wet and steaming.

Justin grinned. His face was bright red. "And *that's* how you boil an ogre."

Seth blinked and wiped his brow with his sleeve. He felt like a lobster himself. "Not bad," he said. "Never took you for a chef."

Justin shrugged modestly. "One of my many talents." Then he remembered the bomb, and his face became serious. "Enough mucking about. We're against the clock. You remember the way back?"

"We're not going back," said Seth.

"We're not?"

"No. We're going *out*. We'll find a way out of the Deadhouse, on to the battlefield."

Justin stared at him. "You serious?"

"Kady's out there," he said. "Besides . . . you really want to go back home?"

Justin shook his head and smiled. "Knew you wouldn't let me down, mate. Malice all the way." He slapped his friend on the arm. "Let's go."

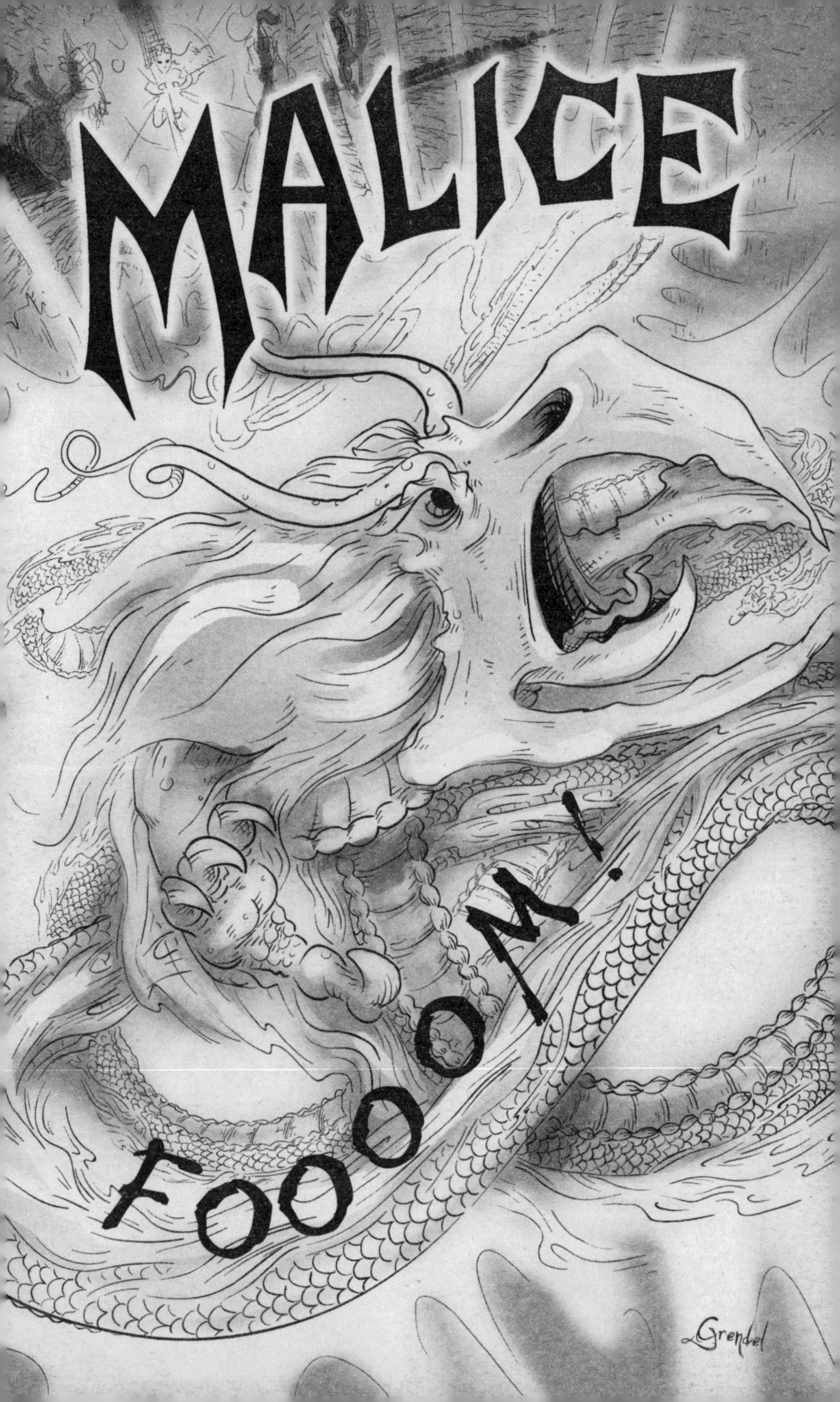
MALICE
FOOOOM!
Grendel

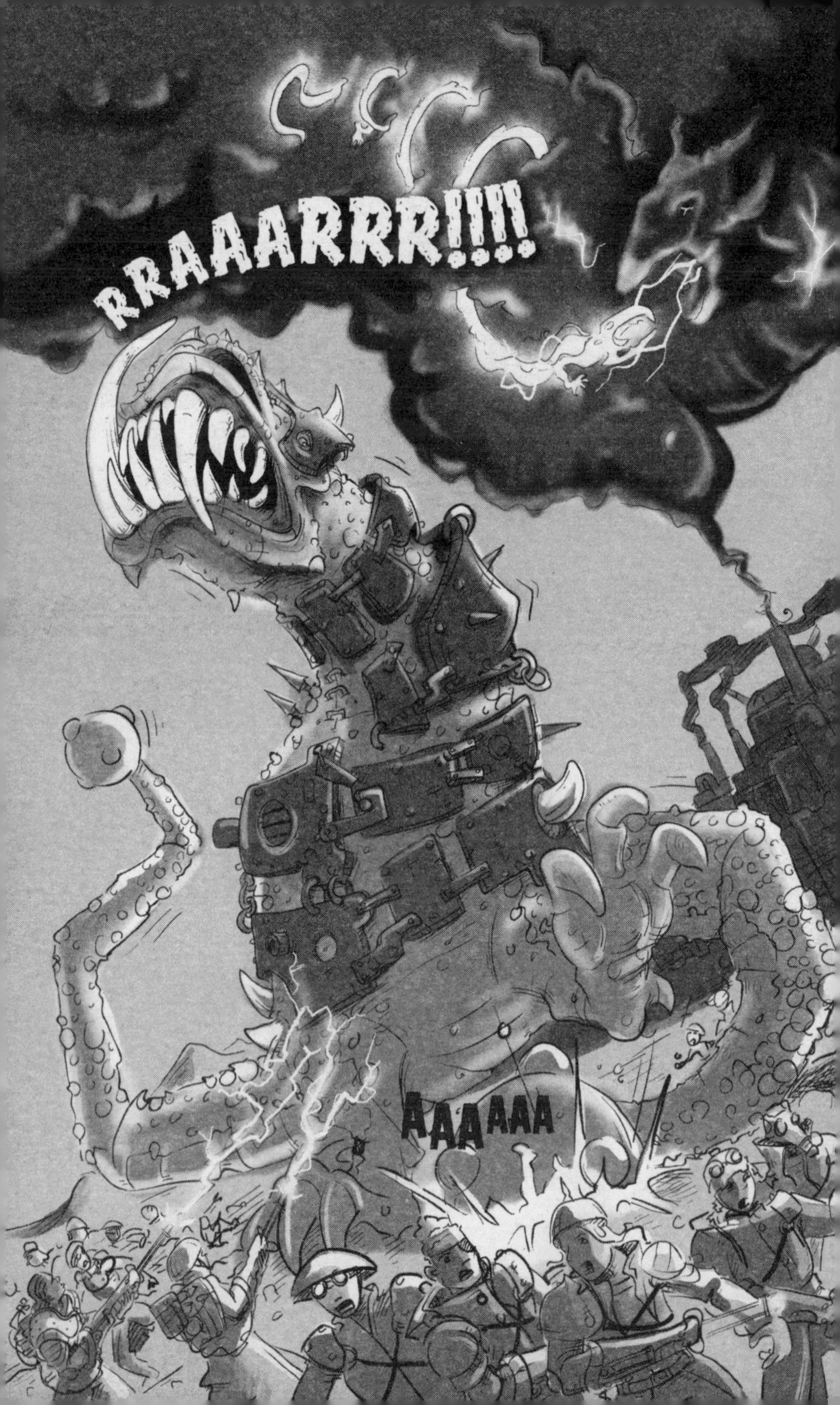
RRAAARRRR!!!!
AAAAAA

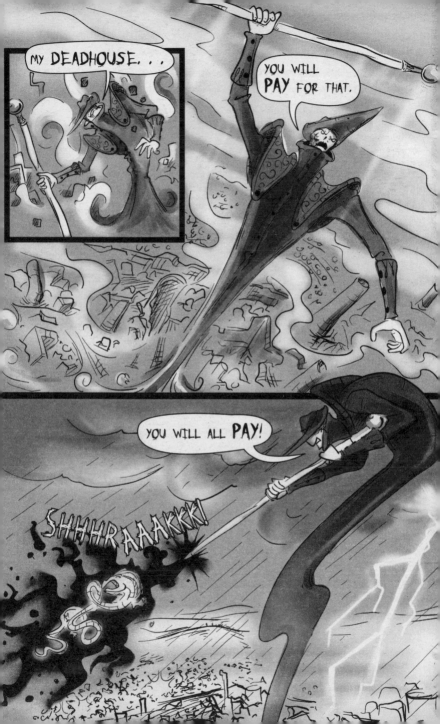

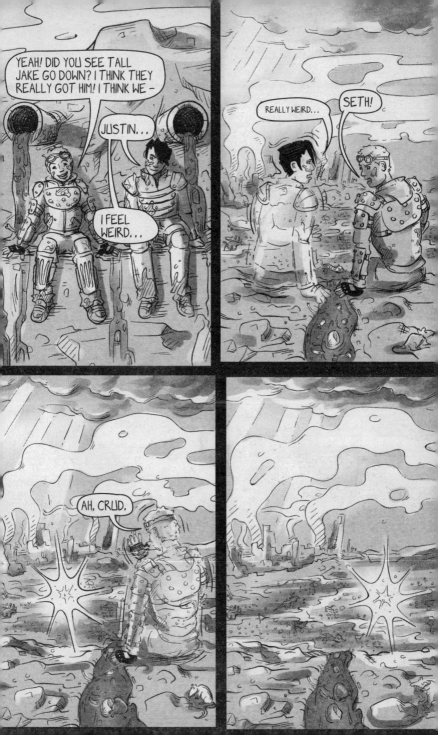

Back to the Attic

1

A moment of darkness, and they were back in their own world.

Seth looked around, a little startled by the change of scenery. One instant he'd been outside, beneath the weak sun of Malice, standing in the smoky ruins of the Deadhouse. The next he was inside, in a large, dusty room with paint flaking off the walls. The windows were covered with wire mesh. A TV, also surrounded by mesh, sat dark in a metal bracket. Mouldy chairs were arranged facing it.

Kady and Justin were with him. They were just as bewildered.

"What is this? A hospital?" Kady asked.

"Looks like the old TV room we had in borstal," said Justin, eyeing the room.

"It's a prison?"

Seth knew what it was. He'd visited this place in a vision once. Though he'd only seen the attic, he recognized the *feel*.

"It's Crouch Hollow," he said.

Kady scratched the back of her neck. "I guess it makes sense. The Lack must have sent us to wherever Tall Jake went. And where else would he run to but his base of operations in our world?"

Something caught her eye. She went over to a doorway, crouched down and picked up a button. She studied it for a few seconds, then tossed it to Seth.

"Looks like it's from a coat," she said.

"Tall Jake's?"

"Couldn't say for sure. I've never seen him up close. But it's a fair bet."

Seth shrugged and gestured towards the doorway. "He went that way."

He headed for the door, but Justin grabbed his arm to stop him.

"Listen, I hate to be a drag or whatever, but what are we going to do when we find him? Even if he *does* have only a tenth of his power, that's plenty enough to turn us all into Egg McMuffins if he feels like it."

"I don't know," said Seth. "We'll work something out."

"Great," said Justin sarcastically. He let Seth go. "Well, I feel better now we've got a plan."

They crept out of the common room and into a corridor. There were bars and gates everywhere in Crouch Hollow. Water dripped, doors creaked, and there was no heating. The cold of a winter morning seeped into them.

Seth knew Justin was worried. He knew they needed a

plan to face Tall Jake. He just didn't want to stop and think right now. There was too much to think about.

What if, by destroying Tall Jake, he was destroying the world of Malice? What if he could never go there again? How could he go back to school, how could he live a normal life knowing what he knew?

Malice had taken his best friend from him, but it had given him a new one in Justin. And it had given him more. It had given him hope. Hope of a world of adventure, a world different to this one. A world where they hadn't polluted the planet. A world where people *spoke* to each other instead of chatting on the internet. A world where there were still things to be discovered.

It wasn't a perfect place – it had good and evil like any other – but it was a *new* one. Seth felt like he'd been born into a world where everything had been done. In Malice, everything was fresh, and waiting for him.

They passed by a row of cells, with circular portholes in them so that people in the corridor could see in. Most of them were ajar, but one was closed. Seth went up to it and peered through the porthole. It was empty.

At least he thought so until a face shot into view, centimetres from his own, fast enough to make him jump.

He staggered back, stifling a yell of surprise. He was even more surprised to recognize the face behind the glass.

"Alicia!"

He released the bolt on the cell door, pulled it open, and there she was. She was thinner than he remembered, her hair was uncombed and she looked worn out with fright.

"What are you doing here?" he said, dumbly.

"What are *you* doing here?" she countered.

"I asked first."

"I got your message," Alicia said.

The message. Of course, the message he'd left on her phone. She'd done what he asked, and it had got her locked up in here. Once again, Seth had managed to get an innocent person tangled up in the world of Malice, just like he had with Kady. He hadn't wanted to involve her, but in the end he'd done it anyway, because he had no other choice. At least now he could try to get her out of it.

She glanced past Seth at his companions. Seth was suddenly aware that their clothes, which were a hybrid of fashions from both worlds, must look very bizarre. Kady gave a little wave. "Hi!"

"Oh, right," said Seth, remembering his manners. "This is Justin and Kady."

"You found her?" Alicia asked, suddenly breaking into a smile. "Well done."

"How did you end up in that cell?" he asked.

"They caught me. It must have been . . . I don't know, two weeks? Three? My parents must be—" She looked suddenly distressed. "Does anyone have a mobile?"

"We all came straight from Malice," Justin said. "Bit hard to find a power point there."

"Wait, they kept you here for *weeks*?" Kady asked Alicia. "Why? Why didn't they just get rid of you?"

"Grendel," Alicia said simply.

"Grendel?" Seth asked. "The artist who draws Malice?"

"Right. He's not what you think. He's just . . . he's like a child. They treat him really badly. But he took a shine to me. I really think they were going to . . . um . . . *get rid* of me, but Grendel kicked up such a fuss when they took me away. He refused to draw, and nothing they could do would make him, and they were desperate to know what you were up to in Malice. So they brought me back to the attic, and they let me sit with him, and he started to draw again. It was his way of making sure I was okay, you see? And every day since, they've taken me up there. He draws, I draw. It keeps him happy."

"That's lovely," said Justin, deadpan. "Really. Now if we're all caught up, can we get on with the job?"

"The job?" Alicia asked Seth, ignoring Justin's tone.

"We're here to take down Tall Jake," Seth explained. "He's wounded. Weak. They drove him out of Malice. Now we have to finish it."

"How?" Alicia asked. "You can't just walk up to him. He'll kill you."

Justin pointed at her. "See? That's what *I* was saying!"

"Besides, Scratch and Miss Benjamin are here too," Alicia said.

Kady went pale at the mention of Miss Benjamin. "Seth, maybe we *should* think this through a bit. . ." she said.

"I vote we burn this place to the ground," said Justin, with sudden enthusiasm.

"No!" Alicia cried. "Grendel's in the attic!"

"So?" Justin said. "He might be your new best friend, but he's nothing to me. As far as I'm concerned, he's part of this."

"He's not! He's an innocent! He doesn't know what he's doing!"

Justin drew breath for a comeback, but Seth put up his hand. "Wait. I've got an idea. Maybe we *don't* have to take on Tall Jake."

Justin crossed his arms and waited for the explanation.

"You think we can get Grendel out of here?" Seth asked Alicia. "You think you can get him to come with you?"

"Maybe, I mean. . ." Alicia said uncertainly. Then she frowned and nodded. "Yes. I'm sure he would. I could persuade him."

"What's your idea, Seth?" Kady asked.

"We take Grendel," said Seth. "No Grendel, no comic. No comic, no more believers. Kids will forget and move on to the next thing. Tall Jake will be starved of power."

"Yes!" Alicia said, catching on. "I overheard him talking. He said he was like a ghost when he first got here."

"The Lack told me the same," said Seth. "Perhaps, without the comic, he'll get weaker and weaker until he just fades away."

"So we go after the *comic*, not the man," Justin mused.

"Not quite as satisfying, but it does involve me not getting killed, so I'm all for it."

"You know where Grendel is?" Kady asked Alicia.

"In the attic," Alicia replied. "Follow me."

2

Alicia knew the trick to the attic stairs by now. "You just have to make sure both doors don't close," she said. "I've seen Scratch and Miss Benjamin do it. Someone holds the door at the bottom, the other keeps the door at the top open."

"What happens if you don't?" Kady asked, looking up the stairs.

Alicia turned on the light and the shadows retreated, clicking and clattering like a swarm of cockroaches. "Something bad."

Justin swore under his breath. "I remember that sound," he said. "From the night when Tall Jake came to take me."

"What are they?" Kady asked.

"I don't know," said Alicia. She shivered as she remembered the horrible feeling of those creatures in her hair, in her nose, on her tongue. Drowning in them. It seemed a long way to the top of those wooden stairs. A single, feeble bulb, hanging from a wire, flickered unsteadily.

"I'll go first," she said. "He knows me." She tapped the door at the bottom of the stairs. "Just don't let this door close, okay?"

Seth held it. "I'll make sure."

Alicia crept up the stairs to the top. As she went, she

wondered at herself. Strange, to find herself here. She'd been imprisoned for weeks now. Her first thought should have been escape. The old Alicia would have made a run for it the moment the door was open.

But that was a girl who had known nothing of Tall Jake, of Malice . . . and of Grendel. It was a different girl who climbed the wooden steps now.

She reached the door at the top of the stairs. The restless darkness stayed in the cracks and corners. She listened for a moment, heard nothing, and opened it.

The attic was as she'd left it last night. Morning light drifted through the skylights on to the paintings and sketches that were scattered around the vast space. Grendel sat at his easel, drawing. He was tranced out again, his favourite steel-tipped pen scratching, scratching, scratching as he detailed another panel of the comic.

She looked down the stairs and beckoned the others up. When they were about halfway, the door at the bottom swung closed. Alicia felt the door she was holding push against her, trying to shut itself, but she held it open until they were all through.

They stared in amazement at Grendel. "Does he know we're here?" Kady asked.

"He sort of *goes away* while he's drawing," Alicia said. "He won't notice you until he's back."

"He's looking into Malice," said Seth. "And drawing what he sees."

Justin moved carefully closer. His face was a picture

of disgust. Alicia felt a surge of anger at him. She knew why Justin had that expression. He couldn't see past the deformity, the misshapen features and warped body.

"That's him?" Justin asked. "The guy who created Malice? *This* guy?"

"Yes. *That* guy," said Alicia, in a tone that dared him to say anything more. Justin got the hint and shut up.

"So what do we do?" Seth asked. "Can we get him out of here?"

"We have to wait till he's done," Alicia said. "He won't move until then."

"Well, how long's *that*?" Justin asked, exasperated.

"As long as it takes!" she snapped. She'd decided very quickly that she didn't like this boy. He'd rubbed her the wrong way from the start.

She went over to stand by Seth, who was gazing in wonder at the pictures that stood all around the attic, on easels or resting against the walls. Among the pencil sketches and charcoal drawings were some enormous paintings. One was a Malice landscape, showing a valley under a cloudy sky. It looked real enough to step into.

Next to it was the life-size painting of Tall Jake. Alicia hated that picture. She always felt that it was watching her.

"So that's Tall Jake's portrait," said Seth. "You know, the Lack told me that he stepped right out of that portrait, into this attic. That was how he came into our world that first time."

Alicia felt goosebumps on her arms at that, and hugged herself.

"Thanks," said Seth. "For what you did. I know it can't have been easy, when you got my message."

She gave him a little smile. "Some things . . . I suppose some things, you can't turn your back on."

She looked over at Grendel. Seth followed her gaze. Kady was standing with him, peering over his shoulder at what he was doing.

"I s'pose not," said Seth, but his eyes were on Kady, not Grendel.

"Hey!" said Kady excitedly. "Come here!"

They walked over to her. Grendel was near the end of a page now, adding detail to the final panel. Alicia craned in to see what had got Kady so worked up. It showed scenes of violence that she didn't much like.

"It's what happened after!" Kady said. "After we left, I mean. Look, there's Dylan and Scotty. And Tatyana!" She looked closer. "Tall Jake's forces are scattering. They're being hunted down and destroyed!" She turned away from the page with a grin. "We've won!"

- Have you, now? -

Alicia went cold at that voice. It was the sound of fingernails scraping the inside of a coffin lid.

From behind a screen of easels stepped Icarus Scratch and Miss Benjamin. And out of the shadows, clotting like blood from the darkness, was a figure she'd hoped never to see. A figure she'd only seen in fleeting glimpses and an awful portrait.

It was Tall Jake himself.

Crossings

1

Tall Jake. Seth stared. Tall Jake was here, right here, in front of them.

The very sight of him felt *wrong*. He was like a hole punched in the world, sucking in light and life. He was dislocated, fractured, not quite there. Not quite real.

But this wasn't the Tall Jake that Seth knew from the comics. This wasn't the same cruel figure that had overseen the death of his friend Luke. His tricorn hat was gone, and his head was exposed. It was bald, white and wrinkled, with straggly worms of lank hair on one side. The other side was even more horrible to look at. The skin there was folded and melted like candle wax: the evidence of his first battle against the Shard. He bore new wounds from his latest battle, too. His coat was ragged and torn, and he walked bent over, clutching his ribs with one hand.

But though he was battered and blasted, he was still a fearful creature. His eyes were yellow star-shaped pupils set in pools of red, and they blazed with hatred. His lips drew back over large white teeth.

- You have proved to be very troublesome, - he snarled.

"Thieves and sneaks, all of you!" Scratch accused. "Vicious little children!"

Seth was terrified, but the more scared he got, the more determined he was not to show it. "How did you know we were coming?" he asked, keeping his voice steady.

- I did not get to be the ruler of Malice without learning to predict my enemies, - Tall Jake replied.

"You didn't predict them blowing your Deadhouse to hell," Justin pointed out defiantly. He was looking around for an escape route of some kind as Scratch and Miss Benjamin closed in on them.

Tall Jake turned his dreadful gaze to Justin. - No, - he said slowly. - I did not. -

Seth and the others had backed up into a tight circle now, near to Grendel. The scratch, scratch, scratch of his pen went on uninterrupted.

- What do you know of the Lack, really? - Tall Jake asked them. - Or of the Queen of Cats? Do you think they will rule Malice better than I did? Do you think you have ushered in a new age of peace and democracy? - He sneered at them. - Foolish children. You meddle with things you do not understand. -

"I understand you've been snatching children and killing them!" Seth cried angrily. "I understand you killed my friend Luke!"

372

Tall Jake chuckled behind the collar of his coat. – Why is it that your kind never take responsibility for yourselves? It is only ever someone else's fault. –

"It *was* your fault!"

– No. I did not take anyone who did not ask. It was made very clear to all of you: if you perform the ritual, I will take you away. And yet so many of you asked me anyway. You just had to risk it, didn't you? –

"That doesn't excuse you for killing them!"

– I am not asking for your pardon. But I did not kill them. I tested them, as they asked. Some failed. Some, like yourselves, did not. – He'd come close enough now that Seth could smell the musty stink of his coat and the skin beneath. The smell of a corpse. – You must be a bored and desperate breed, to be so eager for my tricks and traps. –

Seth felt a fury building up inside him. All these justifications disgusted him. But what was worse was that he felt this terrible murderer had a *point*. He *had* played fair. Everyone who went to Malice had been warned. It was just that most of them didn't believe the warning. And whose fault was that?

No. It didn't matter. It wasn't right! It just wasn't!

– Your kind like to watch, don't you? You thrill to the risk of a gamble on a game show. You love to see others humiliate themselves. You are hungry for pain. And so you read my comic, and you make me stronger. Soon, you will have made me strong enough to rule this world. – He leaned forward, grinning, and his smile was hideous. – I'm just giving you what you want. What you deserve. –

Seth thought suddenly of his parents, slumped in front of the TV, watching mindless light entertainment while their lives ticked past. God, was that how it worked? If the world was stupid, boring, violent and unfair, was it just because we made it that way? Did we really get what we deserved, in the end?

– You see my point of view, – Tall Jake observed. – We're not so different, you and I. –

At that, Seth wanted to cry out in denial. No! He would never be like Tall Jake! They had nothing in common! But he didn't get the chance. At that moment there was a yell from behind him, and Justin lunged at Tall Jake with a craft knife.

Seth didn't know where he'd got it from. Presumably he'd picked it out of the scattered art supplies and hidden it away before Scratch, Miss Benjamin and Tall Jake revealed themselves. It didn't matter. He didn't get within two feet of Tall Jake anyway.

There was a rattling sound, the clicking of a thousand tiny claws, and thick shadows spewed like tar from the folds of Tall Jake's coat. Tendrils of darkness shot across the gap between Tall Jake and Justin. They wrapped around his limbs and face, spreading over his skin, meeting and joining. He fell to the ground, thrashing, but his legs were tied and the darkness was forcing its way through his lips, up his nose, into his eyes. He tried to scream but he could only manage a gurgle.

"Stop it!" Seth cried, and because he didn't know what else to do he swung a fist at Tall Jake. But Tall Jake saw it coming, and the black substance that tormented Justin enwrapped his fingers. Seth felt himself seized by an icy grip, and then he was thrown away. Suddenly, the blackness was all over him, swarming over his skin, a million unseen insects all ticking and rattling. He fought to wipe them off but they were already under his clothes, spreading out from his collar over his chin. He could hear everyone screaming, and then something forced apart his jaw, and suddenly his mouth was full of insects. He coughed and gagged but there was no air in his lungs. The dark shrouded his eyes and he went blind.

Help me! Help me! **Somebody help me!**

But there was nobody to help him.

Suddenly the darkness was gone, and he could see again. The insects had disappeared. It was as if they'd never been there, a nightmare that vanished upon waking. But Tall Jake was still standing in front of him, so the nightmare was far from over yet.

Seth sucked in deep breaths. The memory of the repulsive things that lived in Tall Jake's darkness made him want to throw up. To his right, Justin was lying on his back, wheezing. The girls were crying. Grendel's pen had stopped scratching.

‑ It will not be quick, children, ‑ said Tall Jake. ‑ You have cost me too much for a merciful death. ‑

Tall Jake held out one hand and clenched it into a fist. Seth had barely caught his breath before he was wracked with the most shocking agony he'd ever experienced in his life. It felt like his lungs and heart and guts were all being crushed into a tiny ball. What was worse, he could hear Kady shrieking too. Kady, and Alicia, and Justin too. All of them were suffering the same terrible pain.

Not Kady! Do it to me, but not to her!

The words never made it through his gritted teeth. The next wave of pain stole his thoughts away, and this one seemed like it would never end.

When it did, they were left gasping, beached on the shore of a sea of agony. Seth's ears rang and his eyes wouldn't focus. He lay on his back, staring at the pale rectangle of a skylight. Breathe in, breathe out.

Gradually, he became aware that one of them hadn't stopped screaming. It was a strange sound, like a wounded animal.

"Will you shut up, you feeble-minded moron?" Scratch howled, and Seth realized it was Grendel he was addressing, Grendel who was screaming. Seth turned his head and saw that Grendel was kneeling next to Alicia, cradling her head roughly, trying to hug her to him. His face was twisted in horror.

Tall Jake was paying him no attention. He wasn't finished yet. ‑ You have driven me from my world, so I shall take yours. I may not have my armies now, but I have my believers. My power grows every time my name is whispered in fear. Soon there will be no one in this weak and dreary realm capable of stopping me! –

Seth braced himself, but it did no good. The pain tore the air from his lungs. He curled into a ball on the floor of the attic. But the pain came from inside him, from his stomach and guts, and he couldn't protect himself against it.

Nonono this can't go on—

Then, relief. Blessed, wonderful relief. Seth lay on his side, panting. Close by, he could hear Grendel's wails. His eyes refocused and he saw what had interrupted Tall Jake.

Grendel was howling and beating at Tall Jake with his fists. Despite Grendel's size and strength, the attack was pitiful and had no effect. It was like an infant thumping his father. Grendel was hysterical, tears running down his lumpen face.

He's defending Alicia.

His efforts were in vain. Tall Jake's brow clenched in anger.

– We have indulged you quite enough, halfwit, – he growled. – You will learn your place! –

He grabbed Grendel's wrist and flung him across the attic as if he weighed nothing at all. Grendel crashed to the ground in an avalanche of paint pots and broken easels, where he lay groaning.

Scratch regarded the fallen artist without interest, then turned to Tall Jake and sighed. "Will you just kill them so we can get on with our lives, please? We still have a world to conquer, and you owe me the British Isles."

– Yes, – said Tall Jake. – There is little satisfaction in tormenting these pathetic children. – He stooped down to peer at Seth, then tutted and shook his head. – Look at them. How did they come to cause me such trouble? Well, no matter. They will trouble me no longer. –

It was Seth's last chance, and he knew it, but he found himself helpless. There was nothing he could do to fight Tall Jake. He was far too powerful.

Alicia was right. We're just kids. What can kids do?

Then the pain hit, and this time it was the worst of all. Shocking, terrifying, desperate agony. His insides were on fire. His ears squealed. He couldn't breathe, he couldn't think, he could barely see. The suffering was unbelievable.

I wanted . . . I wanted to save everyone . . . save her . . . and I got so close. . .

He was dimly aware of the others in the room. His friends, writhing and shrieking. Scratch and Miss Benjamin, looking on eagerly. And Grendel . . . Grendel, unseen by anyone, getting to his feet, moving across the attic with something in his hand. . .

But not towards Tall Jake. Towards Tall Jake's portrait.

Seth saw blackness around the edges of his vision. He was on the verge of passing out. If he slipped into unconsciousness, the pain would stop . . . but so would his life.

He ground his teeth together and held on. And just

when he thought he couldn't hold on any longer, the torture stopped and the attic plunged into chaos.

2

Seth lay brokenly on the floor, stunned by the pain and the sudden relief. He'd been sure this was it. He'd been sure there would be no release this time. And yet. . .

There was shouting and movement everywhere. Grendel was roaring. Scratch and Miss Benjamin were yelling at each other. And something else. . .

Tall Jake. Tall Jake was howling.

Seth fought to get to his hands and knees. At first he saw only colourful blurs, but as his vision came back he began to make sense of what was going on in the room.

Tall Jake was staggering about in front of him, clutching his eyes. There was something wrong with his face. Where there had been wrinkled white skin, now it was black and smouldering. Terrible cries came from his throat as he fumbled this way and that, blinded.

Seth looked past him and saw Scratch and Miss Benjamin struggling with Grendel in front of Tall Jake's portrait. An angry streak of black had been painted across Tall Jake's face. Grendel had a dripping brush in his hand.

Miss Benjamin and Scratch were trying to hold him back, but he was too strong for them. He flung Miss Benjamin away and swiped his paintbrush across the portrait once again. This time it was across the chest. Right before Seth's eyes, a black and smouldering line, thick as a tyre track, appeared on Tall Jake's body. It looked like paper thrown on a fire that had crinkled to a dark, glowing mass. Tall Jake shrieked, flailing at himself.

– Stop him! Stop him! – he demanded of Scratch and Miss Benjamin. His creator was trying to cross him out, and Tall Jake was desperate to prevent it. They redoubled their efforts, and this time they managed to wrestle the paintbrush out of Grendel's hand.

Seeing that Grendel would be overpowered, Seth looked around frantically for some way to help. He remembered the craft knife that Justin had, but he couldn't see it anywhere.

The only thing his eye fell on was Grendel's pen. His steel-tipped pen, that had been scratch, scratch, scratching all the while. It lay on the floor near Seth.

There was no strength in his body. Even getting to his feet seemed impossible. But then another sound came to his ears. The sound of Kady crying. She was lying on the floor, curled into a ball, sobbing into her hands.

A fury ignited in him. Tall Jake had hurt her. He wouldn't allow *anyone* to hurt her. He concentrated his hatred, staggered upright and reached for the pen.

There was a crash as Scratch and Miss Benjamin pulled Grendel to the floor. "We've got him!" Scratch cried.

Tall Jake was still stumbling blindly. – I'll kill him! I'll kill him! Where is he? Bring him here! –

Seth's hand closed around the pen. "You've killed enough," he said. He ran at Tall Jake with the pen in his hand like a dagger. Tall Jake heard him coming, turned towards him, and Seth plunged the pen through his collar and deep into the side of his neck.

Everything in the attic went still. Tall Jake just stood there, stunned. Blind eyes stared towards Seth from his ruined and burned face. Scratch and Miss Benjamin gaped. Even Grendel stopped struggling, as if he sensed what had just happened.

Then, from where the pen stuck out of his collar, Tall Jake began to smoulder. The same smouldering that Grendel's paintbrush had caused, like he was a ball of paper burning up in the heart of a fire. Tall Jake staggered back and shrieked as the smouldering spread out from his collar, up his face, down his arm, eating him up. He tripped and fell to the ground, pawing at the floor in soundless desperation. But the smouldering was unstoppable. It spread down his back, to his legs, charring him head to foot. He fought and wailed and thrashed, but he was being consumed, and his kickings became feebler and feebler.

Then there was a scream from the other side of the room. Miss Benjamin was staring at her hands, which were turning to dust and crumbling away before her eyes.

"No! No, it's not fair! Not me, too!" she cried. But her protests did no good. As Seth watched, her disguise fell away, and the prim Englishwoman with the stern, ratlike face became the wrinkled, goat-eyed horror that Seth had seen in a lightning flash that night in Hathern. The moment was mercifully brief. She was consumed even quicker than her master, and with a final wail she collapsed in a pile of mud and blood and dust.

Finally, there was silence. Where Tall Jake had been was a heap of ash on the floor. The butt of the steel-tipped pen stuck out of it.

Seth looked down at what was left of his enemy. "That was for Luke," he said.

Justin was getting to his feet in amazement. Kady helped up Alicia. None of them could quite believe their eyes. Was it really over? Was Tall Jake gone at last?

"You terrible brats!" cried Scratch. "You've ruined me! All this time I've looked after that drooling slob, fed him, printed his accursed comic, and now I get nothing! I was supposed to be king! I was supposed to rule this land!" His eyes glittered crazily. In his hand was the craft knife that had fallen from Justin's grip earlier. "I'll carve you all to pieces!"

He lunged towards Seth with the knife, but before he'd got three steps, he was intercepted. Grendel grabbed him from behind, pinning his arms to his sides. Scratch swore and struggled, kicking and writhing, but he wouldn't let go of the knife as Grendel dragged him backwards and away from the children.

"Get off me, you malformed mongrel!" he shrieked. "I'll cut their throats! Let me go!"

Grendel ignored him. He just kept pulling him back and back, towards the enormous landscape painting of Malice that Seth had admired earlier. Scratch was trying to work

382

his arm free so he could stab his captor, but Grendel held him too tight.

"Where are you taking me?" Scratch shrieked. "Where are you taking me?"

Grendel didn't reply. His hunched back was almost touching the painting now. He looked across the attic at Alicia. Behind that huge brow and twisted face, his eyes were sad. In his gaze was a goodbye.

Then, with one great heave, he toppled backwards into the painting, carrying Scratch with him. But the painting didn't rip, or tip over. They fell into it, as if through an open window.

"*Where are you taking meeeee?*" Scratch wailed.

And just like that, they were gone.

Destinations

1

Nobody quite knew what to do next. They looked at one another, and then at the empty room, full of silent paintings. The terror had departed this place now, but so had the life. There was no power here any more. It was just a chilly old attic.

"Where did they go?" Alicia asked at last.

Justin went slowly over to the landscape picture that Scratch and Grendel had disappeared into. He touched it with his hand. Just canvas. He turned back to them and shrugged.

"I guess they went to Malice," said Kady.

"But how?" Alicia looked lost. There were tears in her eyes, behind her glasses.

"I guess. . ." Kady began, then realized she didn't have a good explanation.

"Grendel," said Seth. "He made a world so real that we could all go there. But he never stepped into it himself. Not until now." He smiled faintly at Alicia. "He did it to protect us. To protect *you*. From Scratch."

Alicia bit her lip and stared at the painting. It looked exactly as it had before.

"Well," said Justin, dusting his hands together. "That's that."

That *was* that, but none of them seemed ready to accept it. They were still dazed and shocked from their ordeal. They stood about listlessly. Everything seemed so *normal*.

Eventually Kady said: "We should probably try to find a phone or something. Y'know, to get out of here."

"We have to watch out," Alicia said. "There was a man . . . no, something *else* . . . he was guarding the gatehouse. And he talked about things in the trees. And—"

"You saw what happened to Miss Benjamin," said Seth. "When Tall Jake died, those creatures he created died with him. I don't think we have to worry now."

They left the attic and wandered through the corridors of Crouch Hollow. The feeling of menace was gone. There were no shadows on the attic stairs. Their footsteps rang from the hollow walls of the empty asylum. There was nothing here to frighten them now. It was only a building.

"What happens now, you reckon?" Justin asked. "To Malice?"

"I don't know," he said. "All I know is, no more kids will be taken away."

"What about the ones who are already in there? Scotty and Dylan and that?"

"I don't know," Seth said again. "I suppose, as long as

Malice still exists, they'll be okay. Everything will keep on like it was, except there'll be no Tall Jake and no Regulators and all that. Havoc has Dylan to lead them now. There are still plenty of white tickets hidden all over Malice. There's no reason why the trains would stop just 'cause Tall Jake's gone. If they want to get out of there, they can still catch a train."

"But if Grendel's *in* Malice somewhere, that means it'll *never* end, right? Even if there's no more comic and kids stop reading it," Justin went on. "I mean, how can it end if the bloke who created it is *inside* it?" He was frowning with the effort of getting his head round that idea.

"Is that what you think? That Malice will never end?" asked Seth. He smiled. "I like that idea."

2

They found a phone in the reception. It was hidden behind the counter, an old 1970s plastic phone with a dial on the front instead of keys. Kady snatched up the receiver and her face lit up as she heard a tone.

"I need to call home!" she said, and started dialling in numbers. Seth laid his hand on hers to stop her.

"Kady, don't."

She stared at him. "Why not?"

"Think about it. Think about the questions we'll have to answer. The police. All of that. How are we gonna tell them what happened here?"

"What does it matter? We'll just say. . ." she began, then trailed off. She was thinking how it would sound when they told the police about a deadly underground comic and about Tall Jake. Especially as there was little or no proof left of any of it. "We've not done anything wrong!" she cried, frustrated.

"I know," said Seth. "But they'll put us in padded cells if we start talking about Malice."

Kady angrily slammed the phone down. "So what *do* we say, genius?"

"Nothing," said Seth. "Nothing about Tall Jake or the printworks or a comic or anything. We don't need to. Scratch and Grendel are gone, Tall Jake and Miss Benjamin are dead. The comic will disappear without our help."

"We say *nothing*?"

"Because we don't remember," Seth said. "Just like all those other kids who came back with their memories blanked. Remember how it always happened? The kids who survived Malice would just turn up at home with no idea where they'd been. That's how we do it. If we breathe a word of this, the whole world will think we're crazy."

Kady reluctantly agreed. So did Alicia, although it took some persuading to get her to lie to her parents. Justin only nodded. He'd been getting quieter and quieter ever since they'd left the attic. Something was wrong with him, Seth could tell. He was grim-faced, and all the bounce had gone out of him.

"Okay," said Seth. "To make this work, we have to get home from here without calling the police or anyone we know. Nobody can know where we've been. We just need to turn up on the doorsteps of our homes."

"How do we do that?" Kady asked. "Even if we had money for a taxi, we couldn't call one. We don't know where we are. And none of us can drive."

"We hitch-hike," said Justin.

"We can't do that!" Alicia exclaimed. "There's no telling who might pick us up!"

Justin shrugged. "After what we've been through today, you think I'm worried about that?"

"He's right," said Seth. "It's the only way. How are we gonna explain what we were all doing in Crouch Hollow? We need to get home without leaving a trail."

"Hitch-hiking is dangerous," Alicia insisted.

"We don't have a lot of choice," said Seth.

"There *are* four of us," Kady pointed out.

"Actually, it's gonna be three," said Justin. "I might stick around here for a bit."

They stared at him. "You want to stick around *here*?" Kady asked.

"Why not? Good a place as any." And he walked out of the reception, his shoulders slumped, back into the corridors of Crouch Hollow.

"What's up with him?" Kady asked Seth.

"I'll go find out," he told them, and he headed off after his friend.

3

He caught up with Justin as he was going into an office. It was as run-down and neglected as the rest of the building, with paperwork left to rot on the shelves and filing cabinets that were rusted shut. Justin began rummaging around, turning things over, poking in corners. Seth joined him and started doing the same.

"What are we looking for?" he asked.

Justin didn't answer. He probably didn't know himself.

"You don't want to go home, do you?" Seth asked him.

"I got nothing, mate," Justin said. "I ain't going back. I'll sleep on the street if I have to."

"I won't let that happen."

"I appreciate the sentiment, but what you gonna do? I can hardly stay with you, can I? I mean, there's Social Services. I'll be back with my dad like *that*." He clicked his fingers. "And I bet he's got a year's worth of beatings saved up for making him worry."

Seth laid his hand on Justin's shoulder. "I don't mean that. I mean, we're going back to Malice. I'm gonna see Kady home; I'm gonna check my mum and dad are okay." He reached into his pocket and pulled out two white tickets. Train tickets for Malice. "And then we catch a train."

Justin's jaw dropped. "You got tickets? How'd you get tickets?"

"Found them in the Deadhouse when I was planting the bomb," Seth replied.

"The little box you found behind the pipes!" Justin exclaimed. "I forgot."

"Me too. I'd have shown them to you then, but that ogre turned up. After that, I suppose it slipped my mind. I reckon Tall Jake stashed a couple there for some lucky kid to find after they'd been sucked into the comic and dumped in the Deadhouse." He studied them thoughtfully. "Y'know, considering these things are hidden all over Malice, I'm surprised it took me this long to find some."

"Tall Jake! I always loved that bloke!" Justin beamed. Then he became serious. "Are you sure about this? I mean, going back for good? What about your folks? What about Kady?"

Seth felt some of the good humour drain out of him. "I don't want to leave her," he said. "I don't want to leave *them*. You think I haven't thought about that? I mean, how can I explain to Mum and Dad where I've gone? How I can't even send them a postcard or make a phone call now and then?"

"That's rough," Justin said. "It's easy for me; I mean, I don't have nothin' worth crying about that I'm leaving behind. But you. . ."

Seth sighed. "Kady's gonna be happy here. My parents are happy here . . . or as happy as they get, I suppose. But this place, it isn't for me. I know where I'm supposed to be."

Justin nodded. "Yeah. Me, too." He looked over at his friend. "I'm glad you're coming along, mate. Wouldn't be the same without you."

"Yeah," said Seth. "Likewise."

4

It was dark and a wintry wind was blowing when they got back to Hathern. They'd walked out of Crouch Hollow along country roads until a passer-by gave them a lift to the motorway. From there, it took them a long time to find someone who would take all four of them. Eventually they squeezed into the cab of a truck. When the driver commented on the outlandish clothes that Seth, Kady and Justin were wearing, they told him they'd just come from a music festival. He seemed to think that was great. He offered them sandwiches, which they ate ravenously, and he sang Johnny Cash tunes all the way to the turn-off to Hathern. They walked from there.

They said their goodbyes to Alicia quickly, since she had to walk on to the next village and it was getting late. Only Seth had known her at all; to the others, she was almost a stranger. And yet she'd played an important part in the downfall of Tall Jake, and Seth would miss her.

"You don't have to worry about him coming to take you away any more," said Seth. "Your friend Philip will be safe, too."

"We did a good thing, didn't we?" she asked. He could see that she was still thinking about Grendel.

"You got really fond of that guy, didn't you?" Seth said.

"He needed help," said Alicia. "I just wish I could have helped him."

They hugged briefly, and then she left, walking away down the road towards her home.

The next stop was Seth's house. They crept through the narrow lanes of the village, taking the back ways. Hathern was deserted at night, and they went unobserved. Finally they came to the church at the top of the hill where Seth's house was.

"Wait here," he told the others, and he slipped down the road, keeping to the shadows. He hadn't forgotten the sinister voice he'd heard on the phone, pretending to be his mum. Maybe it was just Tall Jake's trickery, but ever since then he'd been afraid that something might have happened to Mum and Dad. Before he could go back to Malice, he needed to know. He checked that nobody was about and crept closer.

The lights were on in the living-room window. The curtains were drawn, but they hadn't been fully closed. Seth put his eye to the crack and peeped through.

There they were. Dad in Dad's chair, Mum in Mum's chair. They were watching a game show. Mum looked worn and old in her sweatpants; Dad had even less hair on his head. But there they were, unharmed. Seth sighed in relief.

So it had been a trick after all. Tall Jake had never been here. He and his cronies had always been careful about getting adults mixed up in their affairs. He supposed that, with Tall Jake's power, intercepting a phone call was child's play.

Well, he wouldn't be intercepting any more.

In the living room, Mum laughed at something on the TV. Even Dad gave a bit of a smile. The sight made Seth smile too. Their son might be gone, but they still had the TV. At least there was that.

He headed back up the road to the churchyard. Kady's face was surprised when he returned. "You're not going in?"

"What could I say?" Seth replied. "'Hi, I'm leaving again'? 'Third time's a charm'?" He shook his head. "I couldn't do it. And I can't stay."

"So, what, you're not even going to let them know you're safe?"

"I'll phone them. From the train station. Before I go." Seth felt rotten about it. He wished there was some other way, some way he could make them understand. But they just wouldn't get it.

He didn't want to be an irresponsible son. It just always seemed to work out that way, no matter what he did. Maybe they were just too different, in the end.

Just like he and Kady were.

"I guess this is it," said Kady, catching his thought. "I . . . I mean, I have to go home. Mom and Dad . . . I know they must have been dying every second I was away. It's ... I have to go home."

Justin began to shuffle awkwardly. He was aware that Seth and Kady had their goodbyes to say, and he was in the way. "I'll get out of your hair, eh?" he said. "Gimme a hug."

He and Kady held each other. "I'm gonna miss you even more than that stupid tin cat," Justin said.

"Hey! You make sure you find that cat when you get back!" Kady said.

"Will do," said Justin. He let her go. "I'll just be round the corner," he said to Seth. He sloped off across the churchyard, hands in his pockets, hood pulled over his head. Then they were alone in the churchyard, the cold wind rustling in the trees, the glow of the streetlights falling on them.

Kady couldn't meet Seth's eyes. "I'm sorry," she said at last.

"For what?"

"I wish I was like you. I wish I could just throw myself into things. I wish I loved that world like you do."

"Don't be sorry," said Seth. "It's not your fault. And it's not mine. We ... we just want different things."

"I just wish we wanted them *together*," said Kady. "I can say goodbye to Tatyana and Justin, but *you*?" There were tears growing in her eyes. "It just sucks it has to be this way."

Seth looked at the ground. "I can't stay, Kady."

"And I can't go."

"I don't have a ticket for you anyway. I only got two."

Kady half-laughed, half-sobbed. "Such a dummy. Trust you to be practical at a moment like this."

Seth put his arms around her. She squeezed herself against him, hard, as if she might be able to keep him if she held on tight enough. But Seth knew this was the last time they would hold each other for a long while, and it made his throat tight and his chest ache.

"You find some more tickets, and you come visit, okay?" she said.

"I will," he said. "I'll find a way to get back and forth, somehow. And when I do, I'll come back and see you all the time. I'll come back and see Mum and Dad, too."

"You promise?"

"I promise."

Kady buried her head in his shoulder. "Who's gonna look after me now, Sir Knight?" she whispered.

She stepped away from him and wiped her eyes with the back of her hand. Then she gave him a kiss on the cheek and walked away.

It all seemed too quick. Seth wanted to call her back, to do this goodbye *properly*. But he didn't. There was no way they could ever do this properly. No way in which it wouldn't hurt. And Kady wasn't one for goodbyes. So she got it over with quickly, and then she turned her back. She walked out of the churchyard and was gone. Seth heard her sobbing as she went down the lane. But he didn't go after her. He couldn't.

His legs felt like lead as he walked the other way through

the churchyard. Justin was waiting around the corner. Justin saw the way his head hung and patted him on the shoulder.

"C_____" he said, "Y__'ll __ _____ ____."

"I _____

"S_____

up! Th_____

waitin_____

Se_____

infecti_____

"W_____

catch!"_____

396